# deStIny LAne

# destIny LAne

JARED TLC

ISBN: 979-8-88785-049-8 (Paperback)
ISBN: 979-8-88785-050-4 (Hardcover)

Library of Congress Control Number: 2025938387

Any references to historical events, real people, or real
places are used fictitiously. Names, characters, and places
are products of the author's imagination.

Book design by Allison Chernutan.
Edited by Carol Kudeviz and Emily Kudeviz.

Printed in the United States of America.

First printing edition 2025.

emily@fracturedmirrorpublishing.com
Fractured Mirror Publishing
Knoxville, Tennessee

www.fracturedmirrorpublishing.com

FOR SEQUOIA

(& OUR LITTLES)

"IF WE WALK FAR ENOUGH," SAID DOROTHY, "I AM SURE WE SHALL SOMETIME COME TO SOME PLACE."

L. FRANK BAUM
THE WONDERFUL WIZARD OF OZ

**I'M WRITING THIS TO SAVE** myself. To try to make sense of that day that lasted a summer and tried to take our lives. I need to make sure I remember those women and those girls. Especially her.

There are things I wish I could forget. I find myself flinching at the sight or sound of water. An unexpected splash gives me unwelcome flashbacks. Whenever I see a kid with yellow-painted nails, my body starts to shake. It's rare when an hour passes that I don't replay moments from that nightmare. Too often, I wake up in the darkest morning hours, wishing the fear was confined to my sleep.

Maybe I should give up. Maybe I've already lost. *Maybe I'm still there.*

What would have happened if I had just read that sign? Would I have been brave enough to still walk down that street?

I hope so. I like to think I was that person. But I don't think I was. Not yet.

I don't expect you to believe everything as I tell it. Sometimes I have trouble believing it all myself. And I can't even imagine what you've experienced on your side of all this. I'm the last person to accept a story at face value, so don't feel bad if you have questions. Ask them. Get them out. Just like I need to get this out. I hope this confession helps you find the right words to tell your story.

It's funny, as I sit here, pen in my hand, it's really this little ink stick that started everything. It was my seventh birthday. I was in the backseat of Mom's car, feeling myself shrinking in real time. I wanted to disappear. But Mom wasn't going to let me off so easily. She leaned forward, looking into the rearview mirror. There were few feelings like looking directly into her eyes. Those emerald greens weren't of this world. One glance could induce awe. Another, one of the tightened brow variety, could strike terror directly into the hearts of her children.

But this look was one of the softer types. She told me I was safe without saying a word. Mom dug into her pocketbook, fingering through loose change and receipts, looking for something to settle me. A Werther's hard caramel, I imagined. She always had those. Always, except for today. All her hunting hand came up with was this golden pen.

She passed it back to me, its shell glistening against the setting sun.

"Here, take this."

I remember it being lighter than it looked. I ran my thumb against the ridges on its barrel, finding a few speckled chips in its gold veneer. There were words inked onto the clip. The name and address of the Disc Makers factory Mom worked at since she was twenty. The ink, like the factory, was worn.

"Look at the top, that's the best part."

My pointer landed on the button on the end.

"Yup," she nodded, still watching from the mirror. "Now push."

With a press—*Click*.

The point popped out from the bottom as the satisfying snap filled the backseat.

I did it again. *Click*. And again. *Click-click*.

I must have smiled, because she laughed.

"Kinda relaxing, ain't it?"

I nodded. I'm sure I had picked up a click pen before, but something about this gift, in this specific moment, was just what I needed. A necessary distraction.

*Click-click-click*.

She nodded. "Yup. Do that as much as you need to, baby star."

*Click-click-click*.

"Wait till you see what the other end can do."

I held that cheap gilded pen so tight for the rest of my first night in the house, *click-click-click*-ing anytime I felt my nerves getting the best of me.

That night, I met this kid who called himself Lucky. Or at least, this is when I remember meeting him for the first time. He claims that he was at the hospital when I was born. Needless to say, I don't remember this. He was only about five, so this was the type of big event memory a kid usually holds on to. Apparently Lucky went back to his kindergarten class the day after and told everybody his baby sister was born. He was always kind of an oracle like that.

When I woke up from my first sleep in the new house, the golden pen was gone.

I stripped the bed. Pop poked his head under the mattress. We scanned the cracks in the hardwood floor but there was nothing. It was like it was never there.

*Maybe it wasn't*, I started to tell myself.

"You think someone stole it?" Lucky asked.

"Only other person up here is you," Pop said, sending a suspecting glance Lucky's way.

I felt a shiver roll across my shoulders, a sensation I'd eventually grow accustomed to. I wish Pop were right.

Mom came home that night with a bundle of pens from work. These ones were far shinier, with a new sleek Disc Makers logo printed on each. She was excited about them, and thought I'd be too.

I pretended to be, but those green eyes could sense a lie. I don't know what it was, but those pens weren't the same. I eventually started to forget about that golden one and mindlessly picked up hundreds, maybe thousands more over the coming years. I'd dispose of them the way pens were supposed to be disposed of. Mindlessly. Maybe they'd run out of ink. Maybe I'd chew their caps into submission, or maybe I'd just lose them. This is the way it was supposed to be. They're just pens.

*It was just a pen.*

It's better not to form attachments to things. Or people, really. Everything came and went, came and went, and the sooner I learned this, the better.

# chApteR 1

**MOM DIED THE NIGHT I** graduated from eighth grade.

This was the same night I started to feel like someone was watching me.

I know people say they get that feeling a lot, but I promise you, this was different. It was constant. Unshakable.

I wish I could remember which happened first—Mom's death or the invisible watcher. If I knew that, maybe I'd be able to make sense of what happened next. Looking back, everything before the night's final moments feels black-and-white.

I know I graduated because there's still a bent diploma on top of my dresser. I know we went to Penn Queen Diner after the ceremony because I can still hear Poppy yelling at Lucky for sliding into the booth, eyes on his phone, and sitting on top of said diploma.

"Wake up, Lucky!" he snapped his fingers with force.

And, of course, I know it was raining. As I stood in the church, finally wearing the puke-green cap and gown that signified my survival from St. Veronica's, I could hear the drops pattering against the stained-glass dome above.

"Maya Lane the Third."

When Mr. Nelson announced my name, and I shuffled forward from the second pew, the rain made it sound like I had more clapping fans in the crowd than I actually did. I glanced up at the ceiling, and it seemed as though the painted cherubs were applauding my C+/B- average and the fact that I never got caught for last year's bathroom stall bomb threat. Everyone (the baby angels, that is) knew I wasn't going to do anything. And even if I wanted to, I definitely couldn't. I hate chemistry and wouldn't know the first chemical to use in an explosive cocktail. And, as intended, it successfully canceled our frog dissections that day.

In perfect unison, just as I reached the altar, I swore one of the cherubs winked at me and thunder crashed beyond their perfect puff clouds. Goosebumps coated my skin.

I looked out at the pews, trying to ignore the hundreds of eyes staring at me, and found my family. Poppy waved, his smile as bright as his remaining teeth allowed. Lucky gave me a thumbs up that turned into a middle finger when he was sure no one else was looking. Then, I looked to Mom and—

*FLASH.*

Blinding white. The obligatory I-just-shook-the-principal's hand photo. I blinked, trying to regain my vision. I don't remember seeing Mom's smile. I couldn't see her at all. But I like to think she was grinning. Unless she saw Lucky's middle finger, then she was snarling and definitely about to swat his hand into his lap. That scenario was even more satisfying.

I guess there are a few things you should know about my family before we get any further. I'll spell this out quickly and clearly, so we don't have to go back to it:

- Mom is not my mom.
- Poppy is not my dad.
- And my brother Lucky is not my brother.

Who they actually are:

- *Mom is my grandmother. I usually call her Gigi.*
  My birth mother (Mom's only actual daughter) lives across state, and I see her every once and a Christmas. And not in person, mind you, only in cards. There was also a Facetime once.

- *Poppy is my grandpa.*
  Father to the absent mother mentioned above.

- *Lucky is my cousin.*
  Lucky's dad is (was?) my uncle, brother to Mother of the Year. Lucky's parents died in a car accident when we were kids. It was the 4th of July and they were coming back from fireworks in the city when a drunk driver pinned them on the Ben Franklin. I don't remember either of them, but I know Lucky does even if he doesn't talk about them. Lucky's lived with our (grand)parents ever since.

But for all intents and purposes:

- Mom is absolutely my mom.
- Poppy is definitely my dad.
- And I couldn't ask for a better brother than Lucky.

I started calling myself Destiny three days after Mom died. We had the same name, and I got tired of hearing it. Tired of thinking about her every time someone called for me.

The days surrounding the funeral bled together into one terrible blur. I found myself back beneath the baby angel dome at St. Veronica's, but no one was clapping this time. No one asked for this. Even the cherubs above, eyes closed, looked lifeless.

As people filed forward, I wanted to run from what felt like a very terrible, accidental reality. But there was nowhere to go. I couldn't look at the open casket behind me. One glimpse at the body and I could tell it wasn't Gigi. Not anymore.

This makeup-caked, practically masked face behind me wasn't doing anything to erase the one now burned in my brain forever. She looked bloated, slightly yellowed. Like she'd swallowed the puddle I found her in.

Her Final Face was one-part red: the blood dripping from the corner of her lips like a freshly pressed letter seal. Her Final Face was one-part puke-green: the color of a commencement gone wrong. A hue her perfect brown skin never should have been able to turn.

Before me, stranger after stranger pulled me in for a hug, claiming to know me, her, and my Missing Mother. Three women in their Sunday best (one in green, another in blue, and the last in red) approached me like I'd just seen them yesterday.

"I'm sure everyone's telling you how much you look like your mom," Green said.

It didn't matter which mom she was referring to. We're all carbon copies.

"You could be twins!"

"Triplets, even."

"Look at this hair!"

"A crown! Girl, I'd die for these curls."

"It's these genes, I'm tellin' you."

The woman in red reached for my hair, but I took a step back.

"Is she here?" Blue asked.

"Who's that?"

"Your mother, child," Red scoffed.

I wanted to say, um, yeah? Have you seen the casket behind me? She's why we're all here.

But I took a deep breath, trying my best to hold back.

"Probably busy with the baby," Green shrugged.

The word struck like lightning directly at my heart. *Baby?*

"The what?"

The women looked stunned. They huddled closer, touching each other's arms, forming a church lady web.

"Oh, my…You didn't…?"

"I'm so sorry," Blue shook her head, tugging on the others to follow.

But the red friend wasn't budging.

"Hate to be the one to tell you…" I didn't believe she hated anything about this. A slight smirk was forming at the corners of her lips. For some (we all know the type), no bit of gossip is so unsavory that there isn't a spot too sacred to spill it.

Green cut in, unceremoniously. "You've got a sibling."

Sure. I knew that already. I've got Lucky.

Red clarified, as though she were correcting my thoughts. "A baby sister."

Clearly taking some sort of sick joy in this, she reached into her bag, fiddling her long fingers through hard candies, tissues, and lipstick containers, before finding what she was looking for. No one asked for this. She shoved her phone screen in my face, showing me the unwelcome sight.

"*Temple,*" one of them said.

It has a name?

I must have done something to suggest I was uncomfortable because Lucky intervened.

"Aunt Gracie! Meena! Chartreuse!" he engulfed them in his long arms. "Thank you so much for making it."

He ushered them off to their pews, chattering with a smile each step of the way.

"Oh my goodness, your hair is even bigger than hers!"

"And curlier," Lucky joked.

He was so much better at playing along in the moment than me. He got back and his forced smile dissolved in an instant.

"You good?"

"I have a sister," I said. The words felt cold. Empty.

Lucky looked down at the marble floor and bit his thumbnail.

He usually had the right words to say, or at least he'd pretend to. Right now, he struggled to find anything.

"Horrible timing," he wrapped his arm around my shoulder. "Let's chat through this tonight."

Now or later, it didn't matter. The rest of the funeral was spent thinking about my Missing Mother spending time with her new baby, not being here to say goodbye to her mom or hello to the girl that was once her baby. Now, more than ever, I wanted nothing to do with the woman. No question this was another factor in deciding to change my name.

Maybe "deciding" isn't quite the right word. Looking back, it's clear that I didn't really have a say in the matter.

After Gigi's death, I stopped sleeping. I couldn't doze off, no matter how hard I tried. I couldn't go four seconds without seeing her Final Face pressed against the insides of my eyelids.

After a few days, which blended together like dust mites and dead skin, I shaved my head. I didn't feel like washing it, and I definitely didn't feel like untangling it every morning.

Poppy was too tired to care. At first, his eyes popped from behind his wire-framed glasses, but then, after a long-winded sigh, he shrugged it off pretty quickly.

Lucky was, well, Lucky about it. A real dick. He took the rainbow flag off his wall then draped it over my shoulders like a cape.

"I'd like to officially welcome you to the community," he laughed. "No one has quite as much fun as us."

After a few weeks passed without a visit to the shower, Lucky called me out for it by gracefully framing the complaint around the three items of black clothing I owned.

"Okay, okay, enough with the black. We get it. You're mourning. But we don't need to be cliché about it."

He handed me what looked like a yellow blanket. I held it out and it unfurled before me. It was a hoodie with an upside-down smiley face on it.

"No emoji says '*I'm going through it*' quite like the upside-down smiley," Lucky nodded. "But that's not all. Put it on. They were out of mediums, so I went large. Rather go big and be cozy."

I pulled it over my head and weaved my arms through. It was definitely big but Lucky was right about the cozy part. I threw the yellow hood over my buzzed head. Turning to the mirror, I held out my arms like a T, as my skinny legs stuck out from the bottom.

"I look like SpongeBob."

"Be grateful. Robert is an icon." Lucky stepped closer and tilted my head down. "Look."

Looking down, the smiley was now right-side-up.

"While the rest of the world might think you're crazy, this guy is smiling at you. Yellow Hoodie's always got your back."

He pulled me in for a hug, his curls dripping down over my eyes. Lucky's got these long telephone pole arms, kinda like my legs. They coiled around me as I fought back a smile. I didn't want him to think that this was the new normal. It's a known rule in the Lane household that I don't do hugs. I might get hugs here and there, but I don't do the hugging. But even I had to admit, this felt good. I felt safe, and I needed that feeling more than I knew.

When the world had gone mad, as it tended to do every several hours, Lucky was always able to keep the craziness away from our shared third floor. This attic space which felt like our own loft apartment became our home within this old house.

I have to admit, I used to be afraid of Pop and Gigi's house. When I was little, I'd only come here for family parties, and I kept within the bounds of the living room and backyard. I liked that the outside matched my yellow nails, but that was about all I liked about it. The towering building was older than the world I knew, and bigger too. Gigi didn't think lights should be flicked on before sundown, and sometimes she passed out before then. She lined her windows with glass jars full of oil, flowers, leaves, and feathers, and no one dared to ask what she was doing. Pop listened to the same CD set all day, every day: *Motown: The Complete No. 1s.* The many discs came in a little white cardboard house with little blue doors and read *Hitsville, USA.* The music I knew didn't come on silver discs. Sometimes the songs were so old I felt like they were singing underwater.

Looking up at the ancient house, I felt like it leaned over to look back down on me. The only places I knew that had "towers" were castles, and they were exclusively in movies. But Gigi's house had three turrets, as I learned they were called, and they were quite common on the Victorians across town. But back then, they represented mysteries of an older, larger world—things I'd rather not consider at five or six. Things that made me feel impossibly small.

I never went upstairs until the day I moved in. I only had a mini backpack, not even big enough for a book.

"I'm sure we got some old clothes stuffed around here somewhere," Gigi said, leading me up the steps.

The halls were dark and lined with oversized dressers. There were more doors than I could count. I didn't want to be here, and I think Gigi knew it. She held my fingers and rubbed her thumb against the back of my hand. We kept climbing and climbing until we reached the top landing.

The ceiling was slanted, making the space look like a giant triangle. At the center of the triangle, there was a window that filled the space with light. The sun spilled onto the floor which was covered in a circular purple paisley rug. On either side of the purple circle, there were open doors.

"This is Lucky's room," she pointed to the left.

"And this will be yours," she pointed to the right. "It's not much now, but it's got a bed."

She failed to mention that it used to be my mother's room. That was probably for the better.

"It's hard to get big things up here, but Poppy will build anything for you. Some shelves? A desk? We'll make this place all yours."

Poppy did eventually build some shelves and a desk, all specifically designed to fit against the sloping ceilings in the space. And Gigi was right. It did eventually become my room, but on that first day, it was just an empty white room in a dusty old attic.

I didn't sleep much that night. I'm not much of a crier anymore, but I was six (about-to-be-seven), and I was a little different then.

I laid in the dark and empty space, trying to hide my tears beneath the blanket. A metal creak from the weathervane on the roof groaned overhead. I tried to time my louder pouts from when the weathervane's screech was at its peak, but some of my cries slipped through.

*Tap-tap-tap.*

The knock was gentle. Gigi must have heard me. Pretend you're asleep, I told myself. Lie still, don't make a peep, I told myself.

The door creaked open anyway.

Eleven-year-old Lucky stood there. He was only an outline, the light from his room at his back. He was my cousin, but that's all I knew about him. We had never talked before. Not a single word.

"You wanna watch SpongeBob?" were his first words. I had to admit, this was a promising start. "It's the one where Patrick accidentally brings back DoodleBob."

I'd never seen SpongeBob. My mom said it was about drugs and it would make me stupid.

"I'm okay."

"You wanna read something?" he asked. "I got some books with pictures. You like Spider-Man?"

I'd seen Spider-Man shirts on boys and Spider-Man toys at Wal-Mart, but I didn't know if I liked him. I'd never read a book by myself and didn't want to try for the first time tonight.

"I'm okay."

"Well, if you need anything, my door is right there and open."

He went to pull my door shut.

"Stop," I said.

"Stop what?"

"Can you leave mine open too?"

He nodded and pushed my door all the way against the wall.

Okay, I told myself. I'm going to be okay.

I looked across my bed and saw him sitting up in his, watching SpongeBob.

Now, for the last five years, those two doors have remained open. Sometimes I venture across to watch TV with him or borrow a book, but I mostly lay on my bed as he sits on his, and we just chat. Every night, he's the last person I see, and every morning, he's the first person to greet me.

For my tenth birthday, he didn't gift me anything. Instead, he showed me his secret hiding spot. He had told me about its existence for years, and I was shocked to find it was hidden in plain sight. There's a window overlooking the landing between our rooms, just above the purple rug Gigi called her Prince rug. I never put much thought into this particular window considering the old house has dozens of them.

But this window led out to a flat portion of the roof, out of sight from the concerned neighbors who might not take kindly to two kids playing on top of a third-story roof.

"Welcome to Lucky's Lair," he said proudly. "I'll share it with you, but it's still going to be Lucky's Lair."

I stepped out onto the roof and couldn't believe this hideaway had been here the whole time. The rooftop gently sloped beneath my feet. On either side of us, two steep slants showed us the shingled exteriors of our respective rooms. Symmetrical in design, the roofs looked like mirrored mountains overhead.

"Maybe we call it Maya's Valley?"

"Maybe I put a padlock on the window."

"Would that work?"

"I could try," Lucky said, sitting and leaning against the side where his bedroom was. I followed suit on my end, trying to ignore the empty space beyond the edge. His comfort up here dazzled me, something I admired and worked toward. I'd eventually find comfort in Lucky's Lair, but never enough to claim it as my own.

A guardrail would be nice, I thought. A bird flew from beneath us and landed overhead. I knew there was a weathervane above our rooms, but I never saw it up close. This was the source of the occasional screech that accompanied me during my sleep. I'd grown so used to it that I'm not sure I could sleep without its heinous sound.

Rusted green from top to bottom, it looked like it was placed there by the home's original owner.

"1866," Poppy told anyone who knocked on the door. From the mailman to trick-or-treaters. "Our people have been here since the beginning."

At its base, were its directionals—N, S, E, and an absent West, surely lost in a storm. There was an ornamental arrow above the incomplete letters, and above the arrow, a tarnished green fish. This copper carp was slightly askew, regardless of its direction. With a gust of wind, the fish was heading for the clouds, and with another, he was dipping back down toward his death against the pavement—a horrible demise for a fish flying for over 150 years.

Over the years, the majority of Lucky's and my most important conversations happened out here. On summer days, he'd wait for me to wake up, and then we'd head for Lucky's Lair. He usually fixed himself coffee and was itching to smoke by the time I got going. The first time he pulled out his smoke, I was appalled.

"Is that a cigarette?"

He was equally sickened that I would ask such a question.

"Ew. No. I'm not a monster."

I knew most mornings it took a lot of restraint for him not to go out there and start his day without me, joyfully smoking in the wind. But we had our routine, and he respected that. I was needy, and he knew it.

Since Mom died, 30 minutes of consecutive sleep was rare. Dreams of her—ordinary things like her hands pushing a grocery cart, her fingers turning the volume up in the car, her palm open, waiting on me to pass her some Skittles—were enough to jolt me awake.

When I did finally sleep a dreamless sleep, my first night getting eight straight hours, I woke up mumbling the same word, over and over again.

*Destiny…*

*Destiny…*

"Destiny…"

It was like I had never heard the word before. Like it had been gifted to me by some supreme being.

Lucky noticed that I'd finally risen and called across the way. He was going to grab more coffee, he announced. He'd meet me on the roof. When he did, I was still bundled in my blanket, wordless, staring at the spotless blue sky.

Lucky crouched and stepped through the window.

"Shoulda got you a cup, huh? You good?"

*Destiny…* The word slipped from one side of my head to the other. *Destiny…*

"Nice to see you finally got a good night's sleep."

"Good's not the word. I feel like I'm back from the dead."

Poor choice of words, but I still had that foggy morning brain.

"Back?" Lucky raised a brow. "You still look like shit."

We sat down as the sun joined us. A train passed in the distance. Kids chatted on the sidewalk below. I stared up at the clouds, not something I usually cared to do. Lucky lit his bud and joined me.

I think you see what you want to see in the sky. The clouds are a universal personality test, not to be taken too seriously. But there, at the center of the blue, were two long curved clouds that met on their ends to form sideways ovals. Then, strangest of all, a small dot of a cloud in its center.

"Look," Lucky pointed up. "An eye."

Tingles sprouted across my body.

"Cool," I pulled my blanket tighter.

"Super cool," Lucky took another puff, and our eye cloud was gone.

Silence returned.

I'm not a morning person, Lucky knows this. But he also knew me well enough to tell that something was different today. There was a strange air I carried around me and I wanted it to leave. Thoughts swirled around my head, trying to find their way out.

"You goo—"

"Destiny," I said, cutting him off.

"What?"

I shook my head. "Nothing. I'm good."

Lucky sat up. "Why did you just say that?"

Why did I just say that?

I tried to slow down and make sense of my thoughts and what I was trying to say. I tried to remember what happened in my dream, hoping that maybe it would contain an explanation. But it was already long gone. I read somewhere that the longer you stay in your bed after you wake up, the more likely you are to remember your dreams. Something about blood flow to the brain or something, I don't know. I never tried it but suddenly wished I had.

Whatever happened was lost by now.

"I think…" I paused, hearing the words forming in my head. Where did these thoughts come from? They felt foreign, and yet, I hungered to speak them out loud…

"I want you to call me Destiny."

The weathervane groaned overhead. Wind slid across my forearm, sending chills across my skin. Lucky's eyes narrowed. He peered at me like I was a stranger.

Maybe I was.

"Huh?" He raised an eyebrow.

"Destiny," I said it more confidently this time. "I want a new name."

Lucky scoffed, but then no more than a second later, shrugged like he suddenly understood.

"Always trying to be me."

"What?"

"Giving yourself a fresh start, I get it," he took another pull then tried to speak through the smoke circling his mouth. "But I did it first," he coughed.

Sure.

For clarification, Lucky's real name is, or was, Jackson. Some people in the family used to call him Tre because he was the third consecutive Jackson Lane.

"Tragedy naming all y'all the same thing," I remember someone saying at the last reunion. I think it was Uncle

Ken or his son Jojo. It's hard to keep track of the Lanes, and honestly, I haven't bothered trying to remember everyone's name considering we only see them once every five years. "A damn tragedy, Tre."

Lucky puckered his lips around what was left of his blunt and pulled in deep until nothing but a red smolder remained. He exhaled, letting the smoke waft over his face like a nebulous mask.

"I know what you're trying to do, but be careful," he said.

I love Lucky more than anyone, but he has this habit of believing he's in sole possession of the world's absolute truth. He knows everything about everything, and worst of all, feels the need to impart his endless knowledge to others. And by others, I mean me.

"Careful about what?"

"I'm no psychologist…"

I know. You're 17.

"But I've done my fair share of reading…"

Here we go.

"And I think you might be dealing with a case of denial. It's the first stage of—"

"Grief. Yeah, I'm aware." I skimmed the funeral home pamphlets too.

"I'm just saying, maybe this *Destiny* thing is just you trying to—"

"Gigi died a week ago," I cut him off. "I think I'm allowed to grieve."

"Right. No! Absolutely. I'm just worried about you."

"Why?"

"Protective. I'm protective, that's all. I just don't want Destiny taking away my baby sister."

He stared at me like he wanted to say more. He didn't though, and I wish he had.

The rest of the summer sucked. There's no other way to say it. Each day was the same: rise, see Lucky across the Prince rug, join Lucky on the roof, say bye to Lucky as he headed to his boyfriend's house for the rest of the day. Usually I'd read some Angie Thomas, watch some anime, then listen to a lot of Phoebe Bridgers. Looking back, I probably shouldn't have listened to so much Phoebe Bridgers that summer.

"You know you can come to Low's, right?" Lucky would ask me every few days.

"What are you wearing?"

"Oh, this?" Lucky looked down. "I like stealing his shirts. They're kinda cute, right?"

"Pretty sure they're called jerseys, and no. Not cute. Not at all."

Lucky's slinky cigarette arms stuck out the sides of the blue basketball tank. With the number 55 outlined in yellow, a rainbow behind a mountainous cityscape, and the most ridiculous team name I'd ever seen, it was very Lucky.

"Nuggets?"

"Isn't it great?" he spun. "Basketball is so funny."

"Hilarious."

Lucky threw himself on my bed. His beanstalk limbs hanging over the sides.

"I don't know why you won't come. He's got a pool, and his mom makes the best chocolate chip cookies. They're soft but sturdy. A ton of chips and even a little bit of salt. They're next level. She doesn't even care if we smoke."

I nodded with no intention of leaving my room. Third-wheeling wasn't my idea of fun.

"Sounds like a blast. Maybe tomorrow."

I was never going there. Not tomorrow. Not ever. Even if a soft, sturdy, salty, extra-chippy cookie sounded perfect.

After Lucky left, Poppy made a few low-effort attempts to pull me from the attic, and when I say low-effort, I mean the absolute lowest of effort. When he saw me creep into the kitchen to grab some water, he tried to stall me by asking me to count how many apples we had left—a truly riveting task.

"Three, Pop."

"Hmm. Maybe we could run down to McFarlane's later and grab a few more."

"Maybe." I headed back up.

"You wanna watch this episode with me?"

I looked back at the TV. I don't know how it happened, but he'd become addicted to watching this slick-haired televangelist over the past year. Save for Christmas, Easter, and a certain graduation, I'd never seen him step foot in a church, but he longed for the mega one on the screen.

"We call these episodes?"

He shrugged. I waited for him to offer to change the channel, something I may have accepted. But no such offer came. I didn't blame him for his melancholy. We were all grieving in our own way. I preferred to do mine in the privacy of my room.

And so, back in the attic, it was just me and my thoughts, which I didn't have the strength to tell anyone, were getting increasingly dangerous.

I think we're all used to a sort of constant chatter in our heads, but this was worse. Way worse. All of my worst memories took a daily parade around the block of my brain. Whenever I tried to stop them or distract myself, they got louder. It's one thing when it's your voice, but it's something else entirely when you suddenly hear someone else's.

*Destiny*, a woman's voice trickled through my mind.

*Are you ready?* she whispered.

The wind whirled. My knees shook. I looked down and got dizzy.

I don't know how I got there, but suddenly I was standing on the edge of the roof.

Alone. I never go out there alone.

"Destiny?" The voice sounded familiar, but I didn't turn. "Maya!?"

I shook my head and looked back.

It was Lucky.

He held a chocolate cupcake with a single candle stuck atop it. The flame glimmered against his glossy eyes. Tears brimmed from the bottom of his eyelids.

My lips quivered as I fought back tears. Lucky stepped toward me, and I stepped for him. A gust of wind rushed between us, extinguishing the light on the cupcake.

"What's that for?"

"I didn't want you to think I forgot your birthday. Was just trying to surprise you."

Looks like the only person who forgot was me.

I grabbed the cupcake and threw it off the roof.

I felt like I might collapse, but Lucky caught me. I wept and he held me, coughing back tears of his own.

"I'm so sorry," the words poured from me.

This place was reserved for our early-morning and late-night chats. This was our secret, sacred spot, and I desecrated it.

"I wasn't going to…I don't know how I…" I couldn't complete a sentence.

I swore I wasn't thinking about the leap. I told him and myself that I wasn't thinking about the concrete 30 feet below.

I promised.

"I promise you, that wasn't what that was."

I swore.

"I swear. Don't tell Poppy."

I lied.

The thoughts invaded my mind. There was a war going on inside, and I didn't know which side I was on. I pictured the leap and its inevitable outcomes. The only thing that varied was how many bones were broken and how long it took me to bleed out.

"Please don't tell Poppy. Please."

Lucky nodded, silently promising. We both knew it would crush Poppy. He couldn't handle this right now.

"I'll figure this out."

"*We'll* figure this out," he hugged me tighter, pain and promise balanced on his gentle voice. "Both of us."

I don't know if we've figured it out. Weeks have passed and we haven't talked about it since. I think we're both trying to pretend it didn't happen. We've had our rooftop chats, but they've felt tainted. I feel like I messed up what used to be our special space. Even though it's just the two of us there, the memory of that moment lingers. It might look like there's only two of us up there, but I know better.

I look over my shoulder and press my fingers against the chills on my neck. I know someone's watching me.

Go away, go away, go away.

I try to ward off the invisible watcher, but she doesn't take kindly to my requests.

She moves closer, making her presence unquestionable. She turns herself from a hovering shadow into a pressing one, making her way closer and closer until she's wrapped around me like a blanket.

*Destiny…*

*Destiny…*

Until I take a deep breath, reminding myself who I am.

"Destiny."

I speak my new name aloud. Finally, she lets me breathe.

# chApteR 2

**AT THE CENTER OF MY** mind, I see the golden pen.

I try to focus only on the pen, floating in endless black space. It's simple, free of any ornate design, just as I remember it in the backseat of Gigi's car.

I try to find this hidden pen in my head whenever I'm scared or sad in hopes of settling myself. I've been doing this off and on since the day it disappeared. Problem is, I don't always remember it's there. On my worst of days, the days when one bad thing leads to another and the most poisonous of thoughts are there the whole time, the golden pen is nowhere to be found. It's on these days, thoughts layer atop thoughts, and it's not until I'm tucked in bed, and the storm has settled that I even remember how to find it.

I take a deep breath, and another, and another, until it starts to take shape right in the middle of my brain. I reach up into the black space and press my fingers around its barrel. I inhale and exhale, feeling the pen in my hand, until the rest of my body is gone and only my hand and the pen remains.

With the pen in hand, I watch the world pass by without a thought. All the things that were wrong on the outside world might still be wrong when I return, but I'm not actively making them worse with my mental narration. In giving up control, in just being with the golden pen, I feel stronger than ever.

I know it's weird. I don't expect you to understand unless you've found your version of the golden pen, too. I like to think everyone's got a hiding place nestled at their core that certain things help them access. In fact, it might be the only thing we all have in common. My guess is we all picture something unique to us, if we picture something at all. But maybe if we all found our golden pens, and (this is important) never forgot how to find them, things might not be as crazy as they are now.

"Maya," Pop calls from downstairs.

The sun beats down on my face as I shield my eyes. I look across to Lucky's room.

He's gone.

I jump up from my bed, my heart thumping.

His comforter dips onto the floor. It's okay, I tell myself. He's probably downstairs getting coffee.

"Maya," he calls again, his voice weaker this time.

I intentionally ignore him. I'm committed to making him use my new name, just like everyone else. It'd been two months now, which feels like ample time to honor someone's wishes to be addressed by a new name.

But there's pain in his voice. While this is his new normal, it sounds heavier this morning.  I almost head downstairs to avoid the agony of hearing him say that other name again. But then he surprises me.

"Destiny…"

"Yeah, Pop?" I tap down the stairs and stick my head into the living room.

He doesn't know I'm here. His head sinks into the plush tomb that is his La-Z-Boy. His eyes are closed. His mouth gapes.

"You mind taking Tiger for a walking?"

Really? I clench my teeth. When did this become my responsibility?

I don't respond quickly enough, and Poppy interprets my hesitation accurately.

"You'd rather not." He lifts his head, blinking into action. "I get it."

I sigh. Poppy rises from his comfortable demise. Creaks and clicks from his joints echo across the hardwood floors.

"It's just," I try to find the best excuse. "Tiger doesn't listen to me."

Poppy scoffs. "Ha! Tiger doesn't listen to anyone. He's a turtle."

Maybe that was worth mentioning right away. You probably assumed Tiger was a dog, perhaps even a cat with that feline name? The Lanes seem like a strange enough family that they'd walk their cat. But nope. We're even weirder than the cat walkers. Tiger is a turtle. An orange-striped mud turtle who somehow has convinced this family he needs a daily walk around the block.

I peek my head down the hall and into the kitchen. I don't go in there often anymore. The lights are out. It's silent.

"Where's Lucky? He likes walking Tiger."

Poppy waddles toward the corner of the living room where Tiger's cage sits and stinks up the house. "If it's that much of an inconvenience, I'll do it."

It wasn't the worst idea. The only person getting less sun and exercise in this house than me is Poppy. He used to spend his mornings in the backyard garden, then in the afternoon he'd walk to the library, always stopping at Mrs. Ward's garden along the way. His nights consisted of cooking, using veggies from his journey, usually inspired by whatever he read that day. If it was an Agatha Christie mystery, we'd get something like cucumber finger sandwiches inspired by Miss Marple. If he was diving into some Stephen King, we'd get treated to Carrie's Blood Beet Salad.

Now, he's a new person. A new *old* person. Gigi's death aged him at least a decade. He seldom moves from his La-Z-Boy and meals are usually every man for themselves. The channel never changes from its megachurch programming, which only reminds me of that night and the horrible months leading up to it.

There was a time when Poppy never watched TV, let alone some millionaire ministry bullshit. His Motown Classics collections used to overflow from this home, oozing into every corner. Marvin, Stevie, and when he was feeling especially freaky, Rick, would quake the floorboards until, whether you realized it or not, you were dancing.

The house didn't dance anymore. Dust settled in the cracks that used to be full of music. Like me and Poppy, this old wooden house was on the rapid decline.

Shopping bags became trash bags that piled up by the doorways that no one took out upon exiting. The other day (I haven't told anyone this—I'm almost too embarrassed to), I'm pretty sure I found a cockroach.

Maybe it wasn't a cockroach. I'm not a bug expert, but it was gross, that much I know. This thing was a bone-white, jittery little monster that wasn't particularly thrilled that I spotted it. I was sitting on the toilet when I saw it speed-crawling across the bathroom tiles coming directly for me. I didn't think, I didn't scream. I just stood, it tried to turn and flee, but I stomped.

*Splat.*

This thing had way more blood than I thought its body could carry. I promptly cleaned it and tried to forget about it. I prayed it was an isolated incident, and so far, so good.

Trash bag Jenga towers definitely wouldn't have been acceptable under Gigi's rule. Mom made this place sparkle. Even when she was sick, she had no tolerance for filth. This ancient Victorian was her pride and joy and dust was never welcome. Her great-great-great-greatest grandfather built it with his bare hands when the Lanes moved from the South.

For generations, no roach would have made it past the sidewalk.

I walk across the family room, past piles of old Courier Posts, and the plastic bag of empty cans. Coors Lite. That's new. Beneath Poppy's bookshelf is a playpen full of toys— a plastic ball, a jingly-rope, and a plush that looks like a cheeseburger. I don't know how I'm the only person in this house that thinks it's strange that we've got an entire playpen for this turtle. I lean down and scoop up the shelled-back bowling-ball of a beast. I swear this thing gets heavier every time I pick him up, despite a strict diet of carrots and arugula. With Tiger in tow, I head for the door. Poppy slumps back into his tomb with a plop.

"Not so fast."

I turn back.

"Don't forget his leash."

Pop tosses the leash and I catch it midair with my free hand. Calling it a leash is honestly a stretch. What we've got here is a long white shoelace fit for a giant's boot. Why such a sized lace exists, I couldn't tell you. The Lanes are a tall people, but we're no O'Neal's. Why Tiger the turtle needs this string to serve as his leash is beyond me. The old turtle taps out at a whopping 1.1 MPH and I've yet to see him make a run for it. I place Tiger down and tie the shoelace around his neck in a loose knot. The extra cord makes it look like he's wearing a little bow tie which is almost cute. I roll my eyes. Who the hell walks their turtle?

And where is Lucky?

Just as I reach the door, I hear footsteps behind me.

Not a second too soon, Lucky makes his way down the stairs, his hair bouncing with each step.

"Yo."

He wears another one of Low's retro jerseys and is accompanied by a noticeable skunkish scent.

"Morning." I look into Lucky's bloodshot eyes.

He smiles. He knows I'm on to him. I just hope Poppy isn't.

"I should call the feds," Poppy's brows crease.

My heart sinks.

"Pop, I'm sorry," Lucky stutters. "I just—"

"That damn jersey should be against the law. *Jordan?* On the Wizards!? We should've known this timeline was cursed the minute he left Chicago."

Poppy breaks into a laugh as Lucky nervously joins him.

Lucky shrugs, his bony shoulders grazing his curls. "Yeah, you know, basketball things. Nothing better to wear in this heat."

"Well, thanks for gracing us with your presence," Poppy turns up the TV. "Now you can both take Tiger."

"No, I can handle it."

"You sure?" Lucky asks.

Poppy's eyelids tighten. He starts to sniff.

"What is that godawful smell?"

Lucky steps his slippers past me, straight for the door.

"Great idea. We'll be back soon."

Lucky turns the knob and pulls me outside. We make it down the front steps and I place Tiger on the pavement.

"Someone had a nice morning," I say.

"Is it that obvious?"

"It smells like it's growing from your armpits."

"When did you become an expert on weed?"

"I live with you."

"You better not be smoking."

I shrug. Lucky puffs his chest, doing his best Sheriff Big Bro act.

"You're not answering. Why aren't you answering?"

"I smoked one time with Cooper and Iyana after school."

"Cooper? Parker's little brother. Oh, hell no. I hate that kid."

"I didn't even get high."

"Then you're not doing it right. You gotta hold it in when you inhale. Feel it at the pit of your chest before you blow out."

"You're telling me not to smoke while also giving me a tutorial. Which is it?"

"I just know how you are. You're like me. You'll get stuck."

A chill tiptoes across my shoulder. Like someone's brushed a feather down my spine.

"What do you mean, *stuck*?"

"I mean, like, we both overthink things. Next thing you know, you've dipped into a pocket of infinity. Or that's what they feel like to me. One time I was so high I swore I was trapped. It was like I lived a thousand years in twenty minutes."

"Sounds horrible." I think about the possibility of trying on new lives but also being able to come out unscathed. "But also a teeny bit amazing?"

"It was."

"I'm no pro, but that doesn't sound like weed to me."

"Oh, I should have clarified that part. It wasn't. But the principle of the matter remains. You don't need that shit."

We stop in front of our neighbor's house so Tiger can drop a steamer. His little turds look like baby sausage links and smell like decaying fish. I nearly gag.

"I can't pick that up."

"Of course, you can."

"You do it," I cover my mouth. "He's your turtle."

"Turtles can't belong to any man."

"Cool. Pick up the shit."

Lucky was right. Technically, Tiger wasn't his turtle, and he wasn't even the family's. My first winter at Gigi's, there was a big snowstorm and school was cancelled for about a week. We all decided to go sledding down by River Road when Gigi spotted the striped shell in the sea of white. The little guy was almost frozen to death. Poppy pointed out that he was a striped mud turtle, not native to New Jersey, meaning he had to be somebody's pet. After we posted about the turtle on Facebook and no one claimed him, he became yet another oddball outcast living under the Lane roof.

Lucky leans down and reaches for the turd with his bare hands.

"Ew!" I dry heave. "What are you doing?!"

He rips a few pieces of grass from the ground and sprinkles it atop the poo.

"Fertilizer. The turtle belongs to the Earth."

"You ripped grass to grow future grass. Nice. Not sure that's how it's supposed to work."

We turn from Lincoln Lane and make a right onto Jefferson Avenue.

Wind whistles overhead, shaking the leaves on the birch trees. Silence lingers for a second too long between us. Neither of us is too fond of silence these days.

"So, you ready?" Lucky asks.

"For…?"

"School. Big, bad high school."

I shrug.

Lucky keeps going. "You do your summer reading?"

"Two months ago. *The Odyssey*, snooze. *Romeo and Juliet*, pretty fucked up. You?"

"Haven't started. *Heart of Darkness* and *Song of Solomon*."

"Lots of death. Fun. What have you been reading all this time?"

"*Witches, Sluts, & Feminists*. Did you know that, pretty much throughout history, anytime a woman was sexually liberated or even just, like, a little different from the small-town housewife, the white dudes in power would accuse them of being a witch that way they could burn them at the stake?"

"Checks out," I nod.

"Super fucked up. Then I've been making my way back through *Quotations from Chairman Mao*. Everyone really needs to read it. Did you know the Black Panthers—"

"Used to carry their little red copies around?" I break in. "Yes. I did. You told me the first three times you read it."

"And people really have the audacity to call us radical? They have no idea!"

"When are you going to start the books you actually have to read?"

"The books you *want* to read are actually the books you *have* to read."

"Here you go." I roll my eyes.

"I dunno," he shrugs. "I think I'm just gonna watch the movies."

"That's not gonna work."

"It's worked so far. *To Kill a Mockingbird, Lord of the Flies, Gatsby.*"

"Please tell me you didn't watch the one with Jay Z music."

"Don't forget Lana!" he starts crooning. "*Will you still love me, when I'm no longer—*"

"Okay, great. Thanks."

"*…Young and beautiful,*" he does this sort of whispery, raspy thing that's not half bad.

"There's no movie for *Song of Solomon*," I inform him.

"Yeah, there is," he says firmly. "With Oprah and Donald Glover."

"Danny Glover. And no. Still wrong. You're thinking about *Beloved.*"

"No, no, no. The one with Whoopi."

"Yeah, even more wrong. That's the *Color Purple*. Alice Walker, Toni Morrison. They are very different authors, and you are very disrespectful."

"You don't know what you're talking about. I'ma look it up."

"Please do."

Lucky whips out his phone and starts tapping away.

I glance over and see him Google it.

"And?"

He slides his phone back in.

"I got no service."

I laugh.

He hates when I'm right.

"How do you know all this shit?"

"I have no friends and a computer. A dangerous combination."

"You've got friends. There's Cooper…"

Cooper is not my friend after he pulled his penis out in the woods a few months back. I thought things were going well between us before he introduced his little dick without proper invitation. As already noted, Lucky wasn't a fan of Cooper. Weed was one thing, penises were another. There was no need to risk the mortal injury of an incoming freshman at the hands of my unpredictable brother. Plus, if I'm being honest with myself, Cooper wasn't really my type. His older sister is way cuter.

"Iyana…" Lucky continues.

Iyana really took to Cooper's weed. We used to swap *Amulet* books and SpongeBob memes, but we've had less in common these days. No judging though, she seems happy enough. I just don't really feel anything when I've tried it.

I get super sleepy, and my throat gets dry and itchy. Not exactly my idea of fun.

"There's me. And oh, obviously, Tiger."

He listed three humans: two aren't my friends and one is my brother.

"Perfect. Yeah, I'll bring Tiger with me to the first day of class so I have someone to sit with at lunch."

"Shut up. Don't we have the same lunch period?"

"4th."

"5th. Fuck."

"Don't worry. Didn't want to sit with your friends anyway. When was the last time Low showered?"

"Last night. With me." Lucky gyrates and does the old wrap-your-arms-around-yourself-thing to make it look like he's making out.

"Charming."

"Aren't like, ten kids coming over from your class? What about Frankie? Or that girl Chanel?"

"Frankie got held back a year ago and Chanel's going to Catholic. I don't like my class. I don't know how this is news to you."

Lucky scowls, racking his brain. Apparently, my lack of friends is indeed news to him. And it's making him more nervous for me than he already was.

"How are you doing, though? Like, overall."

"It's been two months," I say blankly.

"What's that mean?"

"65 days, if we're being exact."

"Oh shit, let's turn." Lucky spots something ahead.

But a quick pivot wouldn't be so easy. The thing about turtles is, you can't just tug on 'em and they'll follow. Their courses are set long before their steps. I look to where Lucky nervously averted his gaze.

Mrs. Ward has already spotted us and is waving us forward maniacally.

Great.

Before you meet Mrs. Ward, there's a few things you should know. She's our small town's resident gardener. All the hanging plants along Centre Street, all the small squares of public space, that's her domain. In suit, her home garden is the envy of people who care about these things. I am not one of them. But Poppy on the other hand, he gawks at her cantaloupes. He goes on and on about the girth of her zucchinis. It teeters on becoming sexual and it makes me very uncomfortable.

As a personal rule, I try not to talk shit on anyone's looks. We've all got our own weird shit going on. BUT…

All that said, Mrs. Ward's dental hygiene practices look like they've been taken from a pamphlet about George Washington. If I didn't know any better, I'd swear her teeth were made of wood. There's a small part of me that likes to imagine she grew them in her garden.

"Jackson! Maya!"

Lucky politely nods his head, "Mrs. Ward."

She smiles. I can practically hear her teeth creak.

She looks to me, waiting for me to acknowledge her existence.

I don't. She's going to learn like everyone else.

"Lucky. Destiny." I point to each of us respectively.

"I'm so sorry, dear. Every time I see you two, I feel like I've stepped into a time machine. You're both body doubles of your parents."

"I guess he was a pretty handsome guy," Lucky winks.

"No doubt about it! And so well-spoken, too, just like you! Ya know, both of your parents were so sweet with my Johnny before he passed."

"I'm so sorry to hear that," Lucky says.

I nudge him.

"I mean, the Mr. Ward dying part," says Lucky. "It's nice to know our parents were nice."

"And well-spoken," I add, hoping she catches my sarcasm.

After losing someone I love, I should know better. But I have to admit, I'm not sorry Mr. Ward is dead. It didn't take a Black History major to see that fucker was racist. The confederate flag bumper sticker on his F-150 did that. And if that wasn't enough, he had this stare that I still can't shake from my mind. He'd glare at us through his window, as if he was tracking our movements, mapping out what went wrong in the world that led him into a town where we could possibly be his neighbors, and wondering what could be done to fix this.

"How's your grandfather holding up?" she asks.

I clench my fist but resist the urge to clock her timber jaw.

There was a rumor I wasn't supposed to get wind of but overheard Lucky chatting about with Low one night when I was fake sleeping. Folks around town thought Poppy might be sleeping with Mrs. Ward. And we're not talking about something that started in the last 65 days since Gigi died. Or since Mr. Ward died, for that matter. We're talking about a long running, secret garden affair.

I don't believe it though. I refuse. I know Poppy used to be a player based on the black-and-white photos of him in suits with wide white collars sporting a giant smile to match. He was always with a different girl in each picture. I know for certain Mrs. Ward isn't his type because all of those girls had glossy white teeth.

"He's fine," I say sharply, hoping she interprets the not-so-subtle meaning behind my words, which is something like, *"Keep his name out of your oaky, splintery, rotten-ass mouth."*

Mrs. Ward looks to me and blinks. It's almost as though she's heard my thoughts, and they've stopped her in her tracks. When she opens her eyes, it seems as if she's frozen still. Her eyes stare dead into mine. I can only see the soulless center of her eyes. The glaze against the black. She's like a glitch.

I turn to Lucky and in tandem, so does Mrs. Ward. She blinks and goes back to her best version of normal.

"Did your grandfather get the fruit flowers I sent over? My melons are way better than those Edible Arrangements!"

"He did," Lucky says. "Those cantaloupes were gone in seconds."

"Oh!" Mrs. Ward shudders like a ghost just shimmied through her. "Speaking of pumpkins, I've—"

"No one said anything about pumpkins," I whisper to Lucky.

"I've got the most *corpulent* pumpkins in all the Garden State. You two have got to take one. No! Take two! Take two."

"Did she just say corpulent?" I whisper to Lucky.

She turns around and starts plodding across the grass. Lucky looks down at me and shrugs.

"Thanks a lot, Mrs. Ward," Lucky says. "But what are we going to do with a pumpkin?"

Mrs. Ward's face contorts. The question's baffled her as though it were spoken in a foreign tongue. With her eyes uncomfortably wide, she laughs. It's a horrible, wheezing sound that shoots out in quick bursts, almost like a balloon being repeatedly deflated and pinched.

"So many things. Pumpkin pie, pumpkin bread. You can grill it, you can mash it. Roasted pumpkin seeds. Pumpkin chili. *My pumpkin soup is to die for.*"

"That's really nice of you, Mrs. Ward." Lucky taps Tiger with the tip of his slipper. "But we just ate."

Tiger gets the message and starts to crawl ahead. What a brilliant little creature.

"Not to mention," I add for good measure. "Tiger's allergic to pumpkins."

Mrs. Ward gasps and covers her mouth.

"Yup," I nod. "Poppy dropped a seed in his playpen when he was a baby and his whole head inflated. Honestly, tragic. I can't imagine what a drip of soup might do to him. His shell would probably start dissolving or something."

"Tragic indeed," Mrs. Ward slowly nods her head. "Next

time you two come by without the turtle, you each get one plump pumpkin a piece."

"That would be amazing," Lucky says. "Thanks a lot, Mrs. Ward!"

Tiger tugs ahead and we follow. Once we're officially out of earshot, the laughter we've been holding in bursts at the seams. Tears drip down Lucky's cheeks.

"Allergic to pumpkins!?" he yelps. "And who the fuck grows pumpkins in New Jersey?! Listen, I'll tell you who grows pumpkins…"

He pauses, slowly regaining his composure.

"Witches. That's who grows pumpkins."

I roll my eyes. "You love making shit up in your head. Weren't you just talking about how women were labeled witches whenever they decided to do their own thing?"

"Yes, but this is different and that doesn't mean witches don't exist." I laugh, not sure if he's serious.

"You gotta admit there's something witchy about her."

"I mean, she's a little strange. I'd even hear a debate that something supernatural is going on with her teeth—but just because she prefers plants to people doesn't automatically make her a witch."

"You keep talking like that, and people are gonna start thinking you're in a coven."

"There are worse things people could think," I shrug.

We make our way deeper down Jefferson Avenue when Tiger suddenly beelines across a patch of dead crabgrass. He tugs forward, forcing me to tighten my grip.

"Whoa there, bud."

He's never done this before.

We both look up at the house Tiger appears to be lunging for and…

A chill slides down the back of my neck. My stomach starts to boil.

I look up and my eyes land upon 55 Jefferson Avenue.

Everyone in town knows this house. And everyone in town has a different story about it.

With chipped yellow paint, it's almost an alternate-reality version of our home. This version of home exists in a world where there's no Poppy to apply fresh paint every couple of years and there's no Gigi to maintain the defense between the inside and the out. Green ivy engulfs the side, crawling up its gray turrets. The roof is blanketed in broken shingles, and its precisely pointed molding looks more like sharpened teeth. With broken bones and a faulty foundation, the house dips forward, looming over us like a growling beast. If 55 were such a monster, thankfully it's blind. Just above the porch overhang, its two windows that stare down like empty eyes are boarded shut.

"You know that's the same as our house, right?" Lucky points out.

"I've never stared long enough to think about it."

"The same architect did most of the houses in town. Every few are exact models. If you walked through that house, you'd know exactly where everything was."

The bubbling in my stomach starts to work its way up my chest.

"Gross," I say.

I pull back on Tiger, but he's intent on crawling forward, toward the house.

"That's gotta be a bad omen," Lucky chuckles. "Who's gonna tell him? You don't wanna go in there, buddy."

"Can you grab him?"

He laughs. "Too scared to even step on the grass?"

"No, I just—"

Lucky dramatically leaps onto the lifeless yellow grass and pretends to faint upon touching down.

"I can't go on! Call for help!"

"Very funny." I bring my thumb to my lip, nervously gnawing at my nail.

*Ouch.*

My thumbnail slits the bottom of my lip. I dab my tongue against the fresh gash, tasting the metallic sting of my own blood. I pull my sleeve to my lip, blots of red instantly taking to my white shirt.

Suddenly I'm dizzy. It's not the sight of my blood that makes me feel off. It's that now, at this moment, I feel the familiar feeling of someone watching me stronger than ever before.

I try to steady myself, taking in my surroundings.

Through the leaves of a front yard tree, my eyes land upon the attic window—the only one on the old house that's not boarded.

Two eyes look down at me through the glass.

*Destiny,* a voice slips through my head.

My knees shake. I feel my feet give out and I start to fall. Lucky catches me.

"Whoa! You good?"

The cut on my lip throbs. With each pump of blood to the fresh wound, the world around me pulsates in a white blur.

I'm afraid to look back up at the attic window, but I do anyway.

It's empty.

There's nobody standing there. There are no eyes there staring at me.

Lucky scoops Tiger with one arm and throws the other around my shoulder. As soon as he's there, the weight of being watched goes away. The white blur clouding my vision vanishes. I take a deep breath, and another, starting to feel better.

"What happened?"

I try to find the right words, but my raw thoughts blurt out.

"Someone lives there."

Still slightly dizzy, I close my eyes, hoping to regain my balance—

And there she is. Not the two eyes from the attic, but Gigi. Not the smiling version I miss, but the Final Face, bubbling at the mouth. My eyes jolt open. I can't claim a second of peace.

"I just..." I fade.

"You look like shit. You haven't eaten. Probably haven't had any water, either. Let's go back to the house and take it easy."

We head back down Jefferson, turn on Lincoln, and cut behind the church before seeing the sign for Alexander Avenue. With each step closer to home, I start to feel more like myself.

"Don't tell Poppy, okay?"

Lucky nods in agreement. "Nothing to tell."

When we get back, Poppy's asleep at his tomb. Lucky guides me to the couch and throws a blanket over me. I insist I'm feeling better, but he's having none of it. He tucks the blanket around my legs, effectively mummifying me. He fixes me a giant glass of water before settling down himself. "Today's officially an *Us* Day. I'm gonna call Low and tell him today belongs to my sister."

"No, it's fine. I just—"

"Nuh-uh-uh! I'll hear none of it."

Poppy's ministry channel is droning away on the TV. The preacher is on the tail end of a sermon about Jesus and the American Way.

"My daughter, you know little Scarlett, six-years-old, she asked me where Jesus lived, and I had to laugh. The easy answer is heaven. But I told her that a piece of the Lord lives in all of our hearts. I also mentioned that, if Jesus came back to save us all today, he might not be in such a rush to return. I reckon there's a few ranches in Texas he'd love to check out before returning to the Right Hand."

The massive congregation laughs.

"Hell no. Absolutely not." Lucky picks up the remote and tosses it to me. "Find us something good to watch. I'm gonna go pick up some panzies."

I instantly start to salivate. Panzies (short for panzarottis) are a South Jersey delicacy. Imagine a deep-fried pizza turnover, and then whatever you pictured in your head, trust my word that it's 5 to 10 times better than that, depending upon where you got yours. They're crunchy, a tad sweet, and if you value your life in these here South Jersey parts, don't you ever compare it to a weak-ass calzone. This is precisely what the doctor would never order. Eat too many of these, and you'll die at 40. But today, a healing panzarotti is exactly what my body needs.

I surf for less than a minute and settle.

"Are you judging my apples on what they ought to be?" The talking tree slaps Dorothy on the wrist.

I smile, quoting the treemen quietly to myself. "She was hungry! She was hungry!"

*The Wizard of Oz.*

I've lost count of how many times I've watched this. Mostly with Mom. This was her favorite. She knew every word and would test out different versions of every character until she perfected their voices. The Wicked Witch was her finest work.

"*Here, Scarecrow. Wanna play ball?*" She had mastered her delivery, complete with the diabolical cackle.

You ever have memories that you're not sure are real? I forget most of my childhood (and for good reason), but sometimes certain things come sneaking back in dreams.

I remember this one time, I was no older than six or seven, when we cuddled in Gigi's bed and as she was flipping through the channels, we caught Dorothy & Co. on cable. We owned the VHS, DVD, and Blu-ray, but there was always something special about catching it in the wild. Knowing there were a few thousand people watching it at the same time as us, experiencing similar emotions with us in unison felt spiritual in ways I couldn't yet articulate.

But this night, I fell asleep early, and the words from the screen trickled into my ears. It was the first time I realized that dreams were more than just random moving images in my head. They were a reflection of whatever was going on in my mind that I couldn't express anywhere else.

One second I was with Gigi and then suddenly I was on the Yellow Brick Road. On the horizon, there was nothing but lush green fields meeting the robin egg blue sky. Ahead and behind me was a uniform plain. But just like the movie, if you looked close enough, you could see the line where the road met the painted backdrop, destroying the illusion of a land waiting on the other end of the rainbow. But even though I saw this line where the set turned to canvas, a clear marker between real and fake, I couldn't reach it.

The road went on forever. I ran ahead, trying to find someone or something. I loved Oz but preferred it from the comfort of my couch. The cornstalks stood motionless beside me, no wind to ruffle them to life. I needed a way out. Maybe, with just a few more steps, Judy Garland or the fraudulent Wizard would be there to help me. But there was no one. Nothing. No glowing green city of salvation. Just me and the endless road.

I started to panic. I yelled to myself, reminding my sleeping self that this was a dream.

Wake up, I thought. I could still vaguely feel Mom's warm imprint against my sleeping face, and yet I was here. Split between worlds with no exit.

There had to be a way out. With no Scarecrow on a pole to give me ambiguous directions, I had to forge my own path. I went off the brick road, cutting across the cornfields. Their yellow tassels towered over my head. Within a few steps, I was completely surrounded by green. Just keep going, I told myself. There's got to be something. I ran, faster and faster, until *CRUNCH*—

My foot stepped into what felt like brittle stone.

"My," a voice wheezed out beneath me. "Uhhh."

I looked down. My foot rested in the center of a skeletal torso. Its stewy insides caked against my shoe. I pulled back, a piece of freshly-broken rib getting stuck to my shoe.

I tried to scream, but nothing came out.

I tried to turn away but I couldn't.

The body's midsection down to its toes was exposed bone enwrapped in collapsed veins.

From the body's clavicle and up, its skin remained. But barely.

With the body's arms splayed out, dozens of silent crows pecked at the remaining flesh. Their bloody mouths opened to caw and their wings flapped relentlessly, but no sound came forward. Noticing me, they moved in a dazed blur, rising above, and closing in. As their wings overlapped, they appeared to multiply until their stark black overtook the green of the stalks.

Below me, in the center of it all, was her inescapable face—brown eyes wide, terrified, begging to be saved.

My mother.

Not Gigi, the grandmother I rightfully call Mom.

But my birth mother. The one who ran.

"My…" her voice scratched out.

"Mom!" I yelled. The chorus of crows suddenly sounded, drowning out my scream.

Covered in sweat, I leapt awake to safety.

Gigi pulled me close, immediately reminding me, repeating to me, that I was safe.

She asked me about the nightmare, but I told her I couldn't remember it. I lied. It was easier not to explain.

You'd think I'd hate this movie now, but I can't. I love it more now than ever. In a weird way, that nightmare woke me up. It showed me that other worlds are real. They're like Dorothy's Oz or Lucy's Narnia, but they're easier to get to. At the risk of sounding mildly fucked up, there's a part of me that loves the occasional nightmare. They pull back the curtain on things real life is too afraid to show us in the light.

The front door squeaks open and Lucky walks back in. With the panzies in a greasy white bag, he takes one look at the TV.

"Nope, nope, nope. Absolutely not," he snatches the remote and flicks the channel. "I'd rather watch Evil Church. I'm not ready for Oz and I don't know if I'll ever be."

I can't blame him. Every second of this movie holds another memory of Gigi.

At the smell of the panzarottis, Poppy perks right up.

"Rottis?" there's hope in his voice.

"Oh, shit," Lucky says. "Sorry. You were sleeping, and I wasn't sure if you were eating these again."

"You're right," Poppy slumps. "I shouldn't."

Lucky reaches into the bag and pulls out one for me and one for himself. But the bag's not empty. He smiles, then with a theatric plunge of his arm, he digs into the bag and throws a final panzie at Poppy. Our old man beams.

"Obviously, I got you one," Lucky crunches into his. "I'm not a monster."

We all eat. My movie choice is outvoted 2-1 in favor of a documentary about how eating cows is killing not only us, but in turn, devastating the Earth. I'll tell ya—real escapism at its finest. As soon as Poppy's panzarotti is gone, he passes back out, remnants of orange grease-stained into his gray stubble.

We spend the rest of the day on the couch rewatching episodes of Neon Genesis until Lucky tells me to give him 15 then meet him on the roof. I try to straighten up Pop's cave. I gather the Rite-Aid bags he's been using as trash bags then take them outside through the front door to the cans in the back. I toss them over the fence. I haven't used the backdoor or glanced at the backyard since Gigi died.

Progress has been made, but it's still a pigsty. I see another slithery roach making its way across the floor.

I pull off one of my Vans and get ready to strike, just as it slips between a crack in the floorboards. Okay, I see you. You're safe.

*At least for now.*

I finally make my way upstairs, past my grandparents' second floor, and into the attic. The steps in this old Victorian are dangerously steep and creak with any pressure. One slip down these mountainous slopes and there goes your neck.

I hear Lucky on the phone in his room.

"It's nothing to worry about," he whispers.

I turn the corner. His eyes go wide and he gasps.

"You scared the shit out of me," he almost drops the phone.

"Sorry?"

"All good. I'll be done in a sec."

I walk across the Prince rug and slide the window open.

"Wait for me," Lucky pokes his head out the door.

I pull back. He'd rather I didn't go out there alone anymore. I don't blame him.

He says bye to Low. "See you in the morning."

We head out the window, beneath the breaking sky. The rusty fish-vane grinds and whines above. We settle on the roof's flat section, and in tandem, we sit and lean against our shingled slopes.

The sky is streaked with wisps of orange, lavender, and pink. A pearly crescent moon hangs above us, its jagged points cutting through the color. I smile at the sky only summer can provide.

There's a beat of silence.

"Shit was kinda creepy, huh?"

It had been hours, but the chills return, crawling across the back of my arms. I know exactly what he's talking about.

"I was trying to forget."

But I can't. Scarier than the eyes or the weight that accompanied them was that voice in my head. It wasn't my own and yet, it was strangely familiar.

Lucky starts to smoke. He pulls in deep before exhaling.

"My dad wouldn't let me walk past that place." The smoke clears. He stares up at the sky. It almost looks like he's talking to the moon. He never talks about his dad so I lean in closer. I wanna hear this.

"*Ain't nothing but evil at 55,*" he puts on a deep voice, presumably impersonating his dad. "*Not worth going anywhere near there.* I didn't take it seriously. Still don't, honestly. But today, I'm not gonna lie, that was pretty weird."

Silence settles for a bit. I don't want to lose this moment. I think Lucky needs to talk about his dad, so I try to find my way back in.

"I heard there was a family there, back then? Didn't this lady have twins, and only one survived? She drowned one of them in a bathtub or something?"

"Not what I heard," Lucky shakes his head. "When my dad was a kid, it was a foster home. Ton of kids lived there. I'm telling you, like a dozen or something. Maybe more. They seemed happy, according to him. The foster parents were super Christian or something. They always are, right? Might have even been preachers. But they weren't the strict kind that didn't let their kids do anything. They were apparently pretty cool, or at least that's what the foster kids would tell all their classmates. They wanted their foster kids to really feel like their kids. Real kids. They played instruments, sports, everything…

"But this is where it gets weird. Nobody ever saw the mom. The dad could have run for mayor, though. He was this old white guy, super friendly. Everybody knew him. Some people said he was too friendly. He apparently *really* loved kids. Anytime someone said something bad about the parents, the foster kids would get crazy defensive. My dad ignored the rumors and figured they must be good people, the way the kids talked about them.

"So, it turns out, my dad was on the same baseball team as one of the foster kids. They became friends, started hanging out, you know. Then one day after practice, Poppy was supposed to pick up my dad and totally forgot. Completely forgot."

"Shocker." I nod.

"Gigi was still at work, so the kid invited my dad over to the house after practice."

"He went in there?"

"Listen, listen. Yeah. Everything seemed normal enough. The foster dad ordered everyone pizza. They said a prayer around the pizza box, but that was as weird as it got. Nothing crazy…

"But then, after they ate, dad being dad, asked his friend about their foster mom. She lived downstairs, they said. *In the basement.*"

I cross my arms, rubbing out the goosebumps.

"And, I know you don't really remember that much about my dad, but if there was something he wasn't supposed to do, he was going to do it," Lucky smiles.

"So dad asked where the bathroom was, even though he already knew. You been in one of these Victorians across town, and you've pretty much been in 'em all.

"So, surprise, surprise—dad didn't go to the bathroom. He went downstairs. To the basement."

Lucky stops. I notice the blunt in his hand shaking.

He stares up at the sickle knife moon as though it's being held to his lip. As though it's forbidding him from saying more.

"That's it?"

Lucky looks down at his shoes. He steps on a small pebble and scrapes it against the roof.

"He wouldn't tell me more. Whatever was down there changed him. He wasn't a scared kid. But I heard him tell Gigi that he never stopped being afraid after that."

I don't know what to say. I want more.

The story feels wildly incomplete.

We both soak in the silence. In the sunsetting reflection, Lucky's stubble looks like Poppy's grease-stained chin. It's funny how fast someone else's fears become our own, I think. Funny how fast we can transform into our parents.

"I don't know how word got out," Lucky suddenly goes

on. "Dad said it wasn't him. But the police raided 55 a few days later. Downstairs, beneath the floorboards were cement slabs. Beneath the slabs, pit after pit was piled up with bones. Small ones too. Kids. Babies."

My stomach churns.

"All over the basement wall, there were these strange markings. Little eyes with king crowns growing out of them. Some fucked up version of Basquiat or something. Some of the crowns were flipped, looking like tears streaming from the eyes. Some of them only had two points, looking like 'M's."

"So was the mom down there?"

"They never found the mom. But the old white mayor dad was locked up right away. Right before they came to arrest him, this crazy prick carved one of the crown eyes into his forehead like Marilyn Manson."

"Charles Manson."

"Yeah. That one. They've still got newspapers from the next day at the library. This dude is dripping blood in the pics."

"Gross."

"The guy tried to claim it wasn't him in court. He claimed it was all her. The ole' *she made me do it,* and he had nothing to do with it. Nobody even knows if she even existed. But he was definitely fucking nuts. Killed himself like a week or two after being locked up. Dad said he wished another inmate got to him first. They woulda tortured him if they found out what he did to those kids."

Lucky falls silent and turns to the stars.

I don't think, I just say the first thing that comes to my mind.

"Sounds like bullshit," I laugh.

Lucky looks me dead in the eye. His brows crease.

"You think it's true?" I ask, trying to backtrack.

"I know it's true. I told you, I read the articles."

"They online?"

"No. This wasn't national news. You weren't listening. They're only at the library."

Oh, I was listening. And that's why I don't think the story is true. It's bonkers. And something like this totally would have made its way beyond our little town.

But maybe there's a large part of me that doesn't want it to be true. Maybe I don't want to live in a world, or particularly a town for that matter, where something so horrible could possibly happen. I don't want to believe in evil like this. I prefer a world where there's more to the story.

But killing kids and collecting their bones? That seems pretty fucking evil.

I don't want to believe in it. I can't. I won't.

"Let's say this all actually happened. Why didn't they knock down 55?"

"Are you implying that I'm lying? I'm a liar?" Lucky's actually getting heated. "Are you saying my dad's a liar?"

"No, no, not at all. I mean, there just has to be more to it. That's all I'm saying."

Lucky scoffs. He's clearly pissed.

"Imagine being a kid, seeing something so fucked up, so

crazy that you can't tell anyone. And there's gotta be more to the story? You've gotta be kidding me. This fucked up my dad for his entire life. Kids died. I read it. With my eyes. I don't know what else you need to believe me."

This wasn't my intention. I don't want to fight with Lucky. We never fight, and this doesn't seem worth it.

"I do. I just—"

"Exactly," he cuts me off, venom in his voice.

"I don't know what's going on with you." Clearly, there's something else brewing in his mind, bubbling beneath the surface.

"We're all going through shit right now, *Destiny*," he puts some extra spin on my name, as though he's mocking me.

*Destiny*…she echoes through my mind. *Destiny*…

"Look, I don't want to fight with you," I say.

*Destiny*…the word whispers through the wind, slipping into my ear. *Destiny*…

That was out loud. That wasn't in my head.

"Did you hear that?"

Lucky grinds the pebble beneath his heel, clenching his jaw.

*Destiny*…a shiver passes over my body. I gotta go inside.

"I'm gonna head to bed," I announce.

I stand up and head for the window.

I'm almost there when he asks me something he's never asked before.

"You ever wonder why your mom left?"

I turn back. The question feels like a dagger pierced through my spine, jabbing into my heart.

"What?"

"You ever wonder why she ran away?"

"Wh-why would you ask me that?" I stutter.

I don't want to answer this. I don't want to think about it.

But the truth is, I think about it all the time. Not a day passes when I don't think about it. But that doesn't mean I wanted to talk about it.

"You ever think she's smarter than us?" Lucky goes on. "Getting away from Gigi and Poppy when she had the chance?"

"What are you even talking about?" I step back toward him. "You sound fucking nuts. It didn't have anything to do with them."

"It had *everything* to do with them. Shit, when was the last time Pop went out of his way for us? And I'm not talking about this new and depressed version. I'm talking way before Gigi died. It was all about that lame garden and Mrs. Ward."

I exhale and say nothing.

"Don't act dumb. Everyone knows about them. Why do you think Mr. Ward hated us so much?"

"Cause he was racist?"

"That. Yes. But also because our grandpa was fucking his wife."

"Enough, Lucky."

"There's no Mr. Ward. Now there's no Gigi. It's only a matter of time before their gardens combine. Then what happens to us?"

"That's not gonna—"

"Worst part is, I can't even completely blame him. I know no one wants to say anything bad about Mom since she died, but shit, we both know she wasn't a saint."

I feel blood rushing up to my head. My temples start pulsating. The cut on my lip starts to sting again. A harsh wind gusts across my buzzed head, and I'm almost certain it carries my name along with it.

*Destiny…*

The roof rattles and my knees quake. I reach back and grab onto the windowsill. Lucky tries to grip the shingles.

"We should go inside," my voice shakes.

Lucky looks up at me and I swear his eyes are not his own.

Whether it's a strange reflection of the summer sunset, or my fear getting the worst of me, his eyes look rolled back.

All white.

"*Another drink, another drink, another drink,*" he goes on. I can tell he's trying to do Gigi's voice. But it comes out sounding more like the Wicked Witch of the West's.

He doesn't look like himself. His shoulders start to hunch as his arms vibrate. It's like there's a beast burrowed beneath his skin that's itching to break free.

"Lucky?!"

He blinks and just like that he's back. His eyes are back to brown, but a creeping smirk still lingers.

Was that a sick joke?

"What's wrong with you!?"

"Who smuggles a flask into their granddaughter's graduation? In a church, mind you."

I shake my head. "I can't do this right now." Not now, not ever.

"That night was supposed to be about you—"

"Lucky, please. I'm begging you."

"I'm glad you called her out. I'm glad someone finally said—"

"SHUT UP!"

My lips quiver. I feel tears trying to make their way from the bottom of my eyelids. Just as one drips to my cheek, I flick it away with the back of my thumb.

Lucky is silent. At least for now.

I wish I hadn't said anything that night. That really pissed her off. Her stress, which her doctor always said could trigger her episodes, really set her off.

*It wasn't your fault.*

"She shouldn't have been," Lucky mumbles, "…with her medications."

*She shouldn't have been drinking with her…*

"Shut up, shut up, shut up…" I whisper to myself.

Lucky looks up at me. He thinks the words are for him.

"I'm only trying to support you. But you've been acting fucking nuts since she left. I'm trying to be there for you but—"

"You've been at your boyfriend's house. *Running* to your boyfriend's house! You're no better for ignoring it!"

I can't do it anymore. I should have gone before it got worse. I climb through the window.

"Who's running now?"

Why is he doing this? How did this even start? Cause I said I didn't believe his bullshit story?

*Let it pass.*

And I'm about to. I'm about to retreat to my bed, do my best to forget this conversation happened, and then handle it tomorrow. But then…

"I knew," Lucky says.

I look back. I don't ask. I don't want to know what he knew. I'm going to do everything in my power to stop this before it somehow gets worse.

His eyes flash white, looking like a pair of full moons on an alien planet.

I blink and they're back to normal. It must be me. It must be in my head.

"I knew about Temple."

I choke on my own breath. The stars above seem to drop and my knees buckle. Everything feels like it's spinning.

"What?"

"I knew your mom had a baby. I knew you had a little sister."

He stands tall, shoulders wide, proud of his announcement.

I place my palm against my chest. My heart feels like it might burst free.

I want to scream, cry, push him off the roof, or run past him and see if he tries to stop me. I want to punch him and kick him and hug him and weep into his shoulder because he's all I got.

But even that's not true.

*Destiny…*

I've only got me.

The tears flow freely now. I don't pout or make any attempt at wiping them away. I just let them pour, wondering if anyone's ever drowned in their own tears.

I need Lucky to apologize or explain, but for the first time since he invited me to watch DoodleBob, I feel like I don't know who he is. Who is this person wearing my brother's skin and why is he trying to kill me?

I can tell this feeling is mutual. There's no sign of remorse on his face as he turns away from me. He looks up at the moon, and puffs out his smoke.

I slam the window shut and crawl into my bed.

I curl the comforter over my head as the tears blanket my face.

*You're safe now.* A woman's voice slides beneath my sheets. *Breathe…*

I hope sleep erases this moment from my memory. We can figure this all out in the morning with clear heads.

*Breathe…*

If I know Lucky, he'll tap me on the shoulder and apologize in the middle of the night

*Breathe…*

But I don't even know if I want that right now.

*Breathe…*

You're safe now, I tell myself.

*At least for now.*

# chAPteR 3

**I USED TO WRITE EVERY** night as a way to quiet the storm in my head. I didn't have a project or a plan, I just let it spill. Sometimes poems formed, sometimes I'd make lists of things I loved or loathed or simply things I had to do. Every scratch on paper, even those most meaningless, helped.

"Just let it flow," Gigi said.

It didn't matter if it was good. No one was grading it. "Not even God," she said.

This is all for me, I'd remind myself.

I picked up the habit from Gigi. Each night, until her final year or so, she'd sit at the kitchen table and write. She had this leather-bound notebook that never seemed to run out of pages. It was red with a golden heart on the cover. I used to love running my finger across the etching. The heart had these wings that sprouted between its curves then went outward with a swirl. I never asked her what the symbol meant, but it looked like she carved it herself then traced it with gold paint.

She called her practice "saving herself" and didn't exactly love when I called it the same thing when I first joined her.

"Child, you're seven. What on Earth do you need saving from?" she joked. "You're a blank page. You got the space to create!"

I wasn't so sure about that. Creating was too much pressure. Saving, or letting it flow, felt safer. Easier. I had nothing to say, but I took comfort in the quiet moments at that table. Nothing felt better than putting the pen down and hearing nothing in my head. Silence, even if it was just for a few seconds, connected me to the page.

The morning comes. I peel the blanket from my face, nearly blinded by the summer sun flooding through the window. I don't remember falling asleep.

"Destiny!" Poppy calls upstairs. "Can you take Tiger for a walk?"

This again.

"Can't Lucky do it?" I groan.

"I don't care who does it," he says. "Lucky?"

I don't wanna wake up. I wanna sleep forever.

Beneath the sheets, I am safe.

"Lucky?"

Beneath the sheets, nothing can hurt me.

"Lucky?!" Poppy yells.

I roll over, looking across the hall.

My heart leaps from my chest. I spring forward.

Across the hallway, across the purple paisley rug, the door is closed.

That door's never closed, I remind myself.

My feet slap against the hardwood floor. He must have been super pissed at me. He's never done this. That's okay, that's okay. We both could probably apologize to each other and chat it out. No little fight is worth dwelling on. I shuffle across the way and knock on the door—*tap, tap, tap*—just above the Rina Sawayama poster and beneath the President Sanders sticker.

I grip the doorknob and turn. "Lucky?"

Across the room, something moves. I step back and gasp.

The curtains flutter.

I sigh. Relax, relax. It's nothing.

I push the door all the way open to see...

Nothing.

Nothing but an empty bed.

His bed is made. Pillows placed precisely at the top with the edges of the sheet tucked beneath the mattress. He's never made his bed.

He's never up and out of the house before I'm awake. No way one fight would totally topple our six-year routine.

I look down the stairs. Poppy has made his way up to the second floor and is standing on the landing.

"Where's Lucky?" I ask.

"He's not getting coffee?" Poppy shrugs.

I dash downstairs, past him.

"Whoa, slow down there, kiddo.

I leap over a few more steps, making my way all the way downstairs, toward the front door.

"Where are you going?"

"To find Lucky," I yell.

I'm almost at the door.

"Destiny!" his voice booms. "Slow down."

I turn back to Poppy. He pulls his phone out.

"This feels like a simple fix," he taps on his phone.

Poppy is right. Lucky's phone lives in his hand.

I take a deep breath, knowing my panic will soon subside.

He holds the phone to his ear.

"Is it ringing?"

"Not yet," he sighs, "…oh, there it goes."

No…

Up above, I hear a phone beeping.

No. No. No.

I dash past Poppy, back up to our attic. Lucky's phone blares, vibrating atop his nightstand. I grab it and hold it up to Poppy, who has made his way up the steps.

"Hmm. Okay. That's a little weird but I'm sure there's—"

"Something's wrong," I say.

Poppy shakes his head. "Let's cool it. He's probably just with Low. Forgot it, that's all. He'll show up for dinner like always."

"He made his bed."

Poppy's eyes sink. "What do you mean, made his bed? He's never—"

"—made his bed, I know."

He's never made his bed, or closed his door, or left before our mornings on the roof.

We've also never had a fight as big as last night's.

I'm freaked out. Poppy offers to make me breakfast. I decline, but we head back downstairs.

"I've gotta find him. I'll check Low's first, then maybe the library. He mentioned that."

I head for the door.

"Take Tiger with you," Poppy says.

"You're shitting me," I whisper under my breath.

He hears me. "Tiger's about to be *shitting on you* if you don't get him out."

I roll my eyes. Well played. I quickly scoop Tiger and knot his bow tie.

"Don't slow me down," I tap his head with a finger before scampering out the door. He stares blankly at me through half-closed eyelids. He looks like he's about to fall asleep. I consider placing him down, but now is not the time. I will not operate on Tiger's schedule.

I internally map out my stops, ranking the locations first based upon how likely it is that he's there, then second, considering the time it'll take to get there. Are there any low-odds places worth checking on the way?

First: I'll check his boyfriend Low's house. This makes the most sense. Even though he's never stayed there overnight, they're inseparable. Maybe after our fight, Lucky just needed a break. It makes sense. Great. That's at the corner of Lexington and Chestnut, just a few blocks down from us.

Second: If he's not there, I'll cut across the bike path and take Lincoln up to Leslie, which will cut across the entire neighborhood and get me to the library. I glance at my phone for the time. It's almost ten, and I think they're open early on Saturdays. It's Saturday, right? I can never keep track of these things once summer starts.

Third: I'll avoid panic. Or try to. Because he should really be at one of those two places. But I'm thinking I'll loop back and head to Penn Queen Diner if I'm by the library anyway. It'll be a hike, especially with Tiger. Maybe Low will take Tiger for that leg of the journey? Or I'll hide him in the jungle gym by the library. I've never seen anyone use it. But again, hopefully we don't get that far.

I walk straight down Chestnut, turtle in my arms, three blocks to Lexington. I knock on Low's front door, but no one answers. There are no cars in the driveway. I knock again but there's nothing. Then I remember I have Low's number from when Lucky's phone died and they were out together. Perfect.

I scroll through my messages, finding the unsaved number. Tiger squirms in my arms, already over this expedition.

I start calling the phone when I hear movement on the other side. A pair of eyes peek through the glass at the top of the door.

The door swings open, Low's hair brushing against the doorframe. The only person with more Samson-level locks than Low is Lucky. They were made for each other, their lanky selves looking like two stalks of broccoli.

Low wears nothing but an oversized old blue Iverson jersey, and hopefully, boxers. It looks like a dress. This boy's a complete mess.

"Nice fit," I nod.

Low rubs his eyes and catches my sarcasm. "You're really one to talk."

I look down. I've got on my dirty Vans that used to be white. Not gonna lie, they've now taken on the blonde hue of a dehydrated person's piss. R.I.P. I'm wearing my black-and-white checkered flannel pants and my XL yellow hoody with an upside-down smiley. I wear it to bed every night. It's stained. I can't remember the last time I washed it. Come to think of it, I can't think of the last time I washed myself.

"Where's Lucky?" I ask.

"I'm assuming in bed. Like I should be. It's not even eleven."

I shake my head. "He's not. He's gone."

"What do you mean, *gone*?"

"His bed was made."

"His bed was *what*?"

"Made. He made his bed."

"That boy? Make his bed?" Low shakes his head. "This doesn't add up."

"That's why I'm here."

"Have you tried calling him?"

"He left his phone at home."

"Fuck," Low squats on the front step and pulls out a vape. It looks like a car exhaust with Lisa Frank stickers. "No, no, no."

"Why are you no-ing? What do you know?"

He shakes his head. "I mean, well, no."

"What do you mean, *I mean?*"

"Well, I know you two got in a fight last night. But you would also know about that, so that's not exactly news."

I tense up. "It wasn't really a fight."

"I mean, listen, you got your own shit, and I'm not gonna prod. He just wanted me to listen until he didn't anymore. He's like that. We'll talk for hours, get deep and shit. Then he just stops. Like he's fallen off into himself. He's got these invisible walls, and I don't try to crack them."

"He called you?"

"Texted."

"Read it," I say.

Low laughs.

He thinks I'm joking.

"Read the messages."

"That's kinda an invasion of our—"

"Skip the sex stuff," I clarify. "Doesn't apply here."

Low chuckles. "You're crazy."

He's joking, but it stings because it might be true. I clench my jaw.

Low looks down at Tiger and the turtle is already staring at him. The two appear to lock eyes for a moment, and the little shellback beast gets the best of the giant in the vintage jersey. The boy reaches into his pocket and pulls out the phone.

"There was nothing like that last night. This was more about feelings. I don't know how comfortable he's gonna be knowing I told you—"

"Just read it."

Low sighs and starts. "*Maya's being a bitch.*"

"He said that?"

"I told you you weren't gonna like this."

"Not the bitch part. He called me Maya?"

Low shrugs. "Doesn't he always?"

Weird. "Keep going."

"He said you guys got into a fight, I asked how it started, and he said he crossed a line."

Nice to know he knew it was his fault. "What else?"

"Nothing else, really," Low looks down, scrolling. "Something about having to shave—that boy is hairy."

"Nope. Not relevant."

"Something about being hungry, I told him to run to Wawa, offered to walk with him."

"Okay, we're getting somewhere."

"He said he was too tired, plus he was too…oh. Oh? I forgot this part."

Low's face flushes.

"He was too what? What did he say?"

Low shakes his head, his hair bobbing.

"I'm sure it's nothing. He just gets paranoid when he smokes, that's all. Calls it his *Pockets of Infinity*. He swears he's a poet."

I snatch the phone straight from Low's hand.

"Dude!" He stands.

I turn my back to him, reading it myself.

LUCKY
*wawa can wait. i'm too freaked out.*

And another text.

*i still feel like someone's watching me.*

My ears start to ring. The chilly air returns, swallowing me whole.

I feel a pair of unseen eyes looming above me. They pull closer, pressing down on me.

I almost drop the phone, but Low grabs it. I wanna throw up.

Before I realize it, my back is hunched and I'm dry heaving. I can't stop.

"Whoa! Destiny, you good?"

I look up, almost forgetting Low's there.

I try to steady my breath.

"It says 'still.' What did he mean, '*still*?'"

"I just figured you knew about this…" Low trails off.

I try to take in deep breaths and remember that thing at my center. I see the outline of a pen, but it's faint. Its gold is fading.

"It's something he always dealt with," Low says. "Said he felt like something was watching him since he was little. Apparently it got worse when your grandma died."

My knees start to shake.

How can this be? How come he never said anything?

"Hey, come inside. I'll get you some water."

I stumble backward.

"I gotta go. He's got to be at the library. He wanted me to check out some old articles."

"You want me to come with?"

"No. Thank you, really. But no."

There's a slice of me that instantly regrets rejecting his offer. Maybe human company might not be the worst idea.

"Tiger and I got this." I pull the turtle a little closer.

"Text me if you change your mind. Have him call me as soon as he shows up."

I head for the sidewalk. "Thanks, Low."

I pick up Tiger in an effort to move faster. But after a block, my arm is throbbing. This little turd is deceptively heavy. I place him down, running the risk of being slowed down dramatically.

Tiger tugs on his string, trying to veer us to the left. I can't do this. The library is to the right. I mentally run through the texts. Lucky did say he was hungry. Maybe he went on a morning Wawa run or is sitting at Penn Queen Diner right now. Both were to the left. Maybe I should listen to the turtle. Maybe he knows something I don't.

The morning sun creeps higher overhead. Hanging directly above me, four shadows of myself extend in opposing directions. The temperature's already got to be in the low 80s. It's gonna be a brutal one. To the left, the shade of maples and oaks. To the right, the scorched streets leading to the highway.

Fine. Tiger wins.

We start slogging along. Yes, we're moving at turtle speed, but I've gotta give the little guy some credit. He's pulling ahead with a sense of urgency like he's got somewhere to go.

We reach Jefferson Avenue, and he turns with confidence.

"Nope. Not the way."

I gently tug on him, but he doesn't budge. Instead, he powers forward.

I mentally retrace the map. It's not a terrible detour. In fact, it might get us up to Route 130 at the same time. But after yesterday, between Mrs. Ward and 55, Jefferson feels like a bad idea.

"C'mon, Tiger. We're taking Lincoln."

I reach for him, but he scurries ahead, his claws scratching against the pavement.

I leap ahead, cutting him off. I lean down to pick him up and…

Oh my god. I can't.

I grip the bottom of his shell, between his legs and thrust upward. He doesn't budge.

I stand straight up, breathing heavily, and reaching for my back.

"What did you eat, boy?"

I try one more time, wrapping both of my arms around the bottom of him and pulling up.

I might as well be trying to hoist a boulder. This turtle's going nowhere.

I try to catch my breath. Sweat drips down to my eyebrows. I wish I'd worn something other than this hoodie. As I'm standing here, trying to make sense of the situation, Tiger powers past me, his string leash dragging behind him.

Okay, okay. We'll get through this.

I can do this.

I look down at the two-ton turtle. *We* can do this.

We walk ahead. Shaded by a healthy row of trees, Jefferson feels ten degrees cooler than the rest of town. I'm suddenly grateful we took this path. Maybe Tiger knows exactly what he's doing.

I peer ahead, up to Mrs. Ward's house ahead. I see no movement. Great. This is great. This is gonna be fine. Save for the occasional chirping bird and our steps on the pavement, the street is still, almost silent.

We reach the sweet-scented shrubbery of Mrs. Ward's home. Tiger tugs ahead. I hold my breath, hoping she doesn't suddenly materialize from the foliage. Just keep looking ahead. I pull my hood over my face. The ol', "I can't see them/they can't see me" trick. But I wore this same outfit yesterday. She'll know. Whatever, I'm almost there. Just keep your eyes locked in ahead.

I peek out of the corner of my hood, getting a glimpse of her backyard garden. She's nowhere to be seen. Success.

We keep walking. Only one more hurdle on Jefferson, and we'll be on our way. Something about Tiger's bold, confident stride forward makes me hopeful. I think we've got this.

I glance up at the blue sky poking through the branches. A bird whistles as a shard of light lands on my face. I push my hood back and close my eyes, letting the rays flicker against my eyelids.

There's a gentle tapping on the sidewalk. A trickle up above. And then, the tap becomes a patter.

Rain.

I open my eyes. There's nothing. The sky is clear. Not even a drop of dew.

Yet I can still hear it, faint in the distance.

"There's a storm coming, Tiger," I whisper in my best Hagrid impersonation. It's not very good, but thankfully the turtle doesn't get the reference. Tiger trots on. I don't think he believes me. Honestly, I don't really believe me either. I scan the sky. There's not a cloud in sight.

We walk on until I realize we must have passed 55 Jefferson without noticing, for we've reached a street on our right.

"That's strange," I mutter.

I swear I'm standing directly where the cursed murder house should be. But plain as I can see, that's clearly not the case. I slow down, and Tiger's tail stiffens.

I wish I wore my glasses. Across the pavement, standing at the corner, is the gray pole with its green street marker atop. I can't make out a letter of its bold white words.

There's an idea that floats through my mind every so often—particularly moments like this. I think about how

I've lived in the same 400-acre town pretty much my whole life. After 13 years, you'd think I knew every crease and crevice of this pass-through neighborhood. The way the whole town starts to smell like panzarottis at 2 o'clock on Tuesday afternoons in preparation for the weekly sale rush. How no one acknowledges the church bells that ding every hour. The way people cross the street when they see Mrs. Ward because there's only so much to say about vegetables.

But then there are moments like this. Rare moments, to be sure, but magical ones. Like when I found the little park at the dead end on Clinton. Or the time I spotted a single rose growing from the crack in a sidewalk on Jackson Street and there was a butterfly dancing around it. Or this—a street slicing through Jefferson Avenue that I never noticed before.

With less than twenty streets in the entire town, you'd think I'd walked them all. But that's not the case. For the most part, I stick to my block, head to school, and then back to the attic.

Tiger turns the corner, tugging me forward down this unexplored road. I mentally map out where this street must lead. If it curves to the left, worst-case scenario, I end up back near the church and closer to home. If that happens, I drop Tiger off and go on with my day. Best-case scenario, we've just discovered a direct route up to 130, right across from Penn Queen Diner, and we'll be seeing Lucky in no time.

Tiger tugs and I let him lead the way. I step onto the new road, hoping it leads me to Lucky.

Looking back, I wish I had just crossed the black pavement and read that street sign.

Had I read the words on that green marker, it's hard to imagine I would have taken one step down that lane.

# chApteR 4

**AFTER GIGI DIED, I SEARCHED** the entire house for her red book. I tore apart every drawer and rifled through every closet. I even jostled a few of the hardwood slabs of her bedroom floor to see if she had any secret compartments. There was nothing.

She must have taken it with her to the other side. I don't know what I was hoping to find in there and it's probably better I never found it. Or at least, this is the line I say to myself to keep me from wasting more time searching. Even if I did find it, knowing Gigi, I'd probably be left with more questions than answers anyway.

One night, a few years back, I found her up at 3 AM, all alone in the kitchen. My mouth was a desert and so I soon found myself walking down the steps with my eyes closed in search of an icy glass of water. Every lamp in the house was out, but as I approached the kitchen, I noticed a light flickering through the archway. I turned the corner to find Gigi sitting at the table accompanied by a black taper candle.

At first glance, I swore her eyes were closed. She looked like she might be praying or meditating. But then I noticed her hand moving as her pen slid before her, gliding across the page with purpose.

My heart thumped in my chest. The sight scared me, and I'm still not sure why.

"Gigi?"

She opened her emerald eyes and smiled.

Without hesitation she said, "I started a story."

"Right now?"

"That's all there ever is, baby star."

"It's the middle of the night."

"When the page calls, you gotta answer," she wagged her pen. "That's the thing about this craft. It'll take you deep within yourself. You'll end up finding living, breathing people and places right there inside of you, that you didn't even know were there."

Gigi beamed, thrilled at the prospect of mapping out her mind and meeting the people and places she said were living there. The notion of anyone taking up residence in my mind without my approval scared me. Needless to say, it still does.

But when I rummaged for the red book, more than anything else, I found myself thinking about that night. I wanna know who she met in her mind. I want to see the places she dreamed of. Maybe, if I can figure out what's going on in my own head, I'd like to finish the story she started.

I turn the corner and take in a deep breath.

I exhale, feeling lighter. I take a deeper one, savoring the fresh air.

I look up at the trees. They're no different from the birch and maples around the corner. I look up at the Victorian houses, the same as the rest of the town.

But something feels different. Something feels better.

I smile, realizing what it is.

I feel alone. Good alone. Happy alone. No unseen watcher secretly noting my every move, alone. I feel free and relaxed in a way I haven't felt in months.

Tiger stops, looking back at me. I squat down to join him.

"You did this, little buddy," I pat his wrinkly old head. It gently bobs. "Thanks for taking us this way."

I look into his eyes, and he looks back at mine like he understands me. Around his pitch-black pupil, his iris is an iridescent blue that I've never noticed before. The white that encompasses the blue is even more striking. I rub my hand against the back of my arm, feeling goosebumps sprout.

The turtle's human eyes start to tense up. One eyelid rises then the other, back and forth, almost like his eyes might pop out.

"You okay, bud?"

He looks like he's in pain.

"You're gonna be okay," I tap on his shell.

And then, a gaseous explosion from below.

It smells like eggs, broccoli, and death.

I look back.

A splatter of thick green has slopped across one of my Vans.

I backpedal, getting away from the turtle.

I dry heave before turning toward the nearest tree and trying to scrape it off. It only smears, making it worse. I reach down and rip a handful of grass—

"Sorry, Earth."

—and I mean a true handful of grass from the ground. I need to make sure there's three to four layers of grass between my palm and my shoe when I scrape off the remaining feces.

I cover my nose, trying to turn off my brain so I can do what must be done.

Once completed, I toss the grass into the street, then find a fresh patch to wipe my hand across in the event that any trickled through.

There goes my happy street. I look to the pavement where Tiger is. And—

He isn't.

I groan. You've got to be kidding me.

"Tiger?"

Okay, okay. Fine. He's a turtle. There's only so far he could have gone.

"Tiger!"

I look ahead on the sidewalk. There's no shell creeping down the pavement.

I stand in the middle of the street. Nothing.

I peek underneath the first parked car I come across. No turtle.

Okay, this is bad. I really don't have time for this. I now officially have two missing animals to track down. I walk ahead, toward the slight curvature in the road. It gently bends to the right, which makes me hopeful. Perhaps this is a shortcut to the library and a shortcut to Lucky.

Part of me wants to scan every bit of greenery to find Tiger first, because my brother is going to be pissed that I lost his turtle. But does he really have any room to talk? Running off without telling anyone? Not even taking his phone? I'm the one that gets to be mad this time, not him.

Plus, Tiger will be fine. It's not like he's never spent time outdoors. Maybe he saw his chance to return to his wild ways and made a break for it. I can't blame him. We'll find Tiger like we always have. A few times he's wriggled through the edges of his crate and visited the kitchen. One time he made it into the vents, still haven't figured that out, but Tiger is going to Tiger. And he's gonna show up. I think. I hope.

The street curves sharply, then dips left. My hopes for a shortcut are dimming. I look back, wondering if I should take the roads I know. I look ahead—the road looks long. But I know it can't be. Our town's not that big. Inevitably, I'll walk to the end and I'll spot something I know.

I put an extra pep in my step, determined to right the course and figure out where exactly I am. I can't help but notice how the old Victorians look slightly less old on this street. I'm sure the bones are ancient, but the paint is fresher, the windows are polished, and the lawns look crisp. I'm sure Mrs. Ward would be proud to call these folks her neighbors.

Interestingly, I notice cars in nearly every driveway. I'm tempted to say they're all the same, but I'm sure that Car People (people I'm certain I have zero in common with) would ridicule me for such a statement. But they're all relatively boxy, like they're from the '50s or the '80s or the future. It's all the same to me. Must have been a sale exclusive to residents of…whatever street this is.

I wait for someone to come walking outside or to see someone driving by, but no one is on the street. With lawns like these, you'd think someone would be tending to theirs. But there's no one. Near silence. Except for the occasional chirp and…

Thunder, far in the distance. I hear the rain pattering against pavement. But that doesn't make sense.

I shake my head. The sky is perfect.

You're fine. Everything's fine, I tell myself.

"It's all in your head," I say aloud.

I close my eyes and take in a deep breath.

Her Final Face doesn't flash on the insides of my eyelids. It's still there, but now it's more like a faded imprint. Her features bleed into an oval blob that can't scare me. Its vibrance is gone, the reality of the moment eroding. That image won't haunt me forever. I won't let it.

I open my eyes and see someone ahead. A woman. I let

out a sigh of relief. I pick up my speed. I'm not usually one to talk to strangers, but a little clarity on whether this street will take me where I want to go wouldn't hurt. Plus, I could ask if she'd keep an eye out for a roaming turtle.

I approach the woman. She's bent, tending to a patch of weeds in the front of her lawn.

She hears me coming. She turns back, looking me dead in my eyes.

I gasp.

"Destiny!?" my name squawks from her decaying mouth.

"Mrs. Ward?"

"Oh my goodness, Destiny!" She drops the small shovel in her hand and throws her arms around me. I'm too stunned to resist. She smells like parsley, sage, rosemary, and sweat. "I'm so happy to see you. I've been trying to get ahold of your parents all morning."

She releases me from her grip and takes a healthy step back. Fear is plastered across her dirt-smudged face.

"What's wrong?" I ask.

"Lucky's fine."

She's seen Lucky. My heart starts to ram in my chest. "Where's Lucky?"

She closes her eyes and shakes off her panic. But it's too late. It's already spread to me.

"I found him this morning passed out on my front lawn," she points to the grass beside her. "He had some cuts and bruises, but nothing major. It sounds like someone stole his phone and wallet."

"Oh my god. Where is he?"

"I took him in, cleaned him up, and gave him plenty of water. He's resting now but should be ready to roll when I tell him you're here."

Okay, I nod. Okay. This is bad, but not terrible. He's a little beat up, I'm sure he's scared, but he's fine. This is going to be okay. I replay the image of him getting jumped in my head but try to freeze it as it plays. I can't think about this. Fuck! He left the house because we got in a fight.

I break Mrs. Ward's gaze and look down.

"Thanks, Mrs. Ward."

My eyes land upon my shit-stained Vans, toe to toe with Mrs. Ward's impeccable boots. I take in the crisp laces, the clean rubber ridged sole, all blinding white against the light of the sun.

Impossible. My brows furrow.

They should be caked in dirt.

My eyes move beyond her, across the green grass, and to the front yard garden. I look up at the house. I know Mrs. Ward's house, hardly noticeable behind the greenery. The Ward home has brown vinyl, nothing fancy compared to its garden. This giant home is white with tall pillars around its perimeter, running from the lush green grass, through the balcony, up to the amber red shingles.

"Whose house is this?"

"Mine," she says quickly.

"Your—?"

"Well, my sister's," she chuckles. "It's our parents," she

corrects herself again. "We grew up here, but my sister is living here until everything gets sorted out. I still take care of the plants. You know me!"

"Yeah," I force a laugh that sounds more like a grunt. "Save the plants."

"Plants for president!" Mrs. Ward giggles.

I laugh. Genuinely this time. Mrs. Ward is the weirdest human I know.

"How about you come on in and we'll get Lucky up and running."

I take a quick glance at the house I've never seen before. Among our primarily Victorian populated town, there are a few structures like this. The several modern houses stick out like the monstrosities they are, but something like this feels equally out of place but I can't pin it down. Maybe I've actually passed it before, and Mrs. Ward is harmless enough, but I can't tell you the last time I went into a stranger's home. I honestly couldn't tell you the last time I entered a home that wasn't mine.

"I'm fine, Mrs. Ward. Thanks. You can just let him know I'm here."

"Oh, dear," she shakes her head. "At least wait in the backyard. There are chairs in the garden."

"I'm sure it's lovely, but—"

"It is. It's my garden," she says with a proud smile that makes me wish I loved something as much as this woman loves growing things.

"Sure," I concede.

"Just walk around and we'll meet you on the other side," she points to the left of the house and steadily walks toward the front door.

I cut across the grass, no stepping stones in sight. Mrs. Ward turns back, watching my movement. She stops at the front door before going in, still gazing at me. I feel her stare pressing against my skin. I turn to look at her just before reaching the side of the house, breaking eye contact and out of her sight.

What a freak.

I look ahead. Before me is an arched trellis completely overtaken by vines. Flowers sprout everywhere in an explosion of colliding colors and scents. I step ahead and smell the roses before I can spot them. They're white, smaller than any roses I've ever seen before but their scent is unmistakable. I lean closer to them and inhale.

*Almost heaven.*

I smile. I'm tempted to pluck one, but I know better. There's a part of me that thinks Mrs. Ward would know. There's a part of me that believes this small flower and all of these plants are directly grown from the old lady like extensions of herself. The vines are her veins and snipping one could mean death for both of us.

I step through the arch and gasp.

*Definitely heaven.*

I'm flooded with more colors and scents than I've experienced in one place before. Blue cornflowers sit beside yellow buttercups. A patch of purple petunias border a swath of pink peonies. There are red roses next to redder apples. There are oranges more orange than any orange I've ever sliced into. I salivate at their sight. And of course, kudos to Mrs. Ward, there's a pumpkin patch cutting through it all, encircling a koi pond in the center.

A fish springs from the water before splashing back beneath. I take a step closer to get a better look at the koi. I have to admit, if this is anything like Mrs. Ward's home garden, I get the obsession.

The water is clear as quartz and deeper than I could have imagined. More like a well than a pond, I can't even see the bottom. Dozens of orange-striped koi dart and dance, spiraling down as far as I can make out. The pond is impossibly well lit, I figure there's a light fixed at the bottom. Between the shimmering fish and the sun's reflection, the water appears to glow.

"She put the sun at the bottom," a man's voice cuts from across the garden.

I stumble backward, certain I was alone.

He continues, "It's gotta go somewhere."

A bearded man sits on the other side of the pond. His gaze is fixed on a newspaper settled on his lap. He doesn't look up at me, but I can't stop looking at him. He looks so familiar. I know him. I'm almost certain that I know him.

His skin is sun-stained, his beard white as winter. I've seen this man before, but where?

A fish leaps by the edge of the pond. The water splatters against the pavement, and a splash lands on the toes of my shoes.

Strange.

The water is white. Almost like liquid school glue. I lean down to touch it when I hear a door close behind me. I perk back up.

"I figured you might be getting hungry," Mrs. Ward calls from behind. She starts down the patio steps with a porcelain bowl in her hands.

"I saw you didn't bring the turtle, so I figured it was the perfect time to try my pumpkin soup!"

She reaches me at the koi pond as steam rises from her cupped hands.

"It's a little hot for soup?"

"No. Not my soup. It's so sweet, you won't even notice the heat," Mrs. Ward wiggles, proud of her little rhyme.

"That man…" I whisper, "in the chair. Who is that?"

"What man?" Mrs. Ward chuckles.

I scowl at her and she smiles wider before peering over my shoulder.

"Oh, that ole' fart?" she waves her hand, dismissing him. "That's just my husband."

My heart drops.

I know her husband.

We all know her husband.

Mr. Ward. That racist prick died years ago.

This can't be him. It can't be him. But I look back.

He catches my glance, already staring at me like he used to.

But there's a glaze coating his eyes I didn't notice before. Maybe it was always there, but here in the sunlight, he's fully exposed. We both are. I preferred when there was a glass barrier between us.

I rub my forehead, suddenly feeling lightheaded.

"Destiny?" Mrs. Ward tilts her head. "Are you okay, honey?"

She steps forward and I slide aside. I don't like how close she's getting. I swear I can smell the mulch packed between her wooden teeth.

"Where's Lucky?"

Mrs. Ward is persistent. She lurches toward me, raising the soup toward my face.

"He's coming, my dear. Have a sip. Just a teeny sip."

I dodge my head. "He's inside? I'll get him."

"I wouldn't do that," Mrs. Ward forces the bowl at my face.

I swat the bowl without thinking. Mrs. Ward gasps. The thick orange soup spills all over her. The bowl crashes and shatters against the ground.

Mr. Ward stands from his chair. All three of us stare at the scene, unsure of what to do next, waiting for someone else to make the first move.

Mrs. Ward looks down at her pumpkin-stained blouse, the porcelain shards below, then back at me. Her chin quivers, like she might cry. Her eyes get glassy, but she shakes it off and frowns. In a blink, the sadness turns to fury. There's fire in her eyes. She fights back her tears with clenched jaw resolve.

"Well, don't she work fast these days," Mr. Ward sounds from across the pond.

The crystal water from the koi pond starts to dribble

over its edge. It trickles slow, but then bubbles, moving with apparent purpose. It oozes across the stone pavement encircling the pond, instantly turning thick and white in the sunlight. Mrs. Ward shrieks as the liquid nears her.

"She don't like when things don't go in order," Mr. Ward says. "No room for chaos in this corner."

The koi fish leap from the pond, squealing, floundering in air, as though the water is suddenly simmering.

"This wasn't the way it was supposed to go, Destiny." Mrs. Ward tip-toes, trying to find a place to stand without the gunk. But it's spreading faster than either of us can navigate.

At the pond's center, the water is rapidly rising, turning white before my eyes. As some bleeds over the edge, the rest of it coagulates into a bubble. It starts as a gentle dome over the pond, but quickly inflates larger and larger until it's a giant sphere. Each of the fish sink beneath its film with their own sizzle. Mrs. Ward backpedals as the bubble gets larger. I follow Mrs. Ward's lead, trying to get away, but there's nowhere to go. Its shadow looms over us, briefly cutting off the sun until—

The bubble bursts, the white bile cascading downward. Across the way, I see Mr. Ward's knees buckle as the splash completely consumes him. The old man yelps, a noise that sounds more like a deer bleat than anything human.

I run up the slight hill toward the house as the substance slowly inches its way up the grass. I look back as Mrs. Ward screams. She's fallen toward the grass and is getting pulled toward the center of the pond.

"DE-ES-ES—" she moans, her wretched cry sounding like a goat cursed with the ability to speak, "—T-T-TINY!"

Fuck that.

I leap up the steps and swing the door open. A swarm of flies zips out, fleeing for the light. I cough, pulling my hoodie up over my nose. The house reeks of rotting meat and still water. It's impossibly dark, considering the adequate number of windows and the sun beating outside.

Everything in the space is an outline, feeling like an incomplete sketch. Lines of light funnel from the windows, crisscrossing, giving only a glimpse of my surroundings. I try to make out as much as I can. The walls, the counters, the furniture…the person.

The shadow stares back at me. I can't see its eyes, but I feel them.

My heart rattles.

I feel an electricity surge across my body. Everything in me screams RUN.

I've made a big mistake coming in here.

"Lucky?" I speak to the shadow.

It groans, shuffling ever so slightly forward.

It can't be Lucky. The outline isn't right.

*But he might be here.*

I step back and call out. "Lucky?!"

The shadow creeps toward me, the wood beneath us creaking.

It speaks. "Destiny?"

I feel I've been simultaneously sucker punched in the gut and throat. I lose my breath.

I know that voice. *Her* voice.

She still sounds like lemon drenched in honey.

Mom. Gigi.

I fight back tears. "Come on, here. You know I can't see you in the dark."

She steps closer but I step back. I don't trust her. I don't trust it. Even if it's got Gigi's voice.

I back into a wall.

She shuffles forward.

*Crik. Crik. Criiiiik.*

I pray that sound is coming from the floorboards and not her bones.

"My sweet Destiny? It can't be. Is that you?"

Destiny? No. No. Don't be fooled, I tell myself. I won't be tricked. She'd never call me that. She never knew Destiny.

In the corner of my eye, I see the outline of what looks like a doorway. With my back against the wall, I slide for the opening.

"Maya," I correct her. "You'd call me Maya."

I see the shadow shake her head.

"No, baby star. I know better now," she says, a tinge of sadness in her voice. "That was pride that gave you both my name. Silly, small, pride. I'm sorry for that. I'm sorry."

My heart rumbles in my chest as I fight back tears.

*Maybe it is her.*

No. Another thought interjects. Don't believe it.

"Whoever you are, stop it. You're sick."

"And you're free. I'm proud of you, Destiny. Look at you, stepping into your own. Stepping beyond me, beyond your mother."

"That's not what this is about."

She inches closer.

"Of course it is. And I can't blame you. Why would you want to share a name with two people who hurt you so bad?"

Her head slumps. She leans against the wall and cradles her head in both hands.

"*I'm an idiot. Stupid. Fucked up everything,*" she mutters under her breath.

"Gigi?"

"I'm just so sorry, baby star," her voice breaks. "I never meant to mess it all up. I wish I did everything different."

"Not everything," I say.

She whimpers. I hear her fighting back tears, a sound that cuts directly through my bony chest and into my bleeding heart. Her tears remind me just how connected we are and how little I can do about it. At the sight or sound of her pain, I absorb it all. It becomes mine.

I step forward from the wall.

"No," she says, waving a hand. "I'll be okay, always am. You know that."

I clench my jaw. This was a pattern I knew well. A pattern I despised her for. Dump your pain, bring destruction, practically beg to be hugged and healed. Then, just as the sympathy approaches, turn away the open arms.

"It's time for you to be your own woman, Destiny. Escape who we are."

*Escape.*

*…who we are…*

Strangely, it starts in my heels. I try to suppress it, clenching my toes. My feet quiver, sending my legs into a steady rattle. It rises, spreading to the pit of my stomach like a broken jar of ink, spilling and staining everything. In seconds, it's in my chest, then my throat, then just behind my eyes. I can't hold it back.

I burst into tears.

"Destiny, don't. Please."

The tears are soaked in anger, regret, and more truth than I'd like to admit.

"I—" can hardly…

"miss—" spit out…

"you—" the words…

"so much."

"Please, Destiny!" she yells, slamming her shadowed hand against the wall. "Stop!"

Her voice is suddenly, shockingly different. Gone is her honey drenched sound and in its place is a deep, growling wheeze. I recognize parts of it. It's almost a mix between her Wicked Witch impression and her Lion, just before we find out he's Cowardly.

Without warning, the dark outline of her body hurls for the floor, her spine whipping like a slingshot. I search for a scream, but nothing comes out.

She dry heaves, a wretched sound, like a boulder grinding against gravel.

The shadow heaves and grinds, heaves and grinds, her body slinking up and down in the darkness.

This isn't my Mom.

This isn't a human.

There's a splash on the floor between us. I feel a splatter against my ankle.

The shadow falls to all fours, joining the mess on the ground. She heaves once more, but this time it's not dry. I hear liquid pouring from this creature's mouth, battering against the floorboards.

I dash for the doorway, my Vans splashing with each step. The creature shrieks behind me—a cross between a cat wailing in agony and a gator growling for more.

"DEST—" it calls out, its voice shifting from beast back to my Mom's. "…Destiny, wait!"

I'll do no such thing. I don't turn back. Ahead, I see the outline of what looks like a door and boarded up windows, as light leaks through the edges.

I try to run faster but I can't. With each step ahead, I slosh through deeper waters. In seconds, the liquid rises from my ankles and up to my knees.

I'm almost to the door when—

"Destiny!?" another voice I know cries from above.

Lucky.

"Destiny!" he wails. He's never sounded so scared.

I turn, a sliver of light landing upon the steps.

"Is that you!?" he calls.

I want to run up those stairs so bad. But I know better.

Whatever pretended to be Gigi could be trying the same trick twice.

I reach for the doorknob and pull. It won't budge. I twist and turn and tug. The water is up to my waist and I'm struggling to keep my grip.

"Destiny!?" Lucky cries.

*An imposter*, the familiar voice cuts through my head. *He lies.*

Perhaps. But what other choice do I have?

What if it's really him? Lucky is why I'm here.

The water makes the choice for me. It's now up to my chest. In seconds, I'll be under if I don't move. Up is the only way.

I lift my feet from the ground and paddle to the steps, lifting myself up and out of the water. But it's right on my tracks. With each step, I feel it rising just behind me.

"Don't go up there!" the monster with Gigi's voice cackles from below. "You won't like what you find."

I glance back and I see her struggling through the water, making her way for the steps.

I reach the landing and can see clearer now. With a skylight overhead, the hallway I'm standing in is fully illuminated. Surrounding me are four doors, two on either side. Only one is wide open, through which more light shines through. Beyond the open door, across the empty room, I see the green of the trees outside.

Instinct says dash for the light, burst through that window and get out. But—

"Destiny!" Lucky cries out. "This one!"

He bangs on a door but I can't tell which. The water splashing against wood rattles the floorboards, blending with his sound. I try to catch up with my breath. The notion of the shadow closing in makes everything harder.

I reach for the nearest closed door, the one from which I think he sounds, and pull. It's sealed tight. I throw my shoulder into it but it doesn't give.

"This one!" he thumps again, and I'm certain which one he's behind.

I dash across the landing and feel a hand slap across the back of my leg.

I stumble, falling into the milky water with a spatter. I land before the closed door and instantly pull for the handle. I tug with everything I've got. It doesn't budge. I slam against it and—*CRACK!*

The sealed door gives way, immediately breaking from its hinges. More white water cascades forward, crashing down upon me. I sweep beneath the surface, my body slinging downward until I've hit a wall or the floor, I can't tell which. I'm so disoriented and I can't see a thing. I try to swim up but there's nowhere to go. All I see is the glow of light above. I push my body toward it, holding my breath for dear life. As I approach, the light starts to take shape into a square. This is the window. This is the way out.

I poke my head to the surface and not a moment too soon.

The monster masked as Gigi springs from the water, white droplets shimmering off her body. She lands before me, manically swiping for my ankles, water swashing everywhere.

There, just beyond my feet, she looks just as I remember her in the end—with her face down, she lies lifelessly in the water. She twitches and I spring back, the water weighing me down. The window is no more than ten feet away, but it might as well be a mile. With her head still burrowed beneath the surface, she flails her arms, blindly swiping for me.

I hate to leave Lucky here, if he's even here at all, but there's no other option. I'll die if I don't make it to that window. I paddle backward with all my might, each inch forward taking my full strength.

I keep an eye on the beast. With her face still submerged, she kicks her legs and propels herself forward. She moves faster, faster—*Go! Go!*—effortlessly gliding through the water, the back of her bobbing head looks like a prowling shark's fin.

I'm almost to the window—C'mon!—when I shriek. She grips my ankle and pulls me under again. This is it. Water pours into my mouth, tasting like soured eggs, rosewater, and blood. I cough, which only makes it worse. More liquid floods in and I feel like I might choke.

The glimmer of light above is fading. The monster clutches her other hand on my free leg. I don't think—I can't. I just start thrashing my legs, blindly kicking the body that's trying to take my life. Her grip loosens and I pull myself up to the light.

I heave for air, the window within reach.

I glance back and she's there to greet me.

Her nose grazes mine and I pull back. Her breath, which smells as though she's been living off the rotten, bloody water, is enough to make me lightheaded. But its face, her Final Face, jolts me into full focus.

Here, an inch before me, is her Final Face in exact detail as I remember it. Her royal brown skin has turned to decaying green. Her cheeks are bloated, filled with water. Yellow foam drips from the corner of her mouth as her eyes are rolled all the way back, white with lightning strikes of red.

Before I can lunge for the window, she slaps her hand around my neck and pulls me under.

Beneath the surface, here in the murky liquid, she's no longer as I remember her. The white water has filled her body, bloating her beyond the bounds of human flesh. In seconds, she suddenly fills the room, pulling me closer to her bloodshot eyes.

I kick, I punch, making direct contact. But her skin is airy, I might as well be fighting a sheet in the wind. I claw, I bite, my teeth sinking into her fluid flesh. Finally she loosens her grip. We both flail and for a moment I'm free. But the water whirls like an extension of herself. *It is an extension of herself.* Her gossamer thin skin gyrates, bubbling, the water circling and spinning me closer to her.

She pulls me down. Closer. Her mouth opens. Her teeth giant, the size of my arms, are large enough to shred me in three bites. I face her head on and there's no doubt that she's trying to pull me in. But with all the strength left in me, more than I realize, I push my hands against her giant front teeth and propel myself backward, breaking the glass and crashing through the window.

I slam against the roof as the white water gushes out. I land amid shards of shattered glass. I struggle to stand, my legs feeling like timber. I cough, throwing up what feels like gallons of the spoiled water.

I look down from the roof at the front yard and the street ahead. I'm tempted to leap from the roof but my body tells me otherwise. I didn't survive that only to break my legs on a rooftop tumble. To my left is an old birch, the type I've climbed for years. I dash for it and jump, not considering the sizable gap between the roof and the tree.

My body hits the tree with a thump and I start to slide. I kick my leg out, snagging a branch as my hand finds another. Breathe. *Slow down.* You got this.

I steadily scale my way down until I can drop down to the grass.

*Thank*—there's no time to thank God. As my feet hit the ground, I find a second wind. I dash for the street, not looking back, running faster than I've ever run in my life.

I want to stop and cry. I want Lucky and I want to go home.

But I push forward, losing the feeling in my legs.

Behind me, I can still hear the water pouring from the house, dripping down the roof and into the tin gutter. Amid the sound, I hear rain pattering against the pavement behind me.

*Don't look back,* the voice whispers.

"I won't," I say aloud. I can't.

If I want to survive, I can never look back.

# chAPteR 5

**PUTTING THE PEN TO THE** paper is an act of bravery. A leap of faith. It's a declaration of self-love, self-trust, and self-preservation. My thoughts matter. I matter. I might be scared of the world around me, but because I matter, because my words mean something, I put them down on paper to help me get to the other side.

Or at least this is what I try to tell myself. Sometimes I forget. Sometimes I don't believe it.

Above, there's not a cloud in the sky. She's a perfect robin's egg blue. There's not a droplet of rain.

The sound of pattering behind me is not real.

This place, or my perception of it, is betraying me.

It's not real. It can't be.

Wake up, I tell myself. None of this is real.

I wipe the tears away and feel stupid for it. I'm soaking,

stained in wicked waters. The tears are the least of my concerns.

I keep running, heading back down the street the way I came. Return to the roads I know.

Go home, finally get help.

My whole body is heavy, my legs are Jell-O, but there's no stopping.

"Wake up," I tap my face.

The lane goes straight for as long as I can see. Far longer than I remember.

Where's the turn in the road?

I rush forward, refusing to stop or glance back.

I pass houses I've never seen before, going further than I know I traveled.

Did I go the wrong way? Am I confused? Should I have gone the other direction?

*Maybe?*

Doesn't matter. Keep going. The road's gotta come to an end eventually.

I reach a hill.

No, thank you.

I know for certain there was no hill on the street.

Shit.

I gotta admit it. I went the wrong way.

Shit, shit, shit.

I finally stop running, trying to collect my breath and thoughts.

*You're safe*, the voice echoes. *You're exactly where you're supposed to be.*

Not now, I tell myself. Please not now.

I close my eyes and try to make sense of the world around me. The only saving grace is that this isn't real. Not that voice, not this horrible place. None of it. It can't be.

"Of course, it is," a small voice peeps from behind me.

I turn. There on the sidewalk, beneath the shadow of a maple tree, is a small girl. She's no older than seven or eight.

"Excuse me?"

"You said this can't be real." She steps into the sun. She wears denim overall shorts atop a crisp white t-shirt. Matching her shirt, she wears boots more suited for winter, which go all the way up to her shins. "So, I said, of course it is."

"I didn't say that." I shake my head. "I thought that." I think?

"We both said it." Now she's in the street, moving closer to me.

I step back. She notices my fear and giggles at it.

"You don't need to be scared."

After what just happened at that house, I most certainly do. I step back again, reaching into my pockets, feeling for something to protect myself with.

I pull out my phone. It's dripping wet, its slick black screen reflecting my mess of a self back to me.

"I promise." She's now within a few feet. Her hair is split down the center, fluffed out and up into two pom-poms. She looks so familiar. "I've been where you are. The worst is behind you."

She smiles. It seems kinda forced, like she's trying to be nice. But sometimes trying to be nice is enough.

There's a gap in her top two teeth, a little like mine. Her skin glows, nearly gold in the sunlight. She steps closer and my heart skips a beat. She's got a thick scar that I can feel just by looking at it. It runs from beneath her left eye, across her brow, and up to the center of her head where her hair parts. It reminds me of a river, with ridges that look like waves, and slick smooth patches where one could float for eternity.

"Don't worry." She catches me staring. "It happened before I was born."

Before you were born? What does that mean?

She reaches her hand forward to take mine and I instinctively pull back. Her shoulders slink and she looks down to the street, but not before I catch the flash of sadness in her eyes. I feel bad, but it wasn't personal. I'm just not in a rush to trust anyone right now.

She picks at her nails, scratching away some chipped polish.

I get chills.

Her yellow-coated nails sparkle above the black pavement.

It can't be.

I cross my arms, trying to warm myself.

"I've gotta find my brother," I say. "Shit." I remember. "And his turtle."

"One thing at a time. Let's start with the person," she says, a flicker of excitement in her voice, as though I've just invited her on an adventure. "What's his name?"

"Lucky."

"That's not a person name."

"It's his name," I snap, clearly short of patience.

"Lane?"

I raise an eyebrow. "How do you know—"

"Everyone knows Lucky. He cuts through here all the time."

"Did you see him today?"

"Today?" She scratches the back of her neck. "Not sure. That's kinda hard to say."

"Not really. It's a yes or no. It's today or it wasn't."

Her face scrunches. She struggles with her thoughts. She runs her fingers across her forehead, her yellow nails crossing her river scar.

"Sometimes I lose track of these kinda things, that's all. Miss Am's helping me with it, it's just a thing I do. We'll fix it all eventually."

She looks down at the street, kicking her white boots against the black pavement. There's something incredibly sad about her. Whether it's her small, slow movements or just the air around her, I can't tell. But I feel bad for snapping on her.

"You said he cuts through here? He ever tell you where he's going?"

"Isn't it obvious?" she smiles.

"I wish it were. That's why I'm asking."

"*Lucky Lane…*" She turns her hands upwards, like it's the simplest thing and I'm stupid for not getting it.

"Yeah…where's he going?"

"No. You're missing what I'm saying. He's going where he's supposed to be. The place he's destined for: Lucky Lane."

"I'm not really one for riddles—"

"This isn't a riddle. Riddles are hard. This is easy. Lucky Lane is, my guess, on Lucky Lane."

I'm officially pissed. I clench my jaw and turn away from the child to walk away.

"I'm sorry, miss? Did I say something wrong?" she calls out. "You never introduced yourself."

"I know."

I hear her trotting behind me, making her way to my side. Great.

"Some people call me Favorite, but I don't really like that."

"That's a shame." I try to pick up the pace but she's in lockstep.

"You can call me Little."

"Probably won't do that, but cool."

She's silent. For one glorious second, she's silent.

"I don't remember my real name," she blurts.

Jesus Christ. I look down at her. This sad, annoying creature.

"That's messed up. Like, super messed up." I sigh. "I'm sorry."

She shrugs. "It's fine. Now my name is Destiny."

I freeze. My heart drops down to the tip of my toes, trying to crawl from my body and melt on the pavement.

This doesn't make sense. This doesn't make sense.

*Shhh.*

"What's wrong?" She tilts her head.

"Your name's Destiny?"

"Yeah. Of course. Destiny Lane, right where I'm supposed to be. You don't have to call me that though, it gets really confusing."

My head starts to spin. Stars start to streak from the top of the trees, swirling across the blue sky. I might faint. I'm gonna faint. Don't faint!

Did she say *Lane*?

I look down at her. The pom-poms. The front-tooth gap. The chipped yellow nails.

I know this girl.

No. It can't be. It's not.

*Yes. It is.*

I can't believe it.

This girl is me.

"You okay?" she asks.

Her eyes go wide as she tries to read the fear dripping from my face. Our brown eyes stare at each other's and I see a light go off in the center of hers. She's realizing the same thing as me.

But her reaction is quite different.

A smile spreads on her face. A smile so wide, it should be reserved exclusively for Christmas morning when you open up that final, impossible gift. The one gift that's hidden in the back, the one you wanted the most, but as you opened present after present, you've already started to give up the idea of getting it. But then, against all odds, you rip that paper and for a split second, magic exists.

*Magic.*

"Why are you smiling?"

"You have to meet my family. You've got to meet Miss Am!"

"I've gotta go home."

"Yeah. Of course," she nods, whispering back to herself. "You've got to go home."

"Not without Lucky."

"Right. Lucky Lane," she keeps whispering. "I can take you to Lucky Lane. Just don't mention it in front of the girls."

"What girls? I don't really have time to meet—"

"It's the only way. We need to cut through my house."

"But I heard him. Back at that house."

She shakes her head emphatically. "We both know that wasn't your brother."

I don't want to admit that I think she's right. But how do we know?

"He called for me. He was in pain."

"The Looker was just trying to scare you. It makes everything easier if you're scared."

"The Looker?" I let out a nervous laugh and she shushes me.

"Shh. Shh! Not so loud. Don't repeat that! Don't repeat anything I say. He could be looking right now. He owns all of Lucky Lane, but Miss Am protects us here."

I shake my head. This child is crazy.

We reach a slope in the road. I turn back, looking at the road from which I ran. I must've missed my turn.

"What are you looking for?"

"I told you," I'm short on patience. "Lucky."

I could have sworn the road bent. I should be back on Jefferson by now.

"There's no bend in the road," she says. "Not for a while."

I look back at her, fuming. I know I didn't say anything about the turn out loud.

"Whatever you're doing, stop it."

"Your home is this way." She starts up the hill and waves me forward.

I have no interest in following this imaginative child.

She looks back and sees that I haven't budged. She smiles, her gap darker than the road beneath us.

"I get it. We've all been there," she speaks like she's much older than her age suggests. There are few things more annoying than kids that think they've seen it all. I roll my eyes. She seems to enjoy my frustration, grinning wider.

"Look." She points up the hill.

I groan as I step forward. I squint, trying to see what she's pointing at.

"Here, closer." She waves me ahead. "Stand here."

I slowly join her, accidentally brushing her arm. She doesn't notice. She's still looking ahead.

"Now crouch."

I look up at the path ahead. Both sides of the street are lined with dozens of Victorian houses—a promising sign that we're not far from home.

"Between that blue house and the green one…"

In the distance, at the hilltop, jutting between the two homes, I see a familiar yellow turret.

The girl turns to see my reaction before I've even processed it.

I gasp and she giggles.

No more than the size of a pin, the fish-shaped weathervane shows me the way.

Home.

"Shall we?" she says with a chuckle.

I look down at her. What child says *shall*?

I'd prefer that the girl doesn't join me, but she seems like she'll be hard to shake.

"Sure."

"I just need to stop and ask Am if I can take you."

"You don't need to do all that. I'll be fine."

"Sure I do." She skips ahead. "We don't want you walking into the wrong house again."

"I didn't really have a choice. This water, actually it was more like milk, it started coming out of the pond like it was alive. It was coming for me."

She nods, like she's heard it all before. "Typical Looker tricks. This is why you need me. Once I clear it with Am, we'll be home. Simple."

"Don't forget Lucky."

"Yeah, yeah. But we're not going to mention that part."

We head up the hill. I can't believe I'm following this delusional child. This child that's—

No. She's not you. That makes no sense. That's impossible.

But lots of impossible things have been happening lately, another thought reminds me. Gigi dying, the unseen eye watching my every move, this stranger taking up residency in my head. As we walk forward, I find myself realizing that this feels just like a dream. Not in the sense that I'm watching myself from above as weird, uncontrollable things happen around me. But the other kind, where I at least have some control. It's like that dream I had in the cornfield, and countless dreams since, that opened up doors to places and ideas that shouldn't be real. They couldn't be real. But they were. They are.

Still, it's always felt like there was just a thin curtain separating what I saw in my head from what everyone calls "the real world." But sometimes, the curtain is so thin, I swear I can see through it. Here, in this place, the curtain is gone. These worlds are one and the same.

You sound fucking nuts, one of my thoughts points out. You've lost it.

No, no, no. *You're right where you're supposed to—*

I take a deep breath, trying to center myself and sidestep the storm in my head. I close my eyes and the outline of something small and thin moves into the middle of my mind. At first it appears as no more than a fragmented line. But no. I zero in. It has a button on one end beside a clip, and then on the other end, a point. *A pen.*

"Who hurt you?" The child breaks the silence.

"Excuse me?"

"Oop. I'm sorry. Didn't mean to offend you. You're not ready to talk about it. That's fine. Pretty normal, honestly."

"What are you even talking about?"

"Nothing. I shouldn't say anything. Not my place. Miss Am knows more about the healing process, not me."

"Miss Am. She's like, your mom or something?"

The child laughs. "Okay, definitely don't say that in front of her. She'd hate that. But, honestly, yeah. Kinda. She takes care of all of us. You can call her Miss Am, Aunt Am, or just Am if you guys get close."

I don't plan on getting close. What is this kid on? Talking about a healing process? We are getting in and out of there, finding Lucky, and going back to normal.

"What do you mean, *all of us*?"

"All of the girls, obviously. There's 22 of us."

My jaw drops. "22?"

"Yup. Lots of us were left behind or forgotten. But we're fine now. This is a place where she can keep us safe."

The way she keeps saying *us* makes me uncomfortable. Like she's intent on including me in this *us*. Like we're one and the same.

*We are.*

I rub the chill rolling across the back of my neck. I look over at the girl.

Sure, she looks like me. But as a child. That's not me. And there's one major physical difference.

"How'd you really get that scar?" I blurt out gracelessly. "If you don't mind me asking." I try to soften my delivery.

"I love getting into trouble." She rolls her shoulders and tilts her head. "Accidents happen."

"22 kids is a lot to keep track of."

"Oh. Definitely wasn't her fault."

Strange. "Wasn't even thinking that."

"She's always watching us. I mean, she gives us freedom, but she does a good job at keeping us safe."

Gives us freedom?

"Ya know, Miss Am's always worried I'll say too much. I'll shut up now."

Seems unlikely.

The girl springs ahead, humming a tune to herself. Every couple seconds or so, she sings a word or two, like she's still learning the lyrics. Her voice is soft and sweet when she sings, far less grating than her speaking voice.

"...*Gather blueberries...swan on the lake, swan on the lake...*"

Part of me feels like I know her song. Maybe it's just her voice.

"You have a beautiful singing voice," I tell her.

"You sing?"

"Oh no. Not for me. My voice is—"

"Beautiful. You just haven't let it out."

We smile in unison, like magic mirrors that can see through time.

What did she say she liked being called? Favorite?

"Little," she clarifies.

Please stop doing that.

"Okay."

You're still doing it.

*Whoops.*

I look over at her and scowl. She looks back and grins.

I can't lie. There's a sliver of this kid that's adorable.

And honestly, there's an equal part of her that's pretty scary.

She giggles and hops ahead. Little's every step is a bounce, full of energy, but I try to keep up. We move slowly but steadily ahead, my legs burning against the steep street. The sun beats down, drying my clothes in minutes. My hoodie feels like papier-mâché, stiff and crunchy. We walk in the middle of the street as though cars don't exist. They're parked all around us, but I've yet to see any of them move from their spots. I consider taking off my hoodie until I remember that I left the house straight from my bed, and there's nothing beneath. I could really use a glass of water or a cold shower.

I head for the sidewalk. Little's eyes go wide.

"What are you doing?"

"Anything wrong with some shade?"

"Closer to the grass!?" She's appalled by my change of course.

"Yeah."

"Sure. You could," she scoffs. "But The Looker loves to hide his slitheries in the grass. I can scare most of them away most of the time, but no guarantees."

Slitheries? Okay. Whatever. I'll avoid the imaginary slitheries.

Beneath the shade of the trees, it's impossible to track our progress. I can no longer see the fish-shaped weathervane in the distance. But it feels like we've been walking for a mile, something I haven't done since last year's Presidential Challenge in gym class when I clocked in at a whopping 24 minutes. I don't run anymore. I used to kinda like it. Was pretty good, actually. Now it hurts my knees and my soul.

"We almost there?"

The question's barely out of my mouth and she answers. "Here!"

I dash to join her in the street.

I look up, ready to be home.

"What the hell?"

There's no sign of Washington Street, and yet, beyond an iron gate, sitting atop a grassy hill, there's the yellow house I call home.

With the twin turrets on either side, and the smallest in the center where the angled roofs convene, I know this Victorian facade better than my face in a mirror. Against the sun, the weathervane glistens like gold, seemingly free of rust. Atop the hill, the house has never loomed larger.

We step forward and I wince, shielding my eyes.

That's not my house.

"I know," Little responds.

*It's ours.*

Where my home ends, a monumental white building is pushed up behind it. I struggle to find the words to describe the blinding sight before me. The home I grew up in is merely an entryway for the massive structure that claims the rest of the hill's peak. Picture a giant rectangle laying on its long side, void of windows or molding or any other ornament that might add any character. Save for the yellow home, that looks as out of place as a single tree sprouting from the ocean, this place is an empty slate—entirely void of emotion.

"I'm sorry," Little says. "You thought I meant *your* house? I told you. We need to ask Am."

"And I told you," I yell, "we don't need to do that!"

The small girl looks scared. Her joyful mask drips away, returning to the sad state I found her in. Her lip quivers and she turns away, not wanting me to see her pain.

I roll my eyes. The guilt trip is working.

I sigh. Fine. "I'm sorr—"

"I'm sorry," we say atop each other.

I move closer. Ugh. I can't believe I'm doing this. I put an arm awkwardly around her bony little shoulder.

"You get it, right?" I ask. "I just wanna find my brother."

"I know," she wipes her eyes.

"I'm just scar—"

She cuts me off. "Scared. I know. Me too."

My heart skips a beat as my face scrunches. I'm supposed to be the scared one. What is she afraid of? I can't have this. She knows this place. She's gotta be the brave one.

She looks me dead in the eyes, then quickly glances over her shoulder, back at the gate behind her.

"I'm gonna get you home," she whispers. "And we're gonna get Lucky. You just have to play along."

Play along?

"What does that mean?"

"Hey Destiny!" a child's voice calls from across the street.

We both turn. A small child stands beyond the iron gate, holding a red rubber ball. The child looks like she might be the same age as Little.

"You wanna play grimmball?"

Another child steps in front of the gate, standing beside the girl with the red ball. From across the street, they look like twins.

"Miss Am's looking for you," this child says, a hint of satisfaction in her voice.

Little steps forward, toward the gate. When she realizes I'm not following, she looks back and nods. I take a deep breath and cross the street.

Beyond the gate, the two girls step aside as it opens. On the vast lush lawn, dozens of girls play in small groups. Beyond the children, the building wearing my home as a mask hovers over them.

"Tell her I'm coming."

Little takes me by the hand and pulls me toward the gate. As I'm melting in this heat, Little's flesh is cold to the touch.

Within a step of the gate, I can see the girls' faces clearer now.

My head gets light. My heart batters in my chest, wanting to break through.

Both of the girls have pom-poms, yellow nails, and small gaps between their top two teeth.

My palms get sweaty. My fingers start to twitch. Little rubs her freezing thumb against the back of my hand.

I look down at Little. "She looks just like—"

"You," she cuts me off. She stares into my eyes and nods. "Just play along."

# chApteR 6

**"MY FAVORITE THING ABOUT WRITING,"** Gigi said, not looking up from her red book, "is that it keeps the child in you alive."

Maybe that's why I stopped for so long. I was one of those kids who couldn't wait to grow up. I couldn't wait to cut the cords with the past and just start fresh.

But then there's always those adults who say they wish they could go back. Childhood is the best time of your life! Gross. That's just about the most depressing thing I can imagine. If my past is the best this life has to offer, I understand why some people call it quits.

"Relax," Little says. I don't know whether she's talking to me or herself. Her hand trembles in mine. I notice a glimmer to her glossy brown eyes.

As we pass the brick wall, the double-doored gate swivels

closed behind us. I glance back, and to my relief, I see a control panel from which one of the girls has pressed it closed.

"Don't react," Little whispers.

There's two more, I think, hoping she'll hear me.

"This is just the start." She looks ahead, down the half-mile driveway.

How many did Little say there were? 22? They can't all be—

"Aunt Am's gonna kill you." The girl with the red ball steps closer.

She smirks at Little before turning to me, scanning me from top to bottom. She lingers on my stained Vans for a moment before her eyes dart back up to my face. She wipes the corner of her mouth.

"You're triplets?" I ask, trying to break the silence.

Little shakes her head. Red Ball scrunches her face.

"What do you mean?" the carbon copy asks. "You mean sisters?"

I shrug. "Sure."

"We're all sisters," Red Ball says, motioning to the dozen or so girls spread across the massive lawn.

I look out at the sea of girls and they're all looking back at me. The hairs on the back of my neck stand up straight. They're all wearing the same denim jumper. They all have pom-poms and painted nails. They're all—

"Destiny." This Little clone extends her hand.

I pull to take my hand from Little's but she squeezes it harder, not letting me go.

"Her name is Destiny too," Little says, gesturing to me.

"That's…" Red Ball's eyes go wide. She peers at me and smiles. She's got the gap like the rest of us, but there's something off-putting about her teeth. It's almost like they're sharper. "Fantastic."

"I found her in front of the garden house. Sounds like The Looker was trying to scare her."

"So, she came here by herself?" Red Ball's smile twists.

"No. I found her. I brought her here," Little's voice pitches.

Her hand squeezes mine tighter. It's starting to hurt.

I slip my fingers free but not without her resisting. She grabs for my hand and her yellow nail slides against the side of my hand.

Ouch.

"What the fuck!?"

Her nails are like razors. A thin red line appears on the back of my hand. Blood swells and slips from the cut.

Red Ball breaks into laughter. Little looks mortified.

"She said a no-no word," Red Ball grins wider. "Aunt Am's gonna love her."

"Destiny," she covers her mouth. "I'm so sorry!"

She reaches for my hand, but I step back.

"It's fine." I pull the sleeve of my hoodie over my hand, stopping the flow.

"You found her and you're gonna scare her away all in one day," the mean girl laughs. "Nice job."

Little tries to look me in the eyes but struggles. Her lip trembles. "I swear it was an accident."

"It's whatever," I say. "Forget about it."

"What are we waiting for?" Red Ball elbows Little. "Let's get her to Aunt Am."

"I don't really have time to meet anyone. I gotta find my brother and get home."

"You didn't mention a brother," Red Ball scowls at her sister.

"It's nothing, please. Let's go." Little steps up the driveway, waving us forward.

"You know what she says about brothers." Red Ball shakes her head.

"I don't think it's a big deal," Little speaks quickly. "It's just a brother. She's here now."

*It's* just a brother?

"His name's Lucky," I say.

Little turns back, throwing her hands over her eyes. The sharp girl drops her red ball.

*Pung-pung-pung.* It bounces down the driveway, sputtering off into the grass.

"A Lucky?!" the double howls.

The girls in the field start chattering. Some of them start walking toward us.

"No!" Little yells, trying to wave them off. "It's nothing."

"This is all too perfect," Red Ball says to the gathering girls. "Favorite says she found a new Destiny."

A few of the girls chuckle, closing in.

"Stay away." Little steps in front of me.

"That's not even the best part," the mini-mean continues.

"She's got a brother. *Named Lucky.*"

The girls break into a chorus of laughter.

I'm officially freaked out.

The twenty small Destinys step closer, cackling. Surrounded by these shrunken, twisted versions of myself, I feel like I'm standing at the center of a cursed funhouse.

"She's mine!" Little hollers, stepping in front of me.

I scoff. I'm absolutely no one's.

"What's going on?" I shove Little in the back.

"It's nothing." Her voice suggests otherwise. It's definitely something. "They're gonna try to take you from me."

"No one's going to do anything," Red Ball sneers. "You need this more than any of us."

"What is she talking about?" I try to interject but they're all chattering atop each other.

"Miss Am's never gonna believe you," a voice in the crowd says.

It's clear that I've made a mistake in following Little. I look back at the gate. Could I outrun all of the girls? Probably. But then what? The gate is high. Even on my best day, I couldn't clear that fence. And this is far from my best day.

A few of the girls notice my glance and circle behind me toward the gate. I notice that two of the girls are holding wooden baseball bats. Another holds a bucket of baseballs. I imagine them pummeling me snowball style and I avert my glance from the gate.

Every time I think I've wrapped my head around how many there are, another handful seem to spring up.

A partition of little Destinys line the driveway all the way up to the house. Little said there were 22, but this feels like more. Every time I turn, more seem to materialize.

Before I realize it, Little grabs my hand.  I try to pull back but her grip is iron.

"Please." There's fear in her eyes. "This is the only way."

*Play along*, she said. Is this all part of it?

She tugs me forward and I slowly follow.

Further up the driveway and I'm ready to admit to myself what I've feared for a while now. I'm not in my hometown anymore. Honestly, this might not even be New Jersey. The yard alone is the size of 50 football fields. There's nothing of this magnitude in town. It simply wouldn't fit. I look up at the front of the house posing as my own and I know for certain it's just a disguise. The yellow paint looks crisp, as though it were painted that morning. At the peak, the weathervane is not my own. Its gold glistens, free of rust. As it gently turns, it's silent, missing its trusted groan.

I glance up at the room that should be my own and see a group of older girls in the window. They slide the curtains closed as soon as they realize I've spotted them. Unlike the little girls around me, shadows of my past self, these girls above are my body doubles. With the exception of my oversized hoodie and soaking pajama pants, these girls are my present self. These girls are me.

Hovering over the yellow home, looming over us all, is the white rectangle. The colossal structure wipes out the horizon, blocking out any glimpse of the other side. Looking like a warehouse made of ivory, I can't help but wonder what type of psycho would willingly live in such a bleak building. As I pass the girls on the driveway, they step in a line behind me, ushering me forward. I look back at the sea of little mes.

22, Little said. A rush glides over me. *I make 23.*

"You're gonna love it here," Little nods.

The mean girl with the red ball and sharp teeth butts between us. "You can call me Razor. This one may be the Favorite," she elbows Little, "but I mostly run things."

"Why Razor?"

"I'm the sharpest, fastest—"

"Oh, here she goes," one of the girls cuts her off. A trickle of laughter from the group sets me at ease. I chuckle.

I glance back up at my home, or the part of this house that looks like mine. Our little yellow abode could never hold all these girls. Does each of these girls have their own room, in the giant blank space? Is there a 23rd room, beyond the attic, ready for me?

"What do you think?" Little asks.

"Honestly?"

Little's eyes go wide. She mouths: *No.*

"Familiar. But different?" I shrug. "It's certainly interesting."

"Wait till you see the other side," Razor says.

"I'm not sure I wanna see the other side."

Save for a single laugh behind me, my honesty is ignored.

"It's entirely glass," Little says.

"So we can always see the backyard," Razor adds. "The mountains, the river, the waterfall."

"Mountains?" Now I'm kinda interested.

"Don't forget the Forever Fields," another girl chimes in.

"Fields you can run through forever," Little explains.

Nope. Can't be. This definitely isn't Jersey.

We reach the entrance and the front door I'm expecting has been replaced with a pair of giant wooden slabs with polished golden handles. The double-doors tower over us, more suited for a medieval castle than whatever it is I'm stepping into. Two of the smaller girls skip ahead and pull the doors open as though they're weightless.

Stop. Slow down, I tell myself. What are you doing?

"I'd rather not go in," I lean down and whisper to Little.

"We have to," she mutters back. "Don't worry. It's nothing like the Garden House."

As the doors open, the sun shines through from the far side of the house. Any hint of my home washes away in the crisp light. The space is wide open, with high ceilings and sparkling marble floors. Unlike the last house I entered, there's nothing hiding in the shadows for there are no shadows to be cast. Everything is clean and white. The entire space smells recently polished—a task that must have taken hours to complete. The air is cool, instantly chilling the sweat against my skin. Everything glistens, from winding staircases on either side of the room to the plush welcome mat I've stepped upon.

At the sight of my filthy Vans against the mat, I realize how out of place I am.

I shouldn't be here. I look back just as the girls swing the double-doors shut.

The group gathers in beside me, kicking off their shoes. As they hit the floor, a few of the girls immediately scoop them, pair by pair, and place them on a wooden rack by the wall. Before I can slide mine off, two of the girls are already at my feet, pulling them off for me.

"Oh, oh. I wouldn't touch those."

But they're already gone, tossed amid the pile of shoes.

The mat beneath my bare feet feels like heaven. I could rest here for hours, but Little pulls me ahead. On both sides of us are tall arches leading into wide open rooms. Vines of pink roses line each of the arches and bend, weaving their way upstairs through guardrails. To the left, there's a library with shelves of books stacked to the ceiling. To the right, a game room with flashing lights that looks like an arcade.

"Miss Am gets us games that haven't even come out yet."

The girls dash across the hall, giggling, chattering, seemingly on to their next game. A small pack still lingers around me.

"Here," Razor says, waving forward four more minis. "These girls will show you around."

Little rolls her eyes. Razor heads upstairs to the left, plucking a rose petal from the railing as she passes. Each of the remaining girls introduces themselves. Each of them is identical to Little; identical to my smaller self, save for one or two small features.

"I'm Ace." A girl steps forward to shake my hand. Weird. Her grip is firm, her forearm muscles are slightly defined. Is there a gym here? Are kids supposed to be jacked?

If that weren't strange enough, I notice her dangling black earrings. They're shaped like daggers. Okay, she might be scarier than Razor.

"My name's Violet and this is Daisy," they both flash their hands with weak waves, then smile, turning slightly pink. Identifying them should be easy, for each of them wears a floral headband with their respective flowers. When they try to look up at me, they seem unable to look me in the eye, turning back to each other and breaking down into little giggles. Again, a little weird, but they seem harmless enough.

"And I'm Cupcake," the last of them says. Her voice is gruff, like she's got a stone stuck in it.

"I'm guessing you like cupcakes?"

"Hate 'em," she says. "I break into hives when I eat 'em. The girls think it's funny to poke fun."

"Look!" Ace pulls at Cupcake's shirt collar, revealing a green boil that oozes a thick yellow pus on her neck. I hate to admit it, but it strangely looks like a cupcake. "We had some yesterday!"

All of the girls laugh, including Little. I hope this is part of her act. Cupcake pulls her collar back over the boil, unable to look up from the floor. The girls start walking across the foyer. I lean over to Cupcake.

"Cupcakes are overrated, anyway. Donuts? That's a different story."

"Can't eat those, either," she says.

Damn. "You ever have a panzarotti?"

"A what?"

"It's nothing. Sweets suck, is all I'm trying to say. They're basically poison. You're gonna outlive all of us."

Cupcake's face scrunches. She looks at me like I've just said the stupidest thing imaginable before rolling her eyes.

"Oop!" Little points to the ground. "Don't step on the compass."

I freeze, barefoot in air, then gingerly redirect my step. Etched in gold on the marble floor is a symbol I feel like I've seen before but I can't place it. Little called it a compass, but I've never seen a compass like this before. The image before me looks random. Chaotic.

But that's not quite right either. Surely it has meaning, or it wouldn't cover the floor of this hall. It's gotta be an archaic symbol, the type you'd find carved in a cave. Or one you might see on Ancient Aliens, pressed into a cornfield.

I take in the sight before me, and for a split-second, it feels like time stands still:

Amid a giant circle, three lines meet in a strange pattern that sort of looks like a seven sitting atop a longer slanted wire. Both of the extended lines have two dashes etched on them that look like equal signs. At the end of each line, there's a small circle—four in total. I stare at the circles, and for a moment, it feels like they stare back.

*Eyes.*

I expect chills to wash over me, but they don't. I feel still. A welcome calm. Unlike the all-too-familiar feeling of being watched, when it feels like I'm about to get pounced on, here before the "compass", I feel guarded. Protected.

"It's beautiful," I say.

And scary. But I don't speak that part aloud.

"Am says it's so we can always find our way home."

"This Am says a lot of things, huh?"

Little's eyes turn to daggers that she shoots my way. She quickly tries to change the subject.

"Look at the backyard!" She skips along the edge of the compass.

She leads us from the foyer toward the bright, modern kitchen. I don't stop to take in the details of the sleek stove or new fridge; instead, I'm stunned completely still. My jaw drops.

A gigantic window takes up the entire back wall. Beyond the glass, there's a mountain range. Four identical peaks dot the horizon. I've been told there are mountains in New Jersey, but I've never seen them in person. Mountains exist onscreen. Sure, they were beautiful in movies, but this is impossible. "Purple mountain majesty" made no sense to me before. Mountains couldn't be purple. They're rocks. But here, in the flesh, filtered beneath a blue sky and pink clouds, they dazzle like prehistoric amethysts.

The brain and the heart that the rest of my body are relying on to survive weren't ready for this kind of beauty. I have to pause, reminding myself to breathe. I inhale, exhale, feeling tears welling behind my eyes.

No, thank you. I wipe them away and hope no one notices.

"You thought we were lying?" Little giggles.

I open my mouth but no sound escapes.

The rest of the girls laugh. I feel myself burning up.

Cupcake steps beside me. "Don't feel weird. They remind me why I love it here."

"And look over there," Little points.

To our right, within a few steps of the back porch, several girls run up a grassy knoll. Water gushes from the top, cascading down to a sparkling stream below.

"A waterfall," I whisper to myself, confirming this is real.

Little smiles proudly. "It's all ours."

The girls jump from a ledge, spearing downward then splashing below. Across the stream, there's a platform that more girls are climbing.

"Is that a slide?"

"A waterslide," Violet corrects me.

"We thought it was a good idea," says Daisy.

"Am can't say no to us," Little laughs.

"She can't say no to you," Cupcake corrects.

"Well, you're welcome then."

I smile, remembering the summer days spent with Iyana at the swim club down on River Road. I was too little to use the slide and never got a band to move beyond the kiddie pool, but those days full of Sharks and Minnows and oversized Swedish Fish served in those criss-cross hot dog trays were all I needed from life.

"You want to give it a try?" Ace asks.

"Not yet," a sharp voice calls from above.

We turn back and Razor has made her way back downstairs and into the foyer.

"Aunt Am wants to see her."

"Great," Little swallows hard. "Her room?"

"Not so fast." Razor shakes her head. "*Temple*."

The word zaps me like a lightning rod to my heart.

Strangest of all, I don't know why. My mind tries to map why this particular word stings me, but I come up empty. It's that feeling when *you know* you know something, but when you dig into the ole' brain bank, there's a blank wall with the information you're looking for hidden on the other side.

The girls around us murmur, turning to each other with arched brows and giggly whispers.

"We don't usually do this so soon," I hear Violet say to Daisy.

"What's the temple?"

"Our favorite place in the world," Ace beams.

I turn to Little, who's picking at her nail polish.

"We're talking about the same kind of temple. Like, for praying and stuff?"

Little stares blankly toward the mountainous horizon beyond the glass.

"More or less," Razor says.

I'm hoping it's less. What kids find pleasure in prayer? These girls are weird as fuck.

The whispers of the temple turn to a hollered invite. All the girls from all across the house, even the ones from the waterfall, drop their games at once and gather back in the foyer. Around the etched compass, the girls circle, all of them shoeless. Their naked toes kiss the edge of the strange symbol.

There's a chatter around the compass that a few of the girls try to hush. Everyone links hands with their neighbor and most of them close their eyes. This is a ritual they appear to know well.

I approach their circle with Little and Razor flanking me. The girls side-shuffle to make room for us. To my right, Razor exhales through her nose and closes her eyes. To my right, Little gently smiles and nods. She closes her eyes.

I take one last look around me. Silence sweeps across the bright, airy space. I'm the only one with my eyes still open. Little pops open her left eye, peering at me through her slick scar.

"Waiting on you," she taps her toes.

I'd rather not sacrifice my most trusted sense, but there's likely no harm in trying to quiet my mind for a moment.

I close my eyes, and just as my lashes meet, I feel a rush of wind consume me.

It's almost as though the floor has dropped beneath us. Little squeezes my hand tight and I squeeze back tighter.

I open my eyes and the light is gone.

# chAPteR 7

AFTER THE LONGEST DAYS, GIGI would take to the kitchen earlier.

"The days you don't wanna do it are usually the days you gotta do it the most."

No one asked questions. The home understood. Poppy knew to take care of dinner, which usually meant ordering Chinese food or panzarottis.

The last few years of her life, Gigi stopped taking her best advice. The days got harder, and the red book was replaced with tumbler glasses. Ginger ale and gin were her go-to. Poppy called them Gigi Ales, which made them sound more harmless than they were.

I find myself wondering if things would have ended differently if she kept writing. Maybe it's childish of me to believe a pen and a paper could have saved her.

I try to make sense of my surroundings. One thing is immediately clear—we're no longer in the foyer.

Little and Razor hold my hands firmly. I wriggle but they remain calm.

"What just happened? Where are we?"

The girls nervously whisper. I can only see their outlines around the circle. I'm not particularly fond of figures in the shadows.

"Hey," Little leans closer to me. "I'm here. We're safe."

"Where are we?"

"Temple," Razor says, the frustration palpable in her voice. "We told you."

Beyond the girls, the space isn't completely dark. It's almost as though we're in a tank of some kind. Or is the tank on the other side? The walls of the circular space are made of glass. Beyond the glass, there's nothing but water as far as I can see. A bright yellow fish darts through the crystal blue. Behind the fish, dozens more swim into view.

The sight of the fish steadies my breathing.

One…two…three…

I impulsively start counting them.

"You can be safe in this space," Little whispers directly into my ear. It's as though she speaks for the fish.

Can be?

Little nods, her white eyes hovering in the darkness.

"There's another place. Or a thing, maybe, inside of you that no one else knows about. No one else can touch it. It's always there and always will be. If you remember it, go there."

Go there? *Where is there?*

I close my eyes and try to sink into myself. It's just as dark in there, but there are no pretty fish. I don't know what the hell she's talking about.

Her ghostly eyes sink into mine. *Keep trying*, they say.

I take a deep breath and close my eyes. I take a deeper breath and there's—

*Something.* I see an outline. Something thin. A line? A stick? I know this shape but it's faint. Familiar but fleeting. The image slips away before I can make sense of it.

The chattering from the girls ceases. Without a word, they all bend to the ground. Before Little or Razor can tug me, I follow the pack.

Barely audible, footsteps tap behind me, nearing ever closer. They're soft patters, as though the walker flirts with weightlessness.

The girls sit cross-legged. Some straighten their spines, looking stern. Others slump, with soft smiles. The girls opposite focus their gaze behind me, in the direction of the approaching walker. *Am.* The girls on my left face forward, not turning their necks. I'm tempted. *Am.* My head inches to turn, but Little squeezes my hand.

I sneak a look at Little from the corner of my eye. She doesn't look back. Her eyes are locked straight ahead. She quickly shakes her head, trying to ignore me. *Focus*, she lips.

Before curiosity gets the better of me, the woman steps into the circle and all of the girls bow their heads. I've attended eight years of Catholic school, so I know the drill.

I follow along. Starting with Razor, the woman walks around the compass with an arm extended toward the girls. I try to get a better look at her but can only see that she's wearing a white frock. Like the girls, she's barefoot, grounded to the world beneath her. I don't dare to look up to her face. Not yet. I'm not sure I'm ready to see her.

As she passes the girls, the energy in the room shifts. It's as though something unseen or something I can't understand passes between them. Each of the girls is suddenly filled with joy. Most can't contain it. Wide smiles sweep across their faces. Some of the girls gently giggle. Across the way, one of the girls breaks into tears. I don't know whether to be grossed out or moved. I can't remember a time where I was ever that happy.

The woman in white makes her way around the circle. She's but a few steps over. She's almost to Little...*Breathe. Just breathe...*Almost to me.

The weightless woman lands upon Little and lingers. I don't dare to look over. But she's spending more time with her than any of the others. Should I be nervous? Is everything okay?

Little gasps and I can't help myself.

I turn and Little's already looking at me.

She smiles as a tear trickles down her cheekbone, sliding over her scar, where it slips sideways across her face then drips off her chin.

The woman steps before me. Before I can look up, she crouches, meeting my eye. Her face is within a breath of mine.

"Hi, Destiny," she smiles.

A soft vibration surges over my body. It's as though I'd been shivering, and suddenly I'm being held close. It feels like someone's pushed a hidden button on me and turned me mute. I want to greet her, but I can't. The words won't even form in my head.

I suddenly picture the backyard mountain range and the waterfall where children play without a worry. I remember the first time I went on a rollercoaster, and at its impossible peak, I thought I might scrape the sun. And then my mind jumps to a panther, its coat black and silky. One summer trip to the zoo I locked eyes with one and pretended to be its peer. My heart raced and I swear I could feel its heart doing the same.

Why did these moments flash in my mind? Why now? I guess for each of these fleeting moments, I almost believed in God.

But then I blink, and in the panther's place is a dove, soaring through space, its wings outspread.

This is what looking at Miss Am is like. Beautiful. Impossible. Almost enough to make you believe in heaven.

Her forest brown eyes resemble original land untouched by man. Their black centers look darker than space, like they've seen the origin of time. With her hair pulled back in a simple ponytail, her face is on full display. No blemishes, no wrinkles. She simultaneously looks 23 and older than the Earth.

She notices me taking in her face and smiles. Other than a slight gap between her two front teeth, she's flawless. Part of me suspects she's forced this slight defect upon herself to make herself less perfect. In doing so, it only makes her more so. People aren't supposed to be this beautiful.

"You don't have to say anything," she says. "I'm just happy you're here."

"Thanks, uh," I stammer, "for…having me."

Miss Am smiles, her teeth settled atop her bottom lip. "We're the ones who should be thanking you."

The regal woman stands and everyone mirrors her movement. But her face is fixed on me. Above her, a ring light hums on, crowning her head.

"Thank me for what, exactly?"

The girls giggle. Little places her hand on my knee.

Miss Am smiles at the sound of the girls' laughter. Each of the children looks up at her with adoration, savoring each second her sight lands upon them.

She turns back to me, and I'd be lying if I said otherwise: I feel that same rush.

"For completing us," Miss Am says.

My heart trembles. I don't think it's supposed to do that.

"I'm not sure I understand."

"There's no rush to understand anything," Miss Am nods. "We're all in this together."

Miss Am extends her hand toward me. Razor gasps. The girls break into a buzz. I turn to Little for guidance. Her brows are arched in shock, but after a beat, she nods her head.

I reach up, grasping Am's hand. It's soft, smooth, and warm.

Holding my hand, she leads me across the compass

toward the center of the floor. Her hand engulfs mine. Her fingers remind me of long branches on a willow tree.

Next to her perfect self, I realize how nasty I look in my stained hoodie, pajama pants, and bare feet that are in desperate need of a washing. At the center of the circle, she bends to kneel. She gently pulls on my palms, instructing me to join her. I follow, reflecting her movement.

I try to look her in the eyes, but I can't.

"Yes, you can," she says.

I look up, trembling. I feel like I might fall through the black holes at the center of her eyes.

*Good.*

I know her voice.

*Yes*, she speaks directly in my head. *It's always been—*

No. No. Please, no.

She's the one that's been in my head since Gigi died. She's the one who's been driving me crazy.

*Shhhh…*the sound echoes through my head, trickling down the back of my neck.

*I am the one who's been with you since Gigi died.* She nods. *I am the one who's been keeping you safe.*

Now I can't look away from her deep brown eyes. They look so familiar. Like I've seen them a million times.

*You have,* she says without speaking.

She bows her head, her forehead nearly touching mine.

"I am you, Destiny."

I pull back and shake my head. "No. No. Look at you. You're perfect. I—"

She raises a finger to my mouth, shushing me with a smile on her face. The chorus of little Destinys chuckle.

"Just listen," she continues. "I am you. I am who you become if you stay with us."

"Stay?" My hands start to shake.

The prospect both horrifies and excites me.

"I know," she nods. "It's a lot to take in. But no one's going to rush you to a decision. What you'll quickly learn is that you are accepted here just as you are. Here, your pain is in the past. Your fear will pass." *Your loved ones won't leave you*, she adds.

She leans closer, reaching her hands across and cradling my head in her long fingers, her thumbs softly pressed against my temples.

"Close your eyes," she nods. "You can trust me."

I can't describe why, but I feel safe in her hands. Safer than I've felt in ages. I do as she says.

In a blink, the room gets a little warmer. I hear a single bird chirping. Buzzing below, I can make out the muffled sounds of a TV. There's a voice coming from it with a strong Texan twang. I think he's saying something about God.

"Don't open your eyes until you're ready for what's on the other side."

I hear Miss Am's voice, but I realize I can no longer feel her hands on my head.

"Where are you?"

"The same place I've always been," she whispers. *Right here with you.*

I open my eyes and quickly make sense of the room around me. I know exactly where I am.

Sloped ceilings hover above me. To my left, there's a desk with scattered papers atop. To my right, a bureau with a stack of childhood books. Across the hallway, across the round purple paisley rug, is a closed door.

That door is never closed, I remind myself.

Not only do I know where I am, I know *when* I am.

He's only ever closed that door once.

Without hesitation, I stand and head for the door.

"Destiny!" Poppy calls from below. "Can you take Tiger for a walk?"

My heart skips a beat. I've never been happier to hear Poppy ask me to take that damn turtle for a walk.

"Where's Lucky?" I ask, as though I don't already know the answer to the question. Or at least, part of the answer. I know for certain he's not here.

I lean forward and knock on the door—*tap, tap, tap*— just below his wishful Bernie sticker and the poster of his new favorite popstar adorned in gold.

I grip the doorknob and turn. "Lucky?"

Across the room, the curtains flutter. I don't jump this time, for I know they're coming.

I push the door all the way open, prepared to see the empty bed.

But I don't. It's not empty.

Lucky rolls over, shielding his eyes from the sun. He looks at me through his fingers.

"Hey bud," his voice is hoarse. "This is certainly a first."

"Lucky?" my voice cracks. "What are you doing here?"

"*Here* is my bed." He pushes aside the covers. "Where else would I be?"

He slaps his feet to the hardwood floor and he groans.

I'm stunned silent and frozen still.

"You're being a little weirdo," he says.

I stutter. "Wh-what's new?"

He stretches in an overly-dramatic morning yawn that teeters on becoming a roar, before he swoops forward and embraces me, pulling me in for the tightest, Luckiest of hugs.

I can't help but laugh.

*He's here. He's back. We're safe.*

I lean my head against his chest, and he leans his chin against my buzzed head.

"I'm sorry about last night, Destiny," he says. "About everything. I shouldn't have held that stuff about your mom and everything from you. There's no excuse. I know it doesn't make sense, but I was just trying to protect you and fucked up big time."

I cough, fighting back the tears swelling beneath my eyes.

"I know. It's fine. I mean, it's not fine, but it is. I'm just glad you're safe."

I close my eyes, settling into his cozy arms, fully savoring this moment. Here, now, I want nothing else.

*It's peaceful. It's perfect. It's complete.*

In an instant, the arms embracing me vanish. I have no desire to open my eyes. My brother may be gone, but the feelings don't pass. It's still perfect. *I'm still whole.*

The darkness beneath my eyelids turns to white.

I feel Miss Am's soft hands return to my head and I'm back on my knees.

"He is safe. He is whole. He is gone," I hear Miss Am's calm voice.

*Who is he?*

I take a deep breath and it feels like heaven. I feel refreshed. Revitalized. I feel new in a way I've never felt before.

I open my eyes and Miss Am's gentle gaze is there to greet me.

"You are doing so good, Destiny."

That's me, I nod, suddenly feeling the need to remind myself. *Destiny.*

"Okay, same as last time," she whispers, running her fingers across my scalp, sending chills down my body.

I close my eyes and hear a crowd around me. It's nothing overwhelming, just a few scattered voices and muffled conversations.

"Only open when you are ready," Miss Am says, her touch now gone. "This won't be easy."

My teeth start to chatter. The space is cold. Unwelcoming.

"Maya, you stay right here," an almost-forgotten voice says.

Her sound jolts my eyes open.

No. Please no. Not this.

Once again, I know precisely where and when I am.

"I just need to run to the bathroom," my mother says.

She leans down and tucks a loose strand of hair behind my ear. She raises her cheeks ever-so-slightly, teeth hidden behind sealed lips, in something that resembles a smile.

This time around, I can tell it's forced. I can't believe I ever believed her.

Just as last time, I watch her scurry into the lady's room. She flips her phone open and brings it to her ear. I can't hear what she's says, but it looks like she's screaming into the phone. She turns the corner without looking back at me. Just like that, she's vanished beyond the ceramic tile wall.

This was the last time I saw my birth mother in person.

There was no way for me to know this then.

As though reenacting a memory I wish I'd forgotten, I turn to look at the nearby fish tank. There's more colors than I can take in. There's a pink and blue, a blue and black, a yellow and green, and more combos than I care to consider. Their insides glow in the dark water, their fins flowing as they pass, looking like scattered shooting stars. I remember trying to read the plaque, so I do so again—*Pterophyllum*—more commonly known as angelfish.

The first time I was here, I stared so long at this tank that I counted the angelfish three times over. It wasn't easy, trying to quickly count by section of the tank without any of them squirming across the way. I restarted four times, because one particularly swift yellow fellow wanted to socialize. I figured he must be the mayor running for re-election, or perhaps more of a Paul Revere type, warning of impending doom.

22. The number of angelfish is stamped on my brain forever. Yet, with passing time and perspective, it looks like there's more. I'm tempted to count again. My eyes catch

hold of the yellow Revere when I see my reflection against the glass. I gasp.

I'm seven again. Well, six. Tomorrow would be my birthday.

I look down at my hands, my nails painted lemon yellow. They're shiny and flawless. My mother took great care painting them earlier that morning. She promised this was gonna be the best birthday ever. Now I can't stand to look at them. I want to scrape the paint off and forget the color ever existed.

What was taking her so long? I thought. Maybe she'd forgotten. Or I missed a direction. That was probably it. It must've been my fault. She probably told me to meet her somewhere. At the octopus tank or the stingray pool. This was on me. I was so mad at myself for not listening better.

It wasn't until an old white lady with glasses asked me if I was lost.

"Are the angelfish watching over you?" she leaned forward with a smile.

I told her I couldn't find my mother.

"Oh dear!" her eyes went wide.

She told me not to panic, but her first reaction said it all. She waved over a nearby aquarium security guard and took me to the front desk. Another security guard, a gargantuan mustached man with herculean shoulders and a golden tortoise pin styled like a police badge, asked me all sorts of questions. My name, of course. Who I came with, how long had I been there. It looked like a few of the other guards watched videos on the screens at their desks. After what felt like a day, my grandma Gigi came to pick me up. She said my mother got sick and had to leave immediately.

"Don't be scared," Gigi said. "Everything's gonna be okay."

I wasn't really scared until Gigi suggested I might be.

"Where is she?"

"The doctor," she said. "She's just a little sick, that's all."

Something about the way she said *that's all* made me know she was lying. I knew that wasn't true, even then.

But here, now, standing before my angelfish friends, *it doesn't have to be this way.*

I can find out the truth.

I can see where she really went and maybe even ask her why.

I look toward the lady's room where she disappeared. There's gotta be an emergency exit in there. Or a small window. Lord knows she's fucking crazy enough to climb through a window to get out of here. Just to get away from me. Anything to run away from being my mother.

It doesn't have to be this way this time, I tell myself.

I turn from my six (about-to-be seven) year-old reflection and head for the bathroom.

I can't believe this is happening. I can't comprehend how bizarre it feels to be back in my old body. My legs touch the ground before my mind is used to. I'm two feet shorter than I've been for years. I stumble, momentarily feeling like a wobbly calf.

I enter the bathroom and a centipede jitters across the blue tile floor.

"Mom?" I call out.

No answer. Someone sneezes behind a stall.

I walk through, gently tapping each door open.

I reach a closed one. I almost knock, but I take a step back to look at the shoes.

Elsa lights up on one shoe as Anna lights up on the other. Definitely not my mother.

A horn honks. It sounds like it's just beyond the wall. I walk over to the sinks and look up. As suspected, there's an open window. She would have had to climb on the sinks and pull herself up, but that's the only clear way out.

A storm works its way from the pit of my stomach, up to the center of my chest. I feel the tears trying to make their way out of my eyeballs. I shake my head. I won't let it happen. Enough tears have been cried over this moment.

"Just get me out of here," I say. The child's voice that comes from my mouth makes me feel nauseous. "Please?"

A toilet flushes behind me.

There's no answer from Miss Am or whoever might be above her. God has always been preoccupied. I can only do so much, but apparently I'll have to do a little more. I pause, take a deep breath, then step back into the aquarium where—

"Destiny," a voice calls from behind me. "Surprise!"

I turn.

There, with a giant dolphin-shaped cake in her hands, is my mother.

She leans down to show me the electric blue icing. Seven candles flicker beneath her grinning face.

I want to melt. I start to shake.

"Sorry I had to sneak away," she smiles, all teeth this time around. "I wanted it to be a big surprise."

She reaches her hand down and grabs mine. I instinctively grab hers as she leads me to a nearby picnic table. She places the cake down on the table then pulls me up into her lap. I forgot what it felt like to sit in a lap.

"Okay, close your eyes and make a wish."

I don't even have to think. I don't hesitate.

I wish for this to be real.

My mother nods, the candles dancing against her dark eyes. "You got this."

I blow them out. *Whoof.* All seven candles flicker out in unison. The smell of melting wax rises with the small stacks of smoke, circulating my nose. I breathe in deep, tasting the fumes.

*This is real.*

My mother wraps her arms around me and pulls me in for a tight hug.

*I've never felt safer.*

The tears I'd been holding back burst above my smile.

"I love you so much, Destiny."

The tears turn into an ugly sob. She's never sounded so sincere, so present. Her words are slow, believable. She means it. I know she means it.

I close my eyes and sink into her embrace.

I didn't realize how much I needed this moment. This is the wish I'd been denying myself. This is all I ever wanted.

With my eyes closed, my small body cozied up against hers, the world fades to white. Her body slowly slips away, sinking into the nothingness, leaving a cool mist in its wake that lingers across my face.

I smile. I could stay here forever.

"You're almost there, Destiny," Miss Am says. "This one will hurt, but you're almost free."

Before I can process her words, before I can process their meaning, lightning strikes and my eyes shoot open.

I'm standing in the kitchen. The lights are out. Behind me, the TV buzzes from the family room, letting in a pulsating glow.

*"Once again, the kingdom of heaven is like a net that was let down into the lake and caught all kinds of fish..."* the tele-pastor reads. *"This is how it will be at the end of the age."*

The only other light comes from the refrigerator. The door is wide open.

*"The angels will come and separate the wicked from the righteous and throw them into the blazing furnace, where there will be weeping and gnashing of teeth."*

*Drip. Drip. Drip.*

*"'Have you understood all these things?' Jesus asked."*

Beyond the window set above the sink, rain batters down. But I almost miss the Schweppes Ginger Ale tipped on its side, slowly depositing its final droplets to the floor. Two liters of soda spread across the tiles, filling every crevice, soaking against the cabinets. I step aside, just before any can slide between my toes.

*"Therefore every teacher of the law who has become a disciple in the kingdom of heaven is like the owner of a house who brings out of his storeroom new treasures as well as old."*

Lightning flashes, filling the kitchen. Everything glows orange for a split-second. I notice the sliding door to the backyard is open. Thunder rattles the room, sending the dishes clanking. The hollow Schweppes bottle clinks to the floor.

We're at the center of the storm.

I step toward the back door while every inner-thought begs me not to. Please no. Please no. Even that night, I knew something was wrong. Now, knowing what awaits me beyond that door, just at the bottom of the patio steps, facedown in an overflowing puddle, I can't bear to see that image one more time. There hasn't been a minute since where it hasn't forced itself back into the center of my mind.

And yet, I step forward.

Please no. Make it stop, I think, hoping Miss Am hears me.

I try to claim control of my body, but it doesn't listen. Closer to the door I go. Step, step, step.

Anything but this, please!

I reach the doorway and try to close my eyes, but they won't budge. It's like they're stapled open. I'm stuck in a loop, guaranteed to turn my head just as I did before, guaranteed for my eyes to land upon the spot that once soothed me. The rain pitters against the puddle, a sound that once offered solace.

My eyes move to the small pool of rain, my heart raging at my core.

I let out a wail that bleeds into the thunder above.

Some memories cut too deep to ever be fully extracted. Memories like this nestle close to your core, making permanent settlement in your soul. I hate this moment so much that it's become my identity.

Just as before, Gigi lies facedown, her hair floating, bobbing at the water's surface. Her feet are strewn apart, a kick away from Poppy's daffodils. Just as before, I rush down the steps. I reach Gigi and tug on her left shoulder, thrusting her body from the puddle. She lands on her back with a thud.

For a moment, it's even worse than I remember. No one should have to see their hero defeated, completely drained of life. Once was bad enough. But now, I catch details I missed before. A pair of daffodil petals stick to her forehead. A tiny worm crawls across the bottom of her chin.

But then I gasp. Something is different.

Gigi coughs. Fluid splatters from her mouth and onto her chin, sending the worm falling below.

She didn't cough last time. *A sign of life.* And then another.

Gigi blinks, gradually opening her eyes. She scans her surroundings before making direct eye contact with me.

This definitely didn't happen before.

"Mom!?" I cry, pulling her upward. I pick the petals from her face and tuck the wet strands of her hair behind her ear.

She wipes her chin. "What's going on?"

"You had, uh," I wipe my tears, trying to compose myself and trying to make sense of the situation.

"Too much to drink?" Gigi says. "Didn't sit well with my meds."

She's never said anything like this before. She's far too proud. Her demons are her demons, and her recent preferred course of exorcism—drown them in poison—have been a private undertaking.

She extends her hand.

"Here, honey. Help me up."

I stand and help pull her to her feet. She's far lighter than I expect.

I don't wait to say what's been on my mind for months.

"I shouldn't have snapped at you," I say, claiming my role in all of this.

I've thought about this a lot. Gigi's unholy trinity was Tanqueray, meds, and stress. I added in the lethal and final ingredient that night—stress.

"That only made it worse." It feels good to finally say something out loud. "I'm so sorry."

"What?" Gigi shakes her head. "That has nothing to do with it. I had no right testing my limits tonight. I'm the only one who should be apologizing."

She moves her hand from mine and up to my shoulder.

"I'll never forgive myself for ruining your night, Destiny."

We make our way up the patio steps.

I can't wipe away the tears fast enough. "I'm just happy you're safe."

"That's not enough," she continues. "You were right. You said it. I've been running away from my problems."

"Let's not worry about that tonight." It seems trivial now. I know how much worse this night could have been.

We're about to step into the backdoor when—

*THUNK.*

It's suddenly closed.

Gigi's head bounces back.

"Oh my god," I wince, reaching for her. "You okay?"

"I'm fine, angel. I'm just sorry I hurt you."

"What? No. Your head."

She steps forward again, like she didn't just walk into the glass.

*THUNK.*

"Mom, wait! It's closed! Wait a second."

Strange. I swore it was open. No. I know I left it open.

I go to pull it open, but it won't budge. It's locked.

"What the—"

"Don't worry about it. I'm just sorry that I hurt you," Gigi says again.

I look into her eyes and her usual forest greens are glazed into a murky, lifeless shade. It feels like she's looking right through me.

"What's happening?"

"What's going on?"

"This has never happened before!"

I hear voices whisper behind me.

I turn back to the yard from where the voices sound. There's no one there. My sight lands upon a giant tree in the center of the yard where an old stump should be.

There's no tree in our backyard. There hasn't been since before I was born. Something's off.

"We've got to move!"

"Oh no!"

"What was that?"

Their words blend together, all from the same voice, speaking atop each other.

"Get her out of there. We've got to getoutofhere. Whatsthatcrack."

*Lookatthatcrackwhatshappening.*

*CanyousaveherCANYOUSAVEHER?*

I look into Gigi's eyes. I know this isn't her. But I'm still afraid to lose her.

"I miss you so much," I cry. "I love you."

"I'm…just…" the words literally drip from her mouth. For every word, milk bubbles from her mouth, sprinkled with the falling rain. "sorry…I…love…"

Lightning strikes behind us.

Her eyes roll back into her head. All white.

I scream.

Everything around me vanishes to bright, blank white. Even me.

All that remains is the feeling of someone cradling my unseen head.

And soon, the sound of girls screaming joins in.

"We've got you, Destiny," I hear Miss Am. "We're gonna get you out of here."

"Aunt Am!" a girl yells. "It's cracking!"

"On three, you'll open your eyes," Miss Am says calmly. "You'll return to your body, and you'll be safe. Once again, you will be Destiny."

"What is that!?" another girl shrieks.

"One…"

"It's coming back!"

"Two…"

"Hurry!"

"Three."

I open my eyes.

Miss Am sits across from me but her focus is elsewhere. She looks over her shoulder at the glass wall behind her. There's now a crack in one of the panes through which water relentlessly flows.

Most of the girls have run from the circle and down the hall from which Miss Am entered. At the end of the corridor, they're crowded, trying to make their way up a stairwell. Little steps from behind me and places a hand on my shoulder.

"You alright?"

Razor comes from my right, pointing out beyond the glass.

"Look! Here it comes again!"

I stand up, trying to see what she's pointing at.

At first, I see nothing. But in seconds, I see something small speeding forward, becoming rapidly bigger.

At first it looks like a stone, then maybe a football, but then, right before it *THUNKS* and crashes against the glass, my brain makes sense of the image.

*A turtle.*

"That bastard," both Miss Am and Razor say in unison.

Before I can comprehend what's happening, the crack in the glass gives way. The entire pane splinters and water gushes through in a wave.

The four of us run down the hallway, water trailing our heels, splashing our way up the steps.

# ChAPteR 8

**I KNELT BESIDE GIGI AS** she bathed the turtle named Tiger in the tub. Poppy sang Marvin Gaye's "I Heard It Through The Grapevine" a floor below us as Lucky belted Taylor Swift's "Cruel Summer" in the attic above. Gigi closed the door and lit a candle—one of her long, black stick ones. She dipped her hand in the water and started slowly circling the flow around Tiger.

"When you need to get rid of all the bad stuff, you wanna spin the water upward to the left. Counter-clockwise, they call it. Like turning back time."

Then she reversed her hand, shifting the water with her.

"Now, when you want to bring something in, like let's say, a blessing or some love, you go the opposite way."

"Clockwise," I said.

"Exactly."

She closed her eyes, and I did my best to follow along, but I kept one eye open. I think I still remember what she said next, word for word.

"Spirits of the Earth,

Water, Air, and Fire,

I ask you to protect and guard this pure creature we call Tiger the Turtle.

Keep this blessed beast from harm's way.

May his sacred presence in this home multiply this protection manifold,

And as a reminder of your Divine Creativity,

Keep us close to you, dear Lord.

As I say, so shall it be.

Amen."

I always knew Gigi said prayers that others might call spells, but this was the only time she spoke one aloud in front of me. If there were memories I could willingly revisit, this would near the top of the list.

When I reach the top of the landing, Miss Am pulls at a handle on the wall revealing a door. It slides over and seals with a resounding click. Except for the little golden handle, the wall looks like there was never a doorway there.

Miss Am, Little, Razor, and I stare at each other trying to catch our breath and make sense of what just happened down there with that turtle. The rest of the girls gather around the room with hung eyes and slumped shoulders. Dread drips from their faces.

For a moment, there is absolute silence.

Until Miss Am breaks into laughter.

Little chuckles. Razor joins in. I can't help but smile.

Soon, all of the girls are laughing.

"What was that?" I ask.

"We have lots of wild animals on the property," Miss Am explains. "Sometimes they'd prefer if we weren't here. It's rare, but things like this do happen."

"Wild animals?"

"Bears, tigers, lions, you name it," Miss Am nods. "Golden nursed an injured python back to health. Now she keeps it in her room."

I turn to Golden and instantly understand why the girl's got the name…her skin is sparkling. Her curls cascade around her face. She's clearly different than the rest of the girls. I think she's one that I saw looking at me from in the window. She's not little, instead, she might even be a year or two older than me. And yet, she's me? Or who I might be if I cleaned up a bit and stopped wearing oversized hoodies and poop-stained Vans.

"It's white-lipped, so no worries," the girl clarifies. "Completely non-venomous. You wanna see it?"

"WHO WANTS TO PLAY SHELTER IN PLACE?" one of the little ones yells.

"No, no, no! How about Blind Dogs Die?!"

All of the young ones chatter over each other.

"I hate that game. Let's play Mother More I!"

"Mother More I!" a few cheer. "Mother More I!"

"You gonna play?" Little asks.

I shrug.

"I think you should," Cupcake tugs on my arm and pulls me toward the door. "It's so much fun."

Violet and Daisy slide the back door open.

"You sure you wanna go with them?"

I turn back. It's Golden. Standing beside her are two more older girls. Triplets, I realize. Next to Miss Am it'd be easy to overlook them, but they're absolutely stunning.

"This is Claws," Golden introduces a girl with long, fire-engine red nails.

"Hey cutie," Claws waves. I can't take my eyes off her fingertips. Her nails are half the length of her fingers.

"She won't scratch," Golden assures. "She runs a beauty vlog, that's all."

Golden wraps her arm around her other sister. This girl wears an oversized white cardigan and big round glasses. "This is Page."

"Or Doc," the girl shrugs. "You can call me whatever you want."

"Nice to meet you guys."

"You wanna come up to Golden's room?" Claws asks.

"We were gonna start the new doc series on the Nephilim crisis at the border," Doc says, clapping her fingers together.

"Golden's room?" I ask. "The one with the python?"

"Twigs is safe. She wouldn't eat a mouse," Golden says. "You'll love her."

I smile. These three are smart, beautiful, and a tad dangerous. They're my dream girls.

"That sounds fun," I nod.

"And I was just telling the girls, I can't wait to get into your hair."

Claws rakes her long nails across my buzzed scalp, sending goosebumps all over my body.

"What hair?" I laugh.

"It's so cute. So chic. It's coming in, but now's the time to have fun with it. Can you imagine all the things we could do with this? Lollipop pink? Slime green with a little yellow swirl? Maybe a soft lavender?! Ugh! I'm getting excited just thinking about it!"

I feel myself blushing. I try to rub the goosebumps on the back of my arm back into my skin. But I can't lie to myself. A little pampering sounds magical right now.

"C'mon, Destiny!" Little calls from just outside the back door.

I look back with hesitation. Little notices me pause. She raises her shoulders as her eyes practically pop from her face.

"What are you doing?" she raises an eyebrow.

"I…uh…" I look back at the older, aspirational girls.

I want to hang out with them. Meet a python named Twigs, watch a documentary, and get my hair done? I feel like I deserve this right now.

Little scowls. I see the younger girls behind her, laughing and running in the yard. I'd love to be one of them too, where the only concern in the world seems to be figuring out which game to play next.

This is tough. I can't let Little down, but there's something drawing me to these girls.

They look just like me.

*They are me…*

Or who I can become, as Miss Am would say. I imagine these three once had to make a similar decision. When do we put aside the games and become something else? Something more? Something better?

Upstairs, I think. Just a few doors down from Miss Am. They are how I become—

"Destiny!" One of the littles grabs my arm while another two push me from behind, moving me toward the backdoor. They've made my choice for me.

I turn back to the Dream Girls. "I'm sorry."

They laugh. "Don't sweat it," Golden says. "Come find us after. We're right next to Am's room."

*Am.* That's cool. When you're one of the Dream Girls, she's just Am.

I step barefoot into the grass and wonder if anyone ever wears shoes here. The grass is plusher than a pillow, bouncy like the cotton ones. The dirt beneath the green is firm enough to stick to my foot, but soft enough to spring each step forward.

If I were asked to describe my ideal day outdoors, it would look a lot like this. Mountains in the distance, a waterfall and stream to my side, with big patches of green beneath a center-of-the-sky sun. Days aren't supposed to be this perfect. But here I am. *And it is.*

The girls jog ahead down a gentle slope. At the bottom, I've never seen so much empty space in my life. These fields go on forever. Deep in the distance, along the tree line, I swear I see a trio of gazelles prance into the woods.

The girls head for a sports field that I don't recognize. It's a giant triangle. At each point, there's a wooden column the size of utility poles. Tied between each of the poles is a thick white rope, serving as boundary lines.

"You remember Run the Bases?" Little whispers in my ear.

I try to find the place in my mind where childhood games should be stored, but I come up short. Weird. "I think so?"

"What about Red Rover?"

I turn to her, trying to confirm that this is actually Little. I look down to her nails. I can see the nail bed peeking through the tips of her yellow nails. She turns her face and I see the scar.

"Red Rover…" I try to remember. "Red Rover…"

"Yes," Little's eyes light up. "Send Destiny over. You remember?"

But I don't. The words mean nothing to me.

"Is this a game you guys made up?"

"No," she deflates. "But Mother More I is a lot like that. We all split up between the three stakes. There's three people—we call them Fates—that patrol the middle of the field. They say, for example, something like 'Mother More, I love ice cream.'"

"Who doesn't love ice cream?"

"Exactly, everyone does. So, if you love ice cream, you have to run across the field to another stake without getting tagged by one of the Fates. If they tag you, you join their team. Obviously, it gets harder to get across the field with the more Fates there are."

"I think I get it. So that last one standing is the winner?"

Little giggles. "I wouldn't say that. Here's another. Mother More, I *hate* swimming. So, since the girls here love swimming, they're going to stay at their stake. They're not going to go running. You only go if it's something that relates to you. That's it."

"Seems simple enough."

We reach the rope. I lift my legs over it as Little dips beneath.

A girl asks Little if she's explained the rules of the game to me.

"She's all caught up," Little nods.

"Great," one of the three girls in the center says. "What do we think, loser has to…what?"

Another of the Fates answers with glee. "Sleep in the coffin!"

The girls laugh. I'm not as amused.

I must have made a face expressing as much, because one of the Fates looks at me and tries to clarify. "She meant *cabin*. We've got a cabin down by the stream."

"Right at the foot of Mount Azrael," Little says. "It's actually super cozy."

"Well, I'm not gonna lose," I smile. "I'm fast."

Little shakes her head. Razor shoves her aside.

"Don't be so sure about that, new girl. We're all fast."

"Okay, so we're all ready?!" one of the Fates yells, a wide grin on her face. "Let's do it!"

Another continues. "Mother More I…hate Miss Am!"

All of the girls groan in unison. No one budges.

"Forgot to tell you," Little says in an aside. "We always start that way. Little tradition."

"Be ready for the next one," Razor says.

"Mother More I…*LOVE* Miss Am!"

The girls scream and the chaos begins.

I don't think.

I just start running.

There's 20 of us. And Razor didn't lie. We're all fast.

It must be because I'm new, but I see all three Fates turn and target me, smirks on their faces.

To my left, two girls run into each other and fall down to the grass. To my right, a line of girls I'd surely be stuck behind. Straight ahead, the Fates. I run right for them.

Their eyes go wide. It's a strategy they weren't ready for.

I turn my legs to the left as my upper half twists to the right. My eyes don't give away my destination, but I hold still for a split second. The Fates stumble atop each other. The girls safely at their stakes gasp in awe. I'm home free. I jog to the stake across the way where I'm greeted with pats on the back and high-fives.

The Fates tag the girls who ran into each other. I think one of them is Little.

The original three callers look at me with fury in their eyes. I've got to be ready…

"Mother More I…am an only child!" one of them screams.

Off to the races. Again, everyone's running, but I feel one step ahead of the pack.

Like a trio of banshees, teeth gritting, arms and fingers outstretched, they come straight for me.

They're watching my eyes, tracking my stride, and trying to cut off my route ahead.

They think they know my next move, but this is child's play. Literally, I feel silly being the oldest one of the bunch, but I'd be lying if I said it wasn't fun.

The Fates are within a breath of me. They swipe for my hips, but I spin, completely altering my course.

An ankle twists. A knee buckles. They groan in pain and self-pity as I'm off and into open space.

The girls already at their stakes laugh.

I glance back.

The Fates are less amused. One among them is slow to get up. The other two help her to her feet.

The newly acquired taggers spent their round successfully snagging a few more. They've multiplied their team. I count ten girls in the middle, meaning there's still ten of us in the running.

The Fates briefly huddle. I see the one that I think is Little glance back at me. She holds her stare, raising her eyebrows, as though she's trying to transmit a message through her irises.

What that message is, I don't know.

Slow down? Get tagged?

Maybe. But this is too much fun.

"Mother More I!" a Fate projects, "I am wearing a dirty, smelly hoodie."

I look down at the yellow stained smile looking back up at me. I had forgotten he was here.

I look back up and they're already converging. I burst ahead. Ten versus one. I shouldn't have a chance. And if any of these girls were my age, I wouldn't. But they're not, so onward I dart.

As I run closer, they try to spread out, careful to cut off the paths by the rope. In doing so, they only create gaps between them.

I zip through, just by Little.

"Stop!" she yells.

And I do.

But the two girls flanking me on either side, raging ahead with their sights set solely on me, don't stop. They collide, heads clunking against each other before falling to the ground.

The girls gasp.

I lean down. "You okay?"

One of them reaches for her mouth. Blood pours from the lips beneath her dagger teeth. It's Razor. Red drips between her fingers.

She swipes for me with her bloody hand, but I backpedal, bumping into the line of Fates.

"I'm bleeding!" Razor stands and spits. "We don't bleed!"

I try not to laugh. I feel bad for hurting her, but she sounds deranged.

"I'm sorry. I was just playing, didn't want to hurt any—"

"WE DON'T BLEED!" she yells, her brows slanted. "You lose!"

I successfully hold back my laughter. "But there's still a bunch of girls left."

"You're too fast!" another of the Fates yells. "You are the loser!"

I can't hold back my laughter. "What? That doesn't even make sense."

"I think we know the rules better than you!"

"It's okay," Little places her hand on mine. "She's still learning."

She looks up in my eyes, trying to transmit another thought into my head. This time, I feel like I understand her.

*Trust me*, she's saying. *Play along.*

"You're the loser," she nods.

I roll my eyes then finally nod. "I guess I'm the loser."

"Good," the bloodied Razor crosses her arms. "If this is going to work, you need to follow the rules."

"I was, I just—" I say sharply. Little squeezes the back of my hand. I change my tone. "I just got a little confused, that's all. I had a lot of fun. Maybe we can play again another time."

"Maybe," Razor spits red onto the green grass. "But for now, the coffin."

"The cabin," Little corrects.

"Whatever," Razor growls. "The cabin."

Little tilts her head and whispers into my ear. "Move fast. *Find what's been stolen.*"

She tries to be discreet, but everyone sees her. Razor watches on, fury in her eyes. She steps forward.

"You know how Am feels about secrets."

"There's no secrets. I have no secrets," Little shakes her head. "I was just asking her if she's okay."

"If she's okay? If *she's* okay!? I'm the one bleeding, Favorite. Try explaining that to Aunt Am when we get back inside!"

"It's just a little blood," Little shrugs.

Razor looks like more blood might boil out from her eyes. "A little blood?!"

Cupcake steps between them.

"Alright, alright, let's all settle. It's getting late and I think we're all tired," Cupcake says. "Who else is tired?"

"I think we're all exhausted," Ace chimes in.

The sun is still beating down, still at its peak in the sky. No sign of nightfall, no preview of the moon. I've walked all day and I'm not even tired. But I'm supposed to play by their rules, right?

"I can't wait for bed," I add.

"So, normally, you'd have your own room," Little explains. "There's plenty of space in the house."

"But since the rules are the rules, for tonight, it's the cabin," Razor cuts in.

"Okay, and where is that again?"

"I can show her," Little volunteers.

Razor breaks into a belly laugh, shaking her head. "Nice try. I don't think so. We've all found it ourselves and she's no different."

"That's right," I nod. "No different at all."

I free my hand from Little's grip.

"I got this."

"Just follow this tree line, until you come to two fallen trees. They're kinda holding each other up, like an X. Crawl beneath the X and listen for the stream. Once you find it, hop across right away, because it gets wide deeper in the woods and you won't be able to do it later. Follow the stream all the way until it reaches a tunnel."

"A tunnel? What are you even talking about?" Razor says. "Just find it, okay?"

"On your left, you'll see a stage."

"A stage?" Razor scoffs.

"A stump, I guess." Little shrugs. "It's a giant stump."

"Where you hide to practice your singing!" Razor cackles and her clan follows.

"Yeah, whatever. Sometimes? Anyway, the way the sun hits it perfectly, it's like a spotlight on a stage. You can't miss it. You climb up there so you can get a good look. Then keep turning until you see the cabin. You'll know it when you see it. Can't miss it from the stage."

Razor rolls her eyes. "You wanna mention the way the leaves flutter when you pass them, and be sure to gently tap them so they know how much you care?"

There's more laughter. Razor looks proud of herself. I clench my fist. I feel no remorse for making her bleed.

"I appreciate it, Little," I say. "I guess I'll see you tomorrow?"

"If we're *lucky*," she says with a wink.

There's a pregnant pause.

The wind whirls between us as a bird chirps in the distance.

Everyone saw her wink. Everyone caught the strange way she said *lucky*…

We all stop and stare at Little.

The birds chirping above suddenly sound like cawing alarms.

What's that supposed to mean, I think.

"What's that supposed to mean?" Razor grits her sharp teeth. She steps closer to Little, suddenly looking down at her. Just moments ago, all of the girls stood the same height except for me. Now Razor appears to tower over Little.

"Be careful, Favorite," blood bubbles between her teeth as she turns back to me. "And you too, *Winner*. Am doesn't like when people don't follow the rules."

I don't understand how, but it's clear that Razor has grown before my eyes.

She stands directly before me, our eyes locked. She clenches her jaw as the tips of her canines poke from her mouth, digging against her lips.

Little steps between us.

"The sooner you get to the cabin the better," Little says.

I turn, looking toward the tree line.

*You can do this*, a voice in my head says. I don't know whether it's me, Am, or Little.

"Don't be afraid," Little whispers. "The cabin is safer than—"

Razor shoves between us, cutting off Little's words of warning.

The bloodied Razor must see a fear in my eyes that I can't hide.

"A night alone has never killed anybody," she says. "Except for, ya know, when it has." Razor laughs and her Fates follow suit. "Good night," she says, sarcasm dripping from her voice. She blows me a kiss, blood dabbing onto her fingertips as they touch her lips.

A mighty gust of wind swirls between us. The girls scream before breaking into laughter. As the Destinys head back for the house, I feel the wind encircle me, pulling me toward the woods. I'm afraid that I'm going to need more than luck for whatever waits beyond the trees, in the cabin confused for a coffin.

# CHAPTER 9

**THE LAST TIME I SAW** Gigi with her red notebook was a few nights before she died.

I passed by her room and glanced in. This wasn't something I'd normally do, but out of the corner of my eye, I caught her on her knees. She held the book over her head, like a priest before communion. She turned to me, and I jumped back. Her smile was bright enough to illuminate the room, but her eyes were like saucers. I'd be lying if I said she didn't look a little crazy.

"Imagine a road map to the past," she chuckled. I swear I could smell the ginger on her breath from across the room. "Imagine using it to navigate your future."

She pulled the book in for a hug. She closed her eyes and squeezed it tight.

You can imagine why I searched so hard for it after her

funeral. I wanted answers. Answers that surely would have led to more questions.

I should have asked Little a few follow-ups after her directions, but I'm sure Razor would have chimed in. How long do I have to walk along this tree line? When does night fall around here? The tree goes on forever and the sun shows no sign of falling. I've got nothing but the mountains and my thoughts to keep me company.

Having this alone time, I realize something strange. Something new.

I feel fresh. *Free.*

My mind feels clear in a way that I can't remember experiencing before. Not recently, at least. I don't remember ever feeling this light. What was it? Why do I feel so…*great?*

A butterfly dips and dances before my nose, fluttering its way into the woods. My heart mirrors its moves and I'm half-tempted to follow the flying bug. Why shouldn't I? I feel free of stress, free from fear. The girls definitely seemed intent on trying to scare me about this cabin, but I can't just ignore the sun in the sky. Just because they said it was nighttime doesn't make that true. Sure, they kept confusing the cabin for a coffin which was admittedly weird. But it's not like I'm just going to hop in a hearse if I see one. I'm still in control. Maybe more so than I've felt in a long time.

My eyes scan the trees, evergreens I think, looking for a pair of fallen ones that have formed an X. I see no such trees, but I'm sure I'll notice when I do. Each and every one of these trees is tall, thick, and beaming with life. The presence of anything decaying will stick out like a broken thumb.

The game with the girls certainly could have gone better, but it was just that. A game. Nothing to stress over. Razor obviously took it more seriously than the rest of the girls, but who cares? She's one out of 22. I can't worry about her.

Everyone else here seems happy enough. There's a shared freedom, a sense of ease that I could get used to. What is this feeling? Is it just me being around new people? Maybe I've avoided making new friends for too long now, and this is what I needed. These girls are different, though. *They understand me.*

Is it Miss Am?

I know it sounds weird, and even I hate to admit this to myself, but her presence was unlike anything I've ever experienced before. It felt calming, sure, but it was more than that. Joyous. Almost blissful.

There's no denying that some people are natural healers. Being around them, simply having their attention or their affection is all you need to push you in the right direction. I can't remember feeling as free as I had with Miss Am. Free from my thoughts, free from my pain, free from distractions.

Here, along the tree line, beneath the sunshine, with the mountains watching over me, I don't need anything else.

*I don't need anything else.*

There's a break in the trees ahead. I pick up my pace, jogging forward. Is this it?

I step closer. Two of these trees have fallen, and yes, they're leaning against each other.

But Little said it looked like an X.

I take a step back, trying to see if I'm missing something.

The way the branches are intertwined, it most certainly looks like a passageway into the woods. But rather than crossing atop each other, they curve into each other. If anything, this looks more like an O.

Maybe she meant O.

Maybe she said O?

I take a step closer.

If I'm safely in the woods, does it matter where exactly I enter?

Now that I'm really looking at it, I mean, I guess it could be an X? There's a few stray twigs hanging, crossed over each other. Those could be an X. Yup, those are definitely an X. Okay, maybe an X.

This must be it. It's gotta be. I step through, crouching to Little size. A few of the loose twigs scratch against my head. I pull my hood over my scalp, making my way to the other side. I step through and stand up straight. The sun flickers through the leaves above, landing upon the forest floor. At first glance, my eyes deceive me. The ground looks coated in snow. After a blink, I realize the forest floor is covered in a blanket of flowers. I pull in a deep breath, taking in the scents of spring. *The promise of new life.*

The white flowers are primarily periwinkles with a sprinkle of tall-standing foamflowers. I surprise myself with this knowledge I didn't realize I'd been storing. Some of Poppy's garden chats must have rubbed off on me.

Little probably should have mentioned the snow-white flowers so I'd know I was in the right place. Looking around, they cover the ground as far as I can see. Maybe she's grown so used to them that she doesn't even think about them anymore. I've noticed that, regardless of how beautiful someone or something is, if you see it every day, people stop seeing the beauty for what it is.

As the sun filters through the forest canopy, I close my eyes and let the rays bathe me. I swear I could stay here forever. There's a sliver of me that wants to fall against the forest floor, curl up in the blanket of periwinkles and call it a day.

But I've got to keep moving. Miss Am mentioned wild animals—*lions, tigers*—but no. She must have been joking? They wouldn't send me into a forest with bears. Would they?

Razor's bloodied smirk flashes in my mind, answering the question for me.

Maybe they would.

I step ahead, trying to remember Little's next direction. What was it? Listen for something. That was it. Follow the sound. But the sound of what…?

Birds chirp from the treetops, but I can't spot them. They converse amongst themselves, surely watching me from their lair above. In between their melodic gossip, the leaves rustle in the wind, and none of these sounds recall Little's next instruction.

*Quiet yourself. Listen.*

I close my eyes once more. C'mon. What was it?

Beneath the birds and my thoughts, I hear something faint. A soft trickle. Water sliding against rocks. *Earth's first song.*

My eyes shoot open. That was it. Follow the stream.

I step toward the sound, crossing the flowered forest floor until I come to the water. She's a tiny stream, slim enough to step across. The water is crystal clear, each and every pebble at the bottom could be counted if I hung around. But I start walking alongside the stream, against the water flow.

Follow it upstream until I come to a drain, or a tunnel, that's what she called it. From there, I'll see the stage. Then at last, I'll see the cabin. In there…what did she say?

I'll find what's been stolen?

What was she talking about? What could have been stolen? I just got here. At the risk of sounding overly simplistic, I feel complete. What could I be missing right now? Other than maybe a basic understanding of how time operates in this place.

I'm not gonna lie, pretending it's nighttime as the sun remains fixed in the center of the sky is strange, but it's ultimately inconsequential. The positives of this day far outweigh the negatives. Sure, the girls are dramatic but they're also protective and fierce and fun. Other than Razor, they've welcomed me with open arms, ready to accept me as one of them.

And Miss Am. I don't think any of us deserve her. But here she is, in this perfect house with that imperfect smile, taking care of 23 kids that aren't hers.

Part of me feels stupid for thinking this, but it's just a thought. A harmless one. No shame in exploring it…

This is the family I've always wanted.

*This is the family I've never had.*

So every once in a while I'll have to sleep in a cabin they call a coffin. They're just playing mind games, trying to scare the new girl. I get it. We'll play games that I don't know the rules to yet, but soon enough, that'll all change. I'll figure out my role in this place, and I'll play along until I'm not playing any more. In no time at all, I'll move in sync with the girls, not sparing a single thought on whether I'm doing this right.

I should have had Little specify exactly how long I'd be walking along this stream. With each step, my skinny legs get closer to expiration. The reality that I've been walking all day starts to weigh on my calves.

What would it matter if I decided to lie right here and curl up in the bed of flowers? They look so cozy, so welcoming. I haven't seen one animal and this sun's not going anywhere. I'm safe enough.

But then I imagine how comfortable the beds back at Miss Am's are. Everything there feels custom built and more luxurious than any home I've been in. I can't imagine what a fancy bed would feel like against my back right now. I'm half tempted to turn around to go find out.

My thoughts stumble onto the triplets. The Dream Girls. Golden, the girl that glows. Claws, the sweet model-to-be. And Page, the doctor in training. They were amazing.

I wouldn't mind spending tomorrow with them, watching documentaries and getting pampered. There are worse ways to spend the day.

What was it that Miss Am said down in the temple? I'm sure she was just being sweet. That she is me? Or she is what I could become? Either way, that beautiful lady was lying through the gap in her teeth. But still, it was a nice thing to say…a nice thing to imagine.

If anything ever so wild were to be true, I'd have to become a Dream Girl next, that much is sure. I'd have to keep my playing with the Littles to a minimum and commit to more polished, sophisticated things. I run my fingers across my buzzed scalp, wondering what color Claws will dye it? What color would Miss Am choose?

With each step, the stream gets a little wider and the water flows a little harder. One might be tempted to call it a river now, but I resist that label. Admitting so would be admitting that I didn't do something right here. I was supposed to cross a stream, not a river.

I'm worried I've done the wrong thing. Should I turn back and try to start from the beginning? How am I going to find the X-trees I entered through? Or was it an O?

The water gushes beside me, louder than my thoughts. I take a step ahead and my heart leaps.

Ahead, there's an apparent end to the forest.

Standing a hundred feet ahead, there's a white marble wall most certainly built by man, but beautiful enough to make Mother Nature jealous. Swirls of silver and specks of sparkling black dot the gigantic slab of a wall. At its center, a tunnel shoots out water, creating the river.

Little mentioned this.

She also said I should be on the other side at this point. It's time to admit I should have crossed earlier.

*SNAP.*

I turn back and hear shuffling. A bird squawks above.

Then silence. Nothing.

Something's behind me. Or someone.

"Hello?" I call out.

Only an echo returns my greeting.

But I feel it. This feeling I know too well. Someone watching.

I turn toward the wall and begin marching forward. But I keep an ear turned back. I won't miss a sound. If someone's behind me, they won't catch me. Tired, sore, having run more today than I have in the last few months combined, I know I've still got some left in the tank if someone wants to test me.

Ahead, I notice that the rocks on the slate wall are slightly sticking out. Okay. I can do this. This wall was meant for scaling. This is rock climbing 101. A practice course.

Of course it's worth noting that I've never rock climbed, even in a gym with the proper safety gear, but how hard can it be? And I don't have to go far. A little up action, just above the hole. Then some side-stepping, which will probably be the hardest part.

But there's no point in overthinking this—a clear *CRUNCH* sounds behind me—definitely not now.

I turn and I swear I see something white slide behind a tree.

My heart swoops and swirls in my chest, just as I reach the wall.

I've gotta move. I grab a rock, just about at eye level, then another with my left hand, before bringing my foot off the ground. I'm officially climbing. Yes, it's only an inch, but we're moving. We're doing this.

I repeat this pattern again. Right foot up, left hand to rock, right hand to rock, left foot up. Success. I look up, finding my next four targets. Right foot, left hand, right hand, left foot. I'm up, maybe a foot and a half, but I'm doing this. I can't slow down.

I let out a deep breath. A few more steps and I'll be higher than the tunnel. Then there's the side-scaling. The hard part. Don't think about that.

The wind murmurs through the trees, gliding against my neck. I swear I hear rustling in the leaves behind me, but I try to block it out. Moving my gaze from these rocks will be my failure.

Just move faster. *Focus.*

I step up, pull, step up, pull. My feet are above the tunnel now.

Now the part I'm dreading. I assess the rocky terrain to my left. Okay, I got this. Same principles that just got me here, now I just gotta apply them sideways. Spot the rocks, left step, left arm, right step, right arm? Don't overanalyze. Just move!

Left, left, right—

My right foot struggles to find its landing as my hands grip for dear life. My flesh digs against the stone.

*Crunch, crunch, crunch.*

There's no way it's just in my head. Clear as I can hear my thoughts, clearer maybe, I hear footsteps on the forest floor below.

Hopefully it's just an animal that isn't concerned about me. Not an animal that's had their fair share of periwinkles and would now prefer people. Worst of all, hopefully it's not a person. No one tracks another person in the woods with good intentions.

I side-step, reach and pull, reach and pull, side-step.

Much smoother. Foot, hand, hand, foot, that's the trick.

Don't look down, just don't look down.

Foot, hand, hand, foot. I'm moving. I'm going to make it across.

I look down. I'm just above the tunnel now.

Foot, hand, hand, foot.

My eyes must be deceiving me, for the water now seems to be pulled into the tunnel, like a drain.

Foot, hand, hand, *CRACK.*

The rock beneath my right foot gives way and so does the rest of my body.

My hood sweeps across my eyes, leaving me blind. I fall, bracing my body for impact.

*SPLASH.*

My body dips beneath the surface. I try to protect my head, fearful of slamming against the bottom.

But that doesn't happen. The water is deeper than I imagined. But also stronger too. I kick my feet and stretch my arms upward, trying to reach the surface.

The water doesn't want me to win. But I pull forward relentlessly, toward the glimmer above. I break through with a gasp.

The world around me is suddenly darker. Ahead, there's a circle of light. I've been pulled into the tunnel. I look back into the dark hole and—

I scream.

A giant emerald eye looks at me from the other end.

It blinks and it's gone. Nothing but black.

Was that real?

No, it wasn't real.

I won't even entertain the thought. Nor is there time to.

I swim against the current, pushing as hard as I can for the water's edge. I reach the stone side and scan for something to grasp. Vines from the forest have spread against the stone, reaching deep into the tunnel like the veins of whatever beast lives within. I grab one and pull myself up. This part is far easier than rock climbing. I sidestep toward the tunnel's opening, hands firmly gripped to the vine.

At last, I've made it across. Definitely not the way Little had recommended, but I'm here now.

The sun still hangs above but it offers me no comfort. The Eye in the Tunnel now sits in the center of my brain. No creature is that large. No creature's eye could look so human. With its moss green iris and specks of yellow dashing around the pupil like an eclipse, I know that eye well.

No, forget it. I try to re-center my thoughts. There's someone on my trail. Get to the cabin.

From the lip of the tunnel, I look for the stage.

Just 30 yards ahead, I see a break in the trees. In the clearing, I can spot a giant stump.

Wanting to get as far away from the tunnel and the footsteps on the other side, I run.

I move faster than I've ever moved in my life. I don't know if safety awaits me on the other end, but it can't be worse than what's stalking me. Ahead, the stage is exactly as Little described.

At the center of the clearing is a giant reminder of a gargantuan tree that once was. The stump itself is more than four feet off the ground and wide enough to sit a small house atop.

Using the bark for traction, I pull myself up. Beneath my feet, I can see every circle down to its ring. If that elementary school factoid about rings on trees equaling their age was true, I couldn't even fathom how old this thing was.

The stump/stage is at least 30 feet across, and that's a modest estimate. Every centimeter, there's another line. Strangest of all, the lines aren't naturally flawed like one would think. Each ring is a perfect circle, more like a computer rendering of a mathematically perfect tree than one grown naturally from the green earth. Even the surface beneath my feet is totally flat. Neither machine nor accident could so cleanly cut a tree of this size.

*Stand atop it and turn*, Little said. I can't get this part wrong. You'll know it when you see the cabin.

Instead of turning, I walk the perimeter. My eyes scan for the cabin and any possible stalker. I occasionally look down, unable to wrap my head around these perfect circles.

I wonder what she knows. The tree, that is. What has she seen? How many girls before me and Little have walked across this solid surface and had similar thoughts? How long would it take me to walk around this tree, following the lines all the way back to its first and smallest circle?

Before I can waste time, my eyes go wide.

Little was right.

I couldn't miss it.

There, framed between two birch trees and underlined by a row of white flowers, a green cabin stands. With the periwinkles encircling it, the cabin almost looks like it's floating on clouds.

It's a green house, but most certainly not a greenhouse. This log cabin is painted from bottom to chimney in one uniform lime green—one might even be tempted to call it slime green. Who would choose to paint a cabin this color, anything this color really, baffles me.

I climb down and head for the cabin. I stumble, tripping over a thick stick. I look down at it. Something inside me tells me to pick it up. Use it if I have to.

I look up at the gross green cabin. The closer I get to the building, the less I want to enter it. The windows are boarded and coated. The plywood down to the nails are the same noxious green. Every shingle, every splinter, this radioactive hue.

I slowly make my way toward the door and my heart goes into hyperspeed.

The door is unlatched, already slightly cracked open.

I don't want to go in this house.

But that feeling returns. The hair on the back of my neck springs up. I know I'm being watched.

I turn and see it.

A figure in white runs toward me.

It moves fast. There's no time to wait.

I push the door open and slam it behind me. The cabin is completely dark, no cracks in the green paint for light to trickle through. I quickly run my hand up the door, hoping to feel a lock.

There's nothing on the knob, nor a bolt above it. I hear shuffling beyond the door. The person in white is right on the other end.

My hands rattle when I finally find something. It's small and cold. It feels like a metal hook. I pinch it and place it in the ring opposite it and not a second too soon.

*THUMP.*

The door thrusts forward, grazing my nose.

*THUMP.*

I spring back. Light spraying the room for a split-second before pulling back.

*THUMP.*

More light than last time. There's no way this door's gonna hold. I grip my walking stick, ready to turn it into a baton when that door breaks.

*THUMP.*

The door cracks, splintering from its hinges and falling forward. I lift the stick over my head, readying to slam it against this person's skull.

# CHAPTER 10



**THE NIGHT I ALMOST DECIDED** to take the leap that would take my life was the night I needed Gigi's wisdom the most. If Lucky didn't catch me while I was still on that roof, I wouldn't be here. Crying in his arms, I remember wishing for Mom's guidance, and then on cue, she answered.

"It's okay to be afraid of yourself," Lucky said as I wept.

It may have been Lucky's voice, but I knew she was using him to speak. I knew that through each of us, Gigi still breathed.

Just as I'm ready to thrust the stick forward, I freeze. While the outline is smaller than I expected, the person is still strong enough to kick down a door. *Don't hesitate. There's no time to waste. Do it.* I lift the stick over my head once more, ready to strike. This time I won't—

"Stop!" the figure raises its hands.

I know her voice.

I lower the stick against my shoulder.

"Little?"

She steps forward, pulling the white hood from her face.

"What are you wearing? Why are you here?"

She doesn't answer. Instead, she brushes me aside and pulls a chain in the room's center. A bulb flickers on, illuminating the cramped and dusty room. The sight of the place in the light instantly makes my stomach churn, as everything is coated in the same poisonous green as the cabin's exterior. Because everything's this uniform color, my eyes don't immediately register the shelves on the wall.

The entire wall is lined with small toys and strange trinkets. There's a carving of a horse, a patchwork teddy bear, a tin robot. There are a few Barbies from different eras with various hairstyles and professions. I see a Mickey Mouse, an Elmo, and—is that a Furby?

Tucked away in one corner of the room is a thin twin bed. Every thread of fabric—from the sheets up to the pillowcase—is green. Across the space, a wooden school desk with the chair built in. Above the desk, there's a bookshelf. Every spine on the shelf is green.

I don't know what it is, perhaps it's this moldy, radioactive green, but the sight of these objects makes me want to hurl. I cover my mouth, certain something's going to come up.

"Quick, we've gotta move." Little bends to the floor, looking under the bed.

"What? I just got here. You said I'd find what I was—"

"Stolen. Yes. I know what I said." She reaches beneath the puke green bed and tugs at something below the mattress. Whatever it is scrapes against the wood floor.

"Can you help me with this?"

She's frazzled, overflowing with a manic energy that she didn't have earlier. I don't ask questions. I join her on my knees, then reach under and pull. Whatever's under here isn't so heavy as much as it is awkward. It snags on the corner of the bed. After a little push and pull, it comes free.

I try to make sense of the object. It's basically just dozens of thin branches tied together with vines. Impressive, yet amateur. Against the slime green, it looks very out of place.

"A raft? For…?"

"For the water? What else?"

"That stream?" I shake my head. "I can't go near there. There was this giant eye—"

"An eye?!" Little throws her hands over her face. "Shit! He knows we're coming."

I remember Little talking about *him* earlier. The one with the funny name. "The Looker?"

"Yes. The further we get away from Miss Am, the more he's able to see."

"Then…we should…go back, yeah?" I suggest.

Little drops the raft and steps right in front of me. She stares into my eyes like she's inspecting an experiment gone wrong. She squints, the slick scar across her eye almost connecting to the other side.

"She really got you good, huh?"

I step back. I don't know what she's talking about.

"We're going to find your brother."

"I don't have a—"

She grabs me with both of her hands and turns me back to the knick-knack wall.

"Which of these things belongs to you?"

"Belongs to me? What are you—? Little, you're scaring me."

"Scaring you? I'm scaring *you*? Well, the feeling's mutual. You're already forgetting who you are."

I scoff. "I know exactly who I am."

"Destiny Lane?" she says mockingly, bobbing her head and bouncing her shoulders.

"That's right," I say, slightly less confident after she said it like that.

"Exactly who Am *wants* you to be."

My heart skips a beat. Little's words stir something in the pit of my stomach. Like a part of me has been sleeping.

"She's been working on you for a long time. Long before your mom died, she spotted you. She knew you'd be susceptible."

No. No. *Don't listen to her.*

The voice in my head. Is that me?

"It never was."

"Don't do that! Please stay out of my head."

"I can't. She's connected us. All of us. I'm trying to help you before it's too late. You don't have to end up like me."

"End up like you? Little, you're like, seven years old."

She leans over and places a finger over my lips.

"Zip. Zip it. Start with what's been stolen. Look, here. Which one of these things belongs to you?"

My eyes return to the godawful shelf. I scan for something that strikes a chord with me. Something I connect with.

Little looks on, arms folded, tapping a foot against the ground.

I roll my eyes. It's all a bunch of junk. There's no rhyme or reason to the collection. There's a brick-sized Gameboy next to conch shell bigger than my head. There's a pair of tattered Chuck Taylors next to a blank green square that reads *The Beatles*.

"None of this…means anything?"

"Don't tell me that. Please don't tell me that!" She swings her arms around and starts circling the space like she's having a breakdown. "Something here has to mean something. Something here has to be yours! Look harder!"

Okay, okay, I tell myself. Focus. Feel it. Listen.

There's a green crystal, a green pair of thick glasses, and green nesting dolls lined in a row.

"I'm sorry. None. I don't know what any of this means."

"This makes no sense," she rubs her brow. "There's no way she dug that deep."

Little sits at the desk and cradles her head in her hands when something rolls across the desk. The item catches my eye right away.

"What's that?"

"What's what?"

"On the desk. By your elbow."

Little looks down and picks it up. It's the only thing in the room that's not green.

"This?" She holds it up.

My whole body starts to tremble. I bring a shaking hand to my chest. My heart feels like a waterfall.

"That's—" I'm having trouble breathing.

"A pen?"

I reach for it and Little places it in my hand. The faux-gold metal is cold against my palm. My brain briefly believes it's smaller now, a common trick of passing time.

I press on the button and—*click-click-click*—the ball point pokes its head from the tip. I press again—*click-click-click*—and I see the outline of a woman handing me the pen.

*My* pen.

"I lost this forever ago."

"No," Little shakes her head. "She stole it."

*Click-click-click.*

The woman in my mind crouches down, and I can see her face in full. She smiles, her glowing gold cheeks looking like mirrored suns hoisted by a sideways yet sparkling crescent moon. Her big green eyes show no trace of white at their edges, but the blacks at the center look like tunnels to eternity. Every glance from her feels like a blessing.

"*Here,*" I hear her only in my mind, handing me the long gold pen. "*I got this for you.*"

I grip the pen in my hand wishing I'd never let it go. My lip quivers as a tear drips down my cheek before I feel it coming.

I remember it all now. I remember what's been stolen.

Now I gotta remember what I'm looking for. I know there's more to my story that I'm missing.

I turn to Little, unafraid that she'll see my tears.

Little smiles and nods. "We're gonna get you back. Completely. Step one, lift that side." She gestures toward the back of the raft. "We've gotta move fast. I've gotta be back before the girls wake up and tell Am or The Looker alerts his slitheries."

I gently slide the pen into my right pocket. I feel it press against my leg, snug in my tight pajama pants.

"You and these slitheries."

"The closer we get to his street, the bigger they are. I'm almost positive he's got a few scouting in these woods."

"I want to go back to the house," I say.

"There's no going back, Destiny. You don't want to."

"Of course, I do. That was the best day I've had in…" I try to remember a day better. There's nothing else that even comes close.

"That's what she wants you to think. This is what happens to all of us."

"What are you saying?"

"No one has a bigger heart than Am, no one's questioning that. She wants to help all of us, she really does. But you can't just erase someone and make them better. That's not how that works."

"What are you talking about? That's not what she's—"

"That's exactly what she's doing. When she went in your head, she took out all the bad stuff and replaced it with happy things. Happy things are easier to take away. We don't spend as much time thinking about them, soaking them in. It might feel like she healed you, but she didn't. Slowly, you'll remember the truth. We all do. But this just keeps us coming back to her over and over again. We all need her, but I think she needs us just as bad."

"I don't understand. Don't lie to me. First it was the game, then those directions. You said an X and I'm pretty sure it was an—"

"No one's lying. Only Miss Am and the other girls. But you're lucky you've got someone looking out for you. When that turtle slammed against the glass, that thing knew what it was doing. You couldn't see it, but it kept going and going, trying to break Am's concentration. And it worked. But there's still a piece of you in there. And now you've got that pen."

I run my hand against my thigh, feeling its outline pressed against my leg.

"The memories that come to mind when you see that thing, those are the ones you need to hold on to. Those are the ones that make you, not the fake stuff Am tries to mold over it."

Little backs into the cabin door and pushes it open. She slides the raft against the ground.

"You gonna help or…?"

I step forward and pick up the other side.

"I could probably carry this myself to be honest," I say.

"I'm sorry we're not all teenage giants. Just grab your ends and let's move."

We step back into the forest, and Little raises her hood. Her robe drapes against the floor, matching the pristine periwinkles. I glance back at the cabin and resist the urge to hurl.

"You weren't gonna mention that the cabin was that nasty green? Feels like that would have made it easy to find."

"Couldn't mention that. It's always changing," she looks back at me, only one eye visible beneath her hood. "Everything here is."

"Well, did you have to stalk me through the woods? You couldn't have just called out—*Hey, it's me! Little?*"

"What?"

"You were following me. Through the woods? I saw you."

Little shakes her head. "That wasn't me. I went a completely different way."

"Now you're lying. Stop playing with me."

"Me stop playing with you? You're freaking me out. If you saw someone else wearing a robe like this here, we could be in real trouble."

"Who else could it have been?"

"I don't want to think about it," she snaps back. "It was probably in your head. These woods will do that to you."

She's probably right. It was in my head like everything else. I have enough going on up here without being in an ever-changing forest.

Little tugs on the front of the raft trying to pull me along faster.

"We gotta move it. It's impossible to say how much time we have. Or how much time *he* has, for that matter?"

*He?* Did she mean The Looker? Or was there someone else out there?

"Why are you doing all this?"

Little sighs but refuses to look back. She chugs along.

"Maybe I feel bad, that's all."

"For bringing me to your super awesome house? Where you guys play games all day and swim beneath waterfalls? I should be thanking you."

"No. Shut up. I got you in this mess. I'm always doing stuff like this, and I just wanted a way out."

"I don't under—"

"I lied, okay? I lied." She drops the raft. "I used Am as a trick to make you think we were closer to your house."

"You didn't trick me."

"I did. I knew what I was doing, and now I wish I hadn't."

"I don't know what you think is bad about your life, but it seems pretty awesome to me."

"Stop! Okay? Believe me. You don't know what you're talking about. Look at all this," she gestures toward the flowers and thick trees that reach for the sun. "When I got here, this place was dark. The sun never came out. Only a little slice of the moon, day after day. There were no mountains, no streams, not even a single flower. Every single one of these trees was dead."

I can tell she's fighting back tears. I step closer to her. One part of me wants to hug her while the other half wants to pull my own hood over my face. I'm so bad at this stuff.

"I've been here forever, but I can still remember my life before," she says. "No matter how many visits to Temple, those memories seep through."

"How did you find this place?"

"I wish I could answer that part. I think it'd be more accurate to say that this place found me."

I think about the street that appeared in the middle of my town. The street I swore wasn't there yesterday. I wonder how similar her situation was.

"C'mon. We gotta keep moving." She picks up the front of the raft and charges ahead.

After a minute with only the birds singing and our feet stomping as the soundtrack, in true Little fashion, she can't help but to keep talking. I listen intently, wanting to hear her story.

"We lived at the beach," there's a trickle of joy in her voice. "A second-floor apartment on the boardwalk. Four of us—Ma, Pa, and Cornelia, my sister. Downstairs, my family ran a butterfly house. People came from all over the state to see our butterflies. The glowing blue morphos were my favorite. We had striped swallowtails that looked like little flying tigers. Cornelia loved those best. Or Pa's favorite, the satyrs. They looked like they had little eyes on their wings. He used to say, '*These little guys are watching you when I'm not here*,'" she chuckles. "There was nothing like our butterfly house at the shore. Nothing like it in the world."

Little goes silent.

"I was too little back then to realize everything eventually ends. I thought *then* was forever."

I'm afraid to ask what happened. Little reaches under her hood, wiping her face.

"There was a fire on the boardwalk a few blocks down." Her voice is suddenly rocksteady, like she's been drained of emotion. "A cafe went up in flames and the whole thing spread in seconds. Cornelia woke me up and pulled me outside her window.

"We waited on the boardwalk, watching the whole strip like a wall of fire, waiting for our parents. Butterflies flapped through the air before falling with their wings on fire. They fell right to our feet. Cornelia couldn't stop crying. Our parents never came out."

"I'm so sorry, Little. I can't even comprehend—"

"But you can," she says. "You've got your own pain. Don't feel bad. It was forever ago."

We reach the stream, and Little slows down. The story took a step out of her speed.

"That's when I started feeling her eyes watching me."

I get chills on the back of my neck that run down my shoulders. I know this feeling well.

"I started hearing her voice in my head. She changed my name and then, worst of all, my sister went missing. I couldn't live without her. She was all I had. So I went looking for her and soon, I ended up here. With you."

My heart drops. Something about her story feels too familiar.

"She targets us cause we're alone," I say. "She thinks we're weak."

"That's right. And our reliance on her only makes her stronger. But Am's known for a while now that she can't fix me. No matter how many times she tries to erase that night and make me think it ended with my family altogether, it doesn't stick. I know what actually happened."

I think about Gigi. I picture her smiling face, but it's quickly replaced with the horrid one, drained of life and dripping in water.

"Wouldn't it be easier? Pretend the happiness is real? Until, maybe it is?"

"It would be a lot easier. But then there's no me," she waves her hands between us. "We're gone. She's won."

"I think we're more than our pain," I say.

"I'm not pretending to know who or what either of us are. But whatever the answer is, our memories are a big part of it. If our memories don't even belong to us, we don't have a chance at ever figuring out who we are."

I smile. "You're smarter than me when I was your age."

"I wish," she sighs. "A while back I asked Am if I brought her a new girl, would she let me go. She agreed. She's ready to get rid of me. That's why when I saw you walking on the street all by yourself, I thought my only prayer had been answered."

"I'm your replacement?"

"You were supposed to be. But I can't leave you here. I'm not gonna do it. I love Am but she lies. Like, all the time. I've been here longer than I would have even been alive across the street. I wouldn't know the old world if I left this one. It's all dead. Cornelia is gone."

I notice her lip start to shiver and a glaze forming over her eyes. She looks away and tosses her end of the raft into the stream. She jumps down with a splash, steadying the raft.

"Here, you get on first."

I'm already drenched. I step into the water then sit on the back end as Little keeps it balanced.

"Are we sure this is safe?"

"The raft? Maybe," she slowly steps on herself, keeping the stick planted in the riverbed. "A trip to the other Lane? Absolutely not."

She stands and pushes the stick, steering us forward, toward the tunnel. The water pulls us in, our speed picking up. I'm afraid to look ahead at what might meet us there, but as Little pushes forward, I can't help but look.

There's nothing. No eye, only blackness.

"How can you see?!" I scream.

"I can't!" she says confidently.

In seconds, the light behind us is gone. The wind whirls and I hold onto the dinky wood raft for dear life. I can't see my hands. Deeper in, and I can't even see Little's outline a few feet before me.

"Little?!" I call out.

I hear nothing but the wind whipping in my ears.

"Little!?"

I swipe my hands forward for her and almost lose my

balance. Don't do that. Definitely don't do that. I clutch the raft with everything I've got.

We whizz forward, the world around us getting blacker than sleep.

I pray that we get out of this. I call for Little again but give up. I can't even hear my own voice.

This is it. This has got to be it.

*Death.*

But it's worse than I imagined it. With the violent wind and quaking water around me, this is far less peaceful.

Just as I'm certain that I've come to an end, ahead, I see a flicker of light.

# chApteR 11



**IT'S NOT OVER JUST BECAUSE** I'm writing this.

Saving yourself is a daily practice.

Gigi stopped. I've stopped. I can't afford to again. Please give me the strength to never forget this day.

I see Little and breathe a sigh of relief. Water splashes against my hands and I look down, grateful to see my fingers. I look ahead and shield my eyes. A circle of white light grows larger ahead when—

*THUMP.*

We hit a bump in the river, and Little flies up. I grab her and pull her down just as we hit another. Our dinky raft rattles, careening back and forth, scraping against the rocky bed below as the water dries up around us.

We slide to a complete halt. The sun sears above, battering against my eyelids.

Little doesn't hesitate. She jumps from the raft, landing upon gravel.

"Let's make this fast and quiet. Am's got her flaws, but she's nothing compared to her brother."

I follow Little's lead, shuffling onto the dirt. She tosses me the stick then drags the raft from the dry ditch where she leans it against the tunnel's lip.

I try to make sense of the world around me, but doing so feels impossible at this point. We stand amid a bone-dry valley, scorched orange sand. This place couldn't be more different than the flowery forest on the other end of the tunnel. The walls around us are almost flat, certainly unclimbable. I look up and get dizzy instantly. They're taller than any skyscrapers I've seen. A thin crack in the orange clifftops above lets through a sliver of a baby blue sky. The sun fits perfectly between the cracks, like a marble rolling down a pipe.

Ahead, a clicking scream echoes through the valley, sending every hair on my body straight. Little looks back at me and I feel the blood drain from my face. I shake my head as she nods hers.

"C'mon," she says. "We got this."

Overhead, the clicking scream returns, sounding like a swarm of cicadas mixed with the bleats of an animal dying from thirst.

"No way," I say. Little pulls my arm, leading me against the wall, behind a sizable boulder.

"What the fu—"

She throws her hand over my mouth.

"Don't. Say. A word," she whispers.

I notice something splattered behind her on the boulder. Dried and hardened, it looks like it's been there for ages.

My eyes follow the markings. They're crudely carved into the stone then haphazardly painted in crimson. It reads:

L—it takes a moment for me to remember the mark as a letter in my mind.

U—stabbed into the stone, looking more like a V.

C—smaller than the rest, surely hard to carve the curve.

K—somewhat tilted, looking like a cross.

Y—like a split road.

L—this one cleaner than the last.

A—the red bleeds across the triangle atop the letter.

N—the red drips down from the bottom corner and onto the boulder, like an executioner's blade.

E—but it's backwards—Ǝ. The carver got excited to reach the finish, and messed the whole thing up.

**LUCKY LANƎ**

The dry click of death reverberates against the stone walls.

"It sounds like they've just started another," Little says.

"Another?"

She doesn't answer.

"Watch your step."

She peeks her head around the boulder then—

"What? Where are—"

She darts across, heading for another boulder across the way.

You're kidding me? Little moves onward, unafraid of what might be ahead. She's moving closer toward that horrid sound.

As though she's heard my thought, Little looks back at me and waves me forward. I poke my head around the boulder. All along the narrow path, I see dozens, maybe even a hundred, perfectly circlular holes. No animal could have been so precise, and certainly no man.

I scurry across the way, weaving between the cavities before reaching Little.

She motions with her hands. "Faster next time."

"I was trying not to fall in."

"Yeah, don't do that. No saving you then. These go on forever."

I scoff. "Forever."

"Pockets of Infinity," Little whispers.

I know those words. I've heard them before, but I can't place them.

"Excuse me?"

"It's where the slitheries store the bodies," Little continues. "Sometimes they wrap them before they're cold. Hopefully, that's what they've done with yours."

Little dips her head around the rock and doesn't flinch. She springs to the next boulder and crouches. I try to emulate Little's bravery and just go for it.

I dash, and just as I'm in the center of the valley, hopping across one of the small holes, their sound returns.

*DL-DL-DL-UNK. DL-DL-DL-UNK. DL-DL-DL-UNK.*

Curiosity gets the best of me. I glance toward the sound.

Standing just a few boulders away, I see the most gruesome figure my mind can comprehend. Far worse than anything I could make up consciously or my worst nightmare could concoct.

Standing across the way are a pair of upright cockroaches, composed of yellowed, sun-scorched bones. From my vantage point, they appear to be my size. There's no question they're taller than Little by a head or two. They walk on large bipedal legs, with long twiggy arms that graze the ground. Along their torsos are hundreds of small, jittery legs like those of a centipede. These legs don't stop moving, furling and unfurling, like electric tendrils. One of them turns and I see they've got tails like slithery bones, maybe an external spine, that runs all the way up to their heads. The monster to the right has something draping from its tail, but I don't stop to stare.

I pull back behind the boulder, nearly tripping on a sizable rock by my foot. "What the fuck are those?"

"Shush!" Little covers my mouth. "I told you. Slitheries!"

"That meant nothing to me."

"Well, it does now! They're dangerous, soulless bugs. They do whatever The Looker tells them to."

Little peeks around the corner and shakes her head.

"Give me the stick!" she demands.

"What are you thinking?"

She stares at me, dead in the eyes. I shake my head.

Nope. Whatever she's thinking, it's a no.

I keep a firm grip on the stick, but she grabs it anyway. There's no struggle. But there may have been if I knew her next move.

Without a thought or deep breath to compose herself, she runs from behind the rock and charges for the slitheries.

I gasp.

They don't see her.

She raises the stick above her head, holding it in one arm like a javelin. She's within a step of the thread-tailed slithery.

It ticks its head to the side, seeing her.

It squeals, nervously clicking, faster, louder.

*DL-DL-DL-UNK. DL-DL-DL-UNK. DL-DL-DL—*

Then silence. Deafening, horrifying silence.

Little jabs the stick forward, jamming it into the creature's neck. The bug's body starts to wobble as yellow pus sprays from its wound. Little doesn't stop pushing. The bug's stick legs crumble, its body collapsing weightlessly to the dirt. For good measure, Little thrusts downward, the stick pinning the beast to the ground.

Before I can process what's happening, the slithery across the way lunges for Little, slamming her beside the bleeding bug.

I scream, but I can't hear myself. Little screams louder.

The creature wraps its boney tail around Little's legs as she tries to kick. Its centipede legs wrap around her torso then it slams down her head, covering her mouth with its fidgety claws.

I don't think. I do what Little would do.

I grab the big rock right by my foot that I almost tripped on. Or rather, I struggle to. It's the size of a bowling ball—one far heavier than I'd ever choose to use and one without its finger holes. This twenty, maybe thirty-pound rock is more than my bony arms can bear.

Little gets out a squeal, but her sound is quickly muffled.

Rock barely in hand, I run, my arms swaying side to side.

Little sees me coming. Her eyes go wide.

I can't lift the rock over my head, but I swing it from my hip, bringing it as high as I can, then slam it against the side of the monster's head.

*CRUNCH.*

Half of its head caves in. It stumbles to the side, freeing Little.

But it's not dead. The slithery turns to me, its punctured eye drooping down its face, slathered in yellow mush. It takes a step but falters. It bends, crawling for me.

It's brave. Or stupid. Or brain-damaged. Okay, clearly all three.

I'm feeling stronger. And more capable. With every muscle fiber straining, I pull the rock over my head.

My arms shake. Please don't drop this, please don't drop this.

The slithery stumbles forward, slower than I have the patience for. I step toward it and slam the stone down—

*SLUNK.*

The bug's brain splatters against the gravel, sprinkling fragments of itself on my blackened Vans. I think they used to be white.

I heave through clenched teeth. "Gross."

"Nice." Little pushes herself from the ground.

She heads over to the first dead bug, the one nailed to the ground. She reaches for the thick thread attached to its tail and starts pulling.

I'm frozen, still in shock at what's just happened. None of this feels real. I look down at my shaking hands, some of the creature's yellow excretion dripping between my fingers. This is definitely real.

"Wake up," Little snaps her fingers. "There's hundreds of those things. And they're the least of our problem. Help me with this."

Like a spider's silk, this rope-like fiber runs from the tip of the slithery's tail and into the nearest pit. I wrap my hands around the thick thread. It's waxy, which at least makes it easy to grip. But whatever's on the other end of this—*I'm not sure I want to know*—isn't making this easy.

We try to pull in tandem, Little counts, "1-2-3!"

And on three, we heave backward, pulling perhaps a foot with each tug.

"1-2-3!"

There's a part of me that already knows what's there.

"1-2-3!"

I just don't want to admit it.

"1-2-3!"

I don't want to imagine it.

"1-2-3!"

But the worst version of what it could look like—what *he* could look like—pops into the front of my head.

"1-2-3!"

I remember his name. *Lucky.* But that's not right either.

"1-2-3!"

We loved to play pretend. We'd make up games and find our own secret hideaways.

"1-2-3!"

Pretend we were people we weren't so we didn't have to be the people we are.

"1-2—"

Little loses her grip and the thread starts to unravel. I grab it with all of my weight, my shoulders searing. I fall to the ground. Little latches me, pulling her arms under mine, holding me tighter than I've ever been held. She reaches forward, getting a firm grip on the thread.

She looks back and exhales. We both want to laugh but there's no energy in us left to make a sound.

Little pokes her head forward, peering into the abyss. Her eyes light up.

"Here! Quick! Pull! We're almost there!"

We abandon the counting system and just tug with every ounce in us. My arms shudder. I can't feel them anymore. They act on their own accord, this act far surpassing anything I've asked of them in the past. Little leans back, digging her heels into the dirt for extra leverage.

We both let out guttural yells as we pull the heavy mass over the lip of the hole.

I stumble backward, on the verge of collapse. Little gasps for breath but she's still more concerned about me. She reaches out her hand.

"You did it," she says.

"We," I wheeze.

I reach for her, our fingertips brushing. The weakest high-fives are the ones you worked hardest for.

I'm afraid to look beyond Little. I'm afraid to face the impossibly heavy object we just impossibly pulled from this impossibly deep hole.

I peer over Little's shoulder. She turns to it herself.

It's a giant cocoon, spun the size of a—

It squirms. I jolt backward.

Little reaches into her boot and pulls out something small and white.

She offers it to me. At first glance it looks like a lipstick container, its polished surface made of pearl. There's a small butterfly etched in gold near the top.

I reach for it, but she pulls back.

"Wait, let me…" she flicks her wrist and a blade flashes out from its side.

"A butterfly knife with a butterfly on it," I say, processing the image of a little girl holding a glistening knife before me.

"Very observant," Little smirks. "We all have one. Different symbols, obviously. The girls are always trying to steal mine."

"Why do you all have butterfly knives?"

The cocoon squirms and lets out a muffled sound. I think it was a cough.

"Go." She thrusts the knife in my hand, careful to place the pearl handle in my palm. "Don't go jabbing. Just swipe at the layers. Gentle."

"I don't—" I shake my head but she shakes hers faster. "I can't—" Her head becomes a nod.

*Yes, you can.*

I head toward the cocoon, knife in hand, knowing only partially what I'll find. Little lingers by my side like a shadow. She knows how much I need her right now.

I bend to my knees and Little puts her hand on my shoulder.

The cobweb coffin squirms once. It lets out another sound. This time I know for sure that it's a cough.

"Its head," Little points. "Start there."

I slowly bring the knife down, my hand trembling. I could never be a surgeon. I could never even dissect an ice-cold frog.

The web sticks to the edge of the blade. Beneath the top layer, moisture has accumulated. It's gooey, likely slithery secretion. I gently swipe and swipe.

*Careful.*

It's like cutting cotton coated in clear syrup.

*Slow down.*

I snip and a thick fiber twangs apart, cracking bits of the hardened shell. I see something.

Golden flesh. Long lashes. A brown eye opens.

I drop the knife and grab each side of the opening. I pull, ripping the cocoon down the center. Tears start forcing their way from beneath my eyes. Little works on the rest of his body, trying to tug his limbs free.

His head is first to come free. His hair is matted, the yellow gunk coating his skin. His mouth is gagged with the slither's thread. I pull back the thread, slip the knife under it and pull. It snaps, freeing his mouth.

His lip quivers. Tears fill his glossed eyes. He's lost. Confused.

"Maya," he whimpers. His voice sounds shattered. A shell of its booming self.

One of his arms breaks free, then the other. He reaches for me.

I break down, throwing myself into his arms.

"Lucky."

Here in each other's arms, we weep.

Here in each other's arms, all of our memories come flooding back in.

In my head, I play a montage of us. From SpongeBob recommendations to rooftop conclaves. From stoned soliloquies to queer pop-star dance parties.

This is my best friend. This is my brother.

I look back at Little, but she stands at a distance. She turns away from us, pulling her hood back over her head. I can't see her face.

"This…this is my Little," I struggle to speak. "She saved us."

"We've got to move," Little says sternly. "Let's go."

Lucky's eyes can't stop moving, taking in everything around him. I help him to his feet. He's wobbly. He wraps one arm around my shoulder as he tries to inch forward. His knees shake like they haven't been used in days. He winces in pain.

"You okay? You got this."

He keeps a hand at his side, pressing at his hip.

"We got this," he grunts.

I look to where he holds his side. He's wounded. His favorite Britney Spears shirt is tattered and stained with yellow goo and red blood.

Little has moved ahead, staying several steps in front of us. Lucky stumbles again. Every step is a challenge. I suggest to him that we stop and take it slow. He nods and tries to catch his breath.

"Any chance we can move any faster?" Little calls back, still not turning to look at us.

She's being odd.

"Any chance you could help us?" I say.

Little scoffs, not slowing her step or glancing back.

Lucky leans against the nearest boulder, slumping his body.

I run up to catch Little, weaving between the death traps.

"Hey," I shove her arm. "What's going on?"

She looks down, stepping ahead. She doesn't answer me.

I step in front of her, facing her head on.

I shove her again. "Why are you being so weird?"

She looks up at me. I can hardly see her beneath the hood, but tears are streaming down her cheeks.

"Oh my god. Little? I'm so—"

"Don't lettemseeme," her words run together, hard to understand. She bursts into tears.

I pull her in for a hug.

"What are you talking about? He knows you helped—"

"He won't get it."

"What do you mean?"

I think I understand. She looks like a younger me. She doesn't want to scare him.

"So what? You look a little like me—"

"To you," she spits out.

"What?"

"He can't see me, Destiny," she weeps. "Don't lettemseeme."

I hold her tighter.

"I won't. I promise I won't."

"I'll scare him," she sobs into my shoulder. She struggles to say the next part. Like this is the worst thing she's ever had to say. "And that'll scare you."

I don't understand at all, but I hold her tight. I see that Lucky has noticed and has tried to work himself up and toward us. I put up my hand, telling him to wait. When Little's calmed herself, she wipes away her tears.

I lean down, trying to look in her eyes but she avoids my gaze.

I cup her face with my hands and bring her eyes to mine. They look like they might burst with tears again.

"This is it," she says. "I know the end."

I shake my head. "No." What is she talking about?

"Yes." She moves my hands from her face, holding them in front of us. "When we come out the other end of that tunnel, this is over. I'm going to give you directions through the woods, back to your home. Your real home."

"Come with us," I blurt.

"I can't."

"Yes, you can. We've got the space. We'll just say you're another one of our cousins."

Little smiles. "You'd let me do that?"

"Let you? I'm asking you. I'm not begging yet, but I will. Come with us, please."

Little glances over her shoulder at Lucky. She pulls her hood back down, all the way over her face.

I can still see her mouth. She smiles. But the edges don't reach her cheeks. I can tell it's forced.

"I'll think about it," she says.

My heart slips down to my stomach. I know she's already decided.

Little asks me to pick up the opposite side of the raft and walk it with her into the tunnel. Once we're deep enough in the ditch, once we've reached the water and only shadows can be seen, Little says it's okay to get Lucky.

He hobbles up to the edge of the tunnel and calls in, seeing if we need help. Little shakes her head at me. I know in my heart that Lucky's far more understanding than Little's giving him credit for, but she doesn't know that and it's not worth fighting over right now. Not in our final moments together.

Once we've reached the water—a dribble across the rocks, a small splash with each step, then it's up to our ankles—we place the raft down and I go back for Lucky.

"Here, I'll keep it still," Little speaks to Lucky for the first time, safely in the darkness. "You sit down, and we'll get this thing going."

"I can help," Lucky insists.

"Help yourself by sitting on this raft," Little directs.

Lucky laughs.

"I see why you like her," he whispers to me.

Lucky lowers himself to the raft as Little and I man the back. We push the raft forward, water splashing around us. Within seconds, the water's up to our knees and the raft is picking up speed, the water pulling us forward.

We hop aboard the back, and not a moment too soon. I struggle, the water gushing around us. Lucky and Little safely pull me up.

"Guys?" Lucky calls out. "Is everyone blind right now or is it just me?"

I reach over and hold his hand.

"Over here."

I wait for Little to respond, but she doesn't.

I reach to my left, feeling for her, but come up empty. I swipe my arm, reaching for her.

"Little?"

A small hand grasps mine. Her touch is cold, almost freezing.

"I'm right here." She leans her head against my shoulder.

Together in the speeding black, I feel every second. Wind

gusts around us, droplets mist against my face. Time is imperceptible, bordering on impossible. Without the light, each speeding moment feels infinite. I close my eyes and it makes no difference. We might as well be soaring through space. A single guiding star wouldn't hurt.

I wrap my arm around Little and squeeze Lucky as hard as I can. I think I hear her whisper something in my ear, but I can't make out the words.

We hit a bump, water splashing across us. We pull each other closer, Little's head tucked against my ribcage, Lucky and my fingers are intertwined so tightly I don't know whose is whose. My heart hammers against my chest. It almost hurts. I need oxygen. How many thirteen-year-olds die from heart attacks? This is it. This is the fucking end.

I struggle to exhale and the rapids suddenly steady. I hear a soft sound from Lucky. A tittering that slightly bounces his body. I hear something similar coming from Little.

"Are you laughing?"

*This was fun, huh?* Her voice echoes in my head.

We zoom forward, into the black.

*Yeah,* I think back. Scary. *But fun.*

# cHApteR 12

**PART OF THE PRACTICE IS** recognizing the ebb and flow of life.

"I won't lie to you, baby star. Healing isn't easy," she said as she drove. I was old enough to sit in the front seat beside her. "Your hardest days are ahead. But so are your best."

Ahead, the ring of light. Ahead, the promise of home.

We zip toward the bright forest faster than any of us are comfortable with. I grip each of their hands, holding on with all of my might, hopeful we don't hit a renegade rock that sends us tumbling. Just as our outlines begin to fill in and I can see my own fingers again, Little frees her hand from my grip.

She scoots herself to the front of the raft, shielding herself from Lucky. Before I can protest, we're out of the tunnel, speeding ahead and—*THWIPP!*

There's a shot of pain across my torso. An electric lash that sends me reeling. I scream and hear Little and Lucky wail in unison.

Before I can make sense of what's happened, I'm thrown back, collapsing backward into the water. My head smacks against the riverbed, completely disorienting me. Water rushes into my nose and mouth. I'm choking. I cough underwater, which only makes it worse. I swipe my arms, trying to find my footing and the surface above. Light shimmers below me and I realize I'm toppled. I curl upward, swimming for the surface, realizing that Little and Lucky are beside me doing the same.

We each emerge almost at the same moment.

I notice a rope tied tightly across the stream. It's definitely what sent us flailing. Eyeing the riverbanks, I see who tied it there.

Standing at the water's edge on either side are the Destinys. All of them. Just like Little, they wear white cloaks, trimmed in gold.

A shriek pierces my ear, sending the hairs on the back of my neck standing.

It's from Lucky. I've never heard him sound like this before. It's a noise that stabs my heart. A scream of nightmares, reserved exclusively for run-ins with death.

I reach for him, but he can't see me. I'm right beside him, but that's not registering for him. His eyes are peeled wide, terror plastered across his face.

"WHAT ARE THEY!? WHAT ARE THEY!?" he screams.

I place a hand on his shoulder, and he flails.

"NO! NO! NO! NO!"

His arms wave, splashing water everywhere. He's lost it. He's completely manic.

Little climbs from the stream as I try to guide Lucky toward the side to do the same.

"NO! NO! NO!" he protests.

The girls laugh, their chorus of pleasure sounding like a swarm of bees.

"Make it stop! Make them stop!"

"Boys are so pathetic," one of the girls chirps.

"What is that? What is it saying?" Lucky shivers.

I pull myself from the water and try to bring Lucky with me. He swipes, completely inconsolable.

"Ugh!" Razor steps forward, rolling her eyes. "Just grab him."

Excited to pounce, five of the girls converge on Lucky.

"Be careful, he's hurt!" I try to step between them, but they brush me aside. The Dream Girl called Golden throws a hand on my shoulder. I try to shrug it off, but Claws grabs my arm, pulling me in.

I look across the water. Little is on her knees and they're tying her hands behind her back.

"What are they doing to her?" I yell. "What the fuck are you doing to her?!"

Lucky's shrieks fill the air, echoing through the forest. The leaves above us jitter. A fleet of birds rise from the treetops as one and head for peace. They want no part of what's unfolding here.

"Gag him!" one of the girls commands.

"Slash his eyes! He can't see us like this!"

"Stop!" I cry. "What are you doing!?"

"No! Don't hurt him." Razor steps toward Lucky, commanding authority. Everyone quiets and looks to her. Thank God. They're not all crazy.

*Not so fast,* Razor looks me dead in the eye. Her face twists into a vampiric smirk, her sharp teeth glinting. "That's Am's favorite part."

I want to punch her in the mouth and make her bleed again. I swing my arms, trying to break free. I manage a moment of freedom and elbow Golden in the jaw with a resounding crack.

She reaches in pain as the other two Dreams dig their nails into my arms.

"Calm down, Destiny." Golden spits out blood. "This has nothing to do with you."

Suddenly, Lucky's screams go silent. I look his way and he's completely limp as several of the girls drag him across the flowers.

"Take him back," Razor directs.

"What did you do to him!?"

"Stay quiet and you'll be fine," Razor walks by and I notice a white object in her hand. A small pearl handle.

Across the way, Little fights but it's useless. They've tied her legs together as a few of the bigger girls step on them to stop her from squirming.

"What are you doing to her?!" I scream.

"Shut her up," Razor points the blade at me.

They move swiftly and succinctly, as though their thoughts are connected. While their bodies are separate, they move as one coordinated machine. Before Razor's done speaking, one of the Claws is holding my head still as Page ties a rope around my mouth.

"Sorry," she says softly. "You'll forget about this tomorrow."

I try to bite her hand but find nothing but the cord. Tears drench my face. The wiry rope digs into the corners of my mouth, and I feel my lips split. Blood slips between the gaps in my teeth.

"We should have known better, ladies," Razor steps forward, calling across the stream. "This Little bug has been trying to get out of here for ages. I can't wait to tell Aunt Am. She's going to kill you."

"I've never taken pleasure in killing," a steady voice booms across the woods, silencing the girls. Her words are soft, yet they fill the space. She stands across the way but she might as well be whispering directly in my ear.

Am steps down from the hill, draped in a white gown. Her movements are smooth, gliding, and effortless. In her white, she almost looks like a floating ghost.

She approaches Little and cups her chin in her hand. Her gold nails frame Little's crying face.

"What has our Little one gotten herself into today?"

Little stops resisting. She looks up at Am, her eyes begging for forgiveness.

"I'm not supposed to have favorites," Am says. "But I've never been good at hiding secrets. It was always you, Destiny.

Maybe that's why we gave you so much freedom. Maybe that's why we gave you so many chances."

Don't hurt her. Please don't hurt her.

Am turns to me, her calmness more chilling than the chaos that erupted just moments ago.

*It won't hurt*, Am says. But she doesn't move her mouth. Her voice seeps through into my brain. *It never does.*

"But you did well, Favorite. You gave us her."

The Destinys turn to me. My skin sears as their countless eyes fall upon me. I want to escape myself.

"I'm afraid I can't hold up my end of the deal." She turns back to Little. "Truth is, I never could. Not in the way you wanted. Deep down you know this. There's no peace for you out there. Your family is gone. Your people are gone. The family is all we have. You've always known this."

The group has fallen still and silent. I notice they've closed their eyes, each of their heads is gently bent.

"But we can't have you anymore. We can't trust you. All the love in the world couldn't fix that."

Little sobs. She opens her mouth to speak but comes up empty. Her lips quiver.

"We'll always love you, Favorite. Never question that. Rest knowing that you are deeply loved."

Her mouth moves but no words come out. She cries harder, looking like she's trying to scream. But she's voiceless. A terrifying silence pours from her open mouth.

"But it's peace you're after." Am strokes her golden thumb against Little's cheek. "And we can't provide that."

Little shakes her head. She thrusts her shoulders forward, pleading.

No, please no!

"We're brought into this world in water," Am's words become melodic, like she's reciting a poem she's spoken a thousand times. "And before the water, blackness and…"

"Peace," the girls speak as one.

Am nods, proudly. "You deserve that peace."

Am looks to the girls standing nearest to Little. Their eyes suddenly open. It takes four of them, but together they lift Little from the ground and carry her toward the water.

I try to scream through the gag but nothing makes it through.

I try to fight but the girls hold me tight.

It's an image a million lifetimes couldn't erase.

They heave Little into the stream.

She dips beneath the surface without much of a splash.

I can't help but fight.

*Be still*, Am speaks to me and only me.

I have no control. My body goes limp. I can't resist.

Am stands at the water's edge and closes her eyes.

Little bobs up, her face fighting for breath.

I want to close my eyes. I can't watch. But my eyelids are fixed open. Tears do the best to block the sight but Am wants me to see.

The crystal water in the stream starts to quake. From the tunnel, white sludge starts pouring out, completely permeating the water and then overtaking it.

Little's eyes go wide before her body jerks, the sludge yanking her beneath the surface.

At last, she lets out a sound. She screams in absolute agony, a sound worse than death, before being swallowed by the white.

Then she's gone.

My eyes turn to Am, who's already waiting for my attention.

You lied, I stare into her eyes, certain that she hears my thoughts. She was in pain.

"No longer," Am says aloud. "Now it is us who are left with the pain."

In moments, the sludge slips downstream and the crystal blue returns. No remnants of the white death linger behind. It's as though it was never there. Not a single sign of Little's struggle.

I look back at Am as she wipes her eyes. A tear?

But then smiles, softly, careful not to show teeth.

I wish I had my own butterfly knife right now. I'd love to jab it in one of her eye sockets.

She nods. She knows how I feel. She knows my thoughts which only makes me hate her more.

"Untie her," Am commands. "This obsession with knives and ropes needs to end."

One of the Dream Girls unflicks her knife and cuts the cords binding my hands and mouth.

"We all need a visit to the Temple from here," Am says.

*Destiny, you're first,* she says just to me.

As though nothing has happened, the girls start chattering.

We start the long walk back to the house. The light hum of their voices sounds like a satisfied song.

Am I the only one who just saw Little die? My knees shake, wanting to buckle. I want to—no, need to collapse. I feel my shoulders start to hunch and then, just as I feel like I might give way, I start moving forward. My legs take on long, swift strides. Strong steps that aren't my own.

Please stop it. Throw me in there too.

*Shh. Quiet, baby star. We will free you of these thoughts.*

When the stream has narrowed and requires no more than a step to cross, the Dream Girls and I make our way to the other side. In what feels like practiced choreography, we file into a line like orderly ants. We walk toward the arched exit from the wood and to the great field outside. The sun halos the center mountain, its rays kissing our skin.

I don't want to take another step. I want to give up. But my legs move faster, toward the front of the line. In short time, I find myself opposite Am, our strides perfectly aligned.

My thoughts can't stop racing. And Am won't stop invading them.

Where's Lucky?

*Who is Lucky?*

Don't fuck with me! Where's my brother?

Without moving her mouth or glancing my way, she chuckles. The sound of someone else's laughter circling your mind would drive anyone mad. Thankfully, I don't think I can get any madder.

*He's safe. You can't concern yourself with those things anymore.*

What are you going to do to him?

*Nothing. I'll return him to where he belongs.*

Where he belongs? We both belong home, away from here.

*You stole him, Destiny. We must rise above such sins.*

Stole him? Sins? He went missing. I found him! He was dying.

*Perhaps the greatest human sin is thinking you own these bodies. Being alive could never be confined to the flesh.*

What the fuck is she talking about? I hate this woman.

I look up at her, and she's already there to meet my eyes. She smiles, her golden cheeks glistening.

*I know. It's been a while since I felt hate. It's almost electric, the way it rattles through the soul. But I will free you of that pain. We can save you.*

I clench my jaw, wanting to bite straight into her face. Rip off whatever I can sink my teeth into. No one this evil deserves to be this beautiful.

"I don't want to be saved," I speak.

"You sound like her," she says. *My favorite,* a hint of sadness in her voice. I don't trust it.

Little's face flashes in my mind.

*"Some people call me Favorite,"* she said, *"but I don't really like that."*

I remember her forced smile and the front-tooth gap that mirrored mine. I see her skin glowing in the sunlight and glimmering across that thick scar.

I know who gave her that wound now, and I want to kill them. All of them.

Am narrows her eyes and nods. *You can try.*

She steps closer to me. I instinctively try to pull away but can't. *Here, walk beside Aunt Am.*

You're not my aunt. You're not my family. You're nothing to me.

*You have no family, Destiny. That's why you're here.*

I feel the urge to cry but I'm disgusted with myself. I try to blink the tears away. She can't see my pain. I can't let her think she's won.

*It was never a battle, Baby Star.*

Stop. Don't call me that. Please.

I'm right next to her. Our shoulders graze. She gently places an arm around me and pulls me in.

"Please stop," I beg. The tears are pouring.

"You don't have to live with this pain," Am says.

My anger toward her is useless next to the truth.

"I don't want to," I admit.

Am pulls me closer and my body betrays my angriest thoughts.

Being held feels good. I feel safe. I know this isn't true, it can't be, but her touch feels like a thousand sleeps. I instantly start to feel new. Refreshed. The memories of the woods are already feeling hazy.

Fight it off, fight it off, I tell myself.

I try to suppress a creeping thought, a whisper so deep, so quiet, that even Am doesn't detect it.

Play along…

# chApteR 13

WE RETURN TO THE SLATE white house. Approaching the glass façade, I'm horrified by my own reflection. I'm wilting before my eyes. Blood drips from the edges of my mouth. I hardly recognize my own skin. I'm pale. Drained of life. My flesh blends in with the white cloaked Destinys behind me. But where they glow, I'm ashen. They look like a legion of angels stripped of their wings.

I scan their faces, searching for a distinction between them. A small reminder that these girls are not the same. Like me, like Little, they used to have their own lives. When I arrived, I saw myself in them. Golden sun-kissed skin, black hole smiles that could give life. Now I can hardly recognize their features in mine.

Are they changing? Or me?

They see me searching for answers in the reflections. As

one, all twenty-one of them smile. The hairs on the back of my neck tickle my spine. I mirror their masks, unsure if the muscles in my face have any say in the matter. I smile, but the blood on my lips makes me look like a monster.

You are a monster.

*You are a monster.*

I'm not a monster.

*I'm the monster.*

Her voice is starting to sound more like mine. I can hardly tell the difference.

Am opens the door ahead and guides me into the house. Through the kitchen, across the etched marbled floor, she welcomes me upstairs. The smaller Destinys turn to the left as Am and the Dream Girls point me down the hall to the right. The corridors are narrow, but the ceilings are high. Painted in all white, everything feels bright and new. At the end of the hallway a stained-glass window takes up the entire wall.

Shards of green, blue, and gold light trickle through the image of an angel. The woman in a simple blue robe stands over a lake, a forest behind her. On her shoulder she holds a clay pot from which icy blue water pours into the lake beneath her. Her long blonde hair flows beside the water, not quite reaching its depths. Almost lost in the image is the divine. Her halo hovers between her arching wings, their golden color faded in comparison to the rest. With her eyes fixed to her left, beyond the window, she seems disinterested with the task at hand.

We step closer. I notice a scroll beneath the water's splash. On it, letters read: *fecunditatem mundo cum amore.*

I butcher the words in my head.

Am looks over her shoulder at me. "Fertilize the world with your love."

She turns and gestures into an open doorway.

I still can't take my sight off of the window. Beneath the scroll, submerged in the lake, dozens of infants stare up at the angel. Their naked hairless bodies match the blue of the water. Their poses are identical. Each reaches toward the surface, for the angel. Less than lost, their faces look blank.

"This is your room," Am smiles. "Right next to mine."

I step in and my heart skips. It's beautiful.

*It's all yours.*

All mine?

The room is all-white, mostly a blank canvas. There's a king size bed, wide enough for six of me, but not much else. One doesn't need much with a wall-wide window that looks out on a trio of mountains.

Imagine waking up to that every morning. I could do that forever.

*That's the idea.*

"We can start decorating this afternoon," Am says. "Make it more personal."

"I love it as is," I admit.

"My room's spotless too," Am smiles.

She suggests I clean up and points me toward my connected bathroom. Its white stone looks and smells freshly cleaned. The fresh scents of lavender and lemon compete with the room's only décor. Five roses stand in a thin glass vase above the toilet.

All mine.

As I shower, lathering my skin, I imagine doing the same to my insides. Each scrub, I polish the impurities only I can see. Bloodstreams become crystal clear, my artery-crowned heart transforms into the simple shape swappable with the word love. Clear of the hate I've been harvesting, my new heart is glass. I place a rose in it for good measure.

Most importantly, I cleanse my thoughts. Warm water against my scalp never felt better. But it drips deeper. I see each droplet slide against my short hair, seeping into my pores. Then, through my skull with ease, the water permeates my brain. I know exactly who else is here, and they can't see what I'm holding on to. And so, the water flushes it.

Where's Lucky?

*Shhh.* Shhh. Lucky is gone now, the warm water says.

Who is Lucky? I smile, letting the shower flush my face.

When I return to the bed, there's a folded white robe waiting for me.

*Destiny.*

I approach the garb with caution, trying my best to erase the images associated with it. Draped against the bed, it looks like a dying ghost. But a glimmer from the setting sun casts a lavender glow on the room. The light takes to the leather robe, almost making it look like its floating, holding on to life.

How many times can a ghost die? I imagine infinite. Everyday trapped in that form has to feel like a fresh death.

Scrunched up beside the ghost robe are my dirty clothes. The brown hoodie that was once yellow, the black pants that used to be checkered. They're disgusting. They belong in the trash. I imagine myself doing just that, balling them up and throwing them in a can. I choose to despise them, pushing these thoughts to the forefront of my mind. Who would wear that stupid ass smile? Pajama pants in the middle of the day? Have you really given up on life at thirteen?

I repeat these thoughts and others like it as I slip the flannel pants on and slide into the grimy hoodie. These are mine. They're not going anywhere. *I'm not going anywhere.*

But shh. Shush. Not yet.

I pick up the glowing robe and hold it outstretched before me. It's heavier than it looks, far nicer than any piece of clothing I've ever worn. With its simple design save for its gold trim, it looks like a cross between a priest's robe and a Viking's tunic. Be at peace, it says. For I might kill you.

I enwrap myself in the leather cloth, but not before silently slipping on my smiley hoodie first. With this extra layer of clothes beneath, it fits me perfectly. I'd be lying if I didn't feel a little cool in this thing. With no mirror, I turn to the window. I see an outline of myself on the glass between me and the mountain.

I gasp.

For a second, I'm seven. My smaller self, complete with pom-poms and yellow nails.

*Little.*

No. Don't stop. I close my eyes and shake the thought.

In a blink, I'm me again. But not quite. I look slightly older than I did just hours ago. What is it? I stare into my outline's eyes. My eyebrows crease. My gaze is strong and fearless. My skin radiates. I reach up and touch my face. My skin is soft. The bags under my eyes have left without me.

I look…good?

I look like one of the Dream Girls.

I smile. My dream self, I consciously think.

I'm one of them now. Destiny.

I turn toward the door and feel something slide in my pocket. I dig into both and feel something in each. I pull out the left. It's a rope. Long and thin like the type for jumping. This isn't for that type of jumping, to be clear. I know exactly what this is for, and I don't want anything to do with it. But I run my thumb across its fibers, pondering its many uses the way I imagine she'd want me to. Games, maybe. But for hunting. Trapping. Hanging. Tying up Destinys who've stepped out of line.

*That's good*, I think.

The rope shakes in my hand. That sounded like her. I slide it back into its pocket and pull out the small, cold item gripped in my right palm. At first it looks like a makeup container, but I made that mistake before. I know exactly what this is. My own butterfly knife. But mine features no butterfly. Engraved in gold on the pearl handle is a fish.

A sick joke.

I clench my teeth. I can't do this anymore. I don't know how much longer I can hold back.

This little fish, not unlike the one Jesus fans slap on their cars, means something else to me. For me, it's a sign of luck and Lucky. It's a sign of home, that rusted weathervane marking our secret lair. I feel a tear rising but I turn to anger instead. This little fish is a reminder of my mother. The day she left me with those 22 angels in the tank.

I rub my palm against the other thing in my pajama pocket, hidden beneath the costume.

Don't—I stop myself. Don't show yourself too soon.

There's a knock on the door followed by a familiar voice.

"Time for Temple," Razor jeers. "Meet you in the foyer."

My fist instinctively clenches at her voice. I close my eyes then take a deep breath. I need to leave my emotions here. Turn off my brain and just go. Don't let out the slightest hint as to how I really feel. Who I really am.

I head downstairs, down to the marble floor. The girls are already gathered, waiting for me around the compass. Their eyes track my every step. They've saved a spot for me, just at the foot of the stairs.

I look at the center, the point where all the lines collide and enclose in a circle. The eye. I feel her watching. I've grown to live with this feeling. With her. Long before I knew she existed.

Our shared existence didn't come without a fight, though. I've wanted to claw my own skin off because of her. When the invisible watcher gained a voice, one that ran rampant in my mind, I turned on myself. I was willing to lose my life if that meant getting rid of her.

But that's what she wants. It's what she's always wanted. Am's been leading me here. Luring me here. Just for this moment, when I'd lose the final bit of myself that I've got left and fully belong to her.

Just as I enter the circle, for a moment, I wonder about the rest of these girls. What was their story before this? Who did they lose? No, I correct myself. Who and what got stolen from them? Who hurt them, transforming them to prey for the predator they lovingly call Am?

But the thoughts pass. I shake them off. Fuck these girls. They killed Little. And maybe Lucky too. God help them if they killed Lucky.

The girls beside me extend their hands for me to hold. I want to rip their arms from their sockets. But this is sure to be a long game. I've already let too much of my true emotions slip to the surface. I've got to be more careful. I force a soft smile and gently hold their hands.

I look again at the alien etchings on the floor. The girls robed in white. I take in the silence, not ready to let it wash over me. I close one eye.

"Kinda scary, huh?" I break the silence.

Some of the girls try to shush me.

"Only if you've got something to be afraid of," a girl says from the other side.

What does that even mean? I scoff. It's a defensive reaction. I don't like how true her words ring for me.

One of the smallest Destinys just a few spots over from me waves, trying to get my attention. Her yellow nails do the trick. I turn to her. She smiles.

"We're supposed to close our eyes," she says with raised brows.

Saying she reminds me of Little would be like saying the person in the mirror looks like me. Obviously, she reminds me of Little. The sight of her small, scarless face makes me want to scream. Pasty white waves roll through my mind. My fingers start to twitch. Why does she deserve to be here, and Little doesn't?

Suppress, suppress. Not now.

I nod my head, inhale through my nose, then close my eyes.

The warm light of the foyer dissipates in a blink. Chills blanket my skin. I open my eyes and we've returned to the Temple.

Am is already standing front and center. She bows her head, a white hood shadowing her eyes. Beyond the circle, the glass has been mended and the fish swim freely. Slivers of colorful life dart through the tank. I try not to think about what Am could do to this clear water.

Without a moment's hesitation, the girls genuflect before her. On a slight delay, I trail the girls' movements, doing my best to keep pace. According to my memory, which isn't worth much these days, my first visit here was different. More relaxed. The girls were joyous, celebrating the sight of the woman before us.

But no one was dead the first go around. Now it feels like we're at church. A cross between a funeral and an exorcism.

Am walks toward me but breaks to my right, starting with the girl beside me. Like last time, she extends her hand above our foreheads. As she passes each Destiny, they're overcome with joy. Blank faces transform into beaming smiles, silence turns to subdued laughter with some girls on the verge of tears.

They're all full of shit.

Am's almost made it all the way around. She's to my left when I suddenly feel Little's imprint beside me. I don't believe in spirits. I'm too afraid to. But after all this, I see no reason to keep lying to myself. For a flash, I swear I can feel her specter right beside me. The chill of the Temple passes.

I feel warm. Genuinely protected, unlike this ruse Am's running.

What are ghosts but trapped memories? Energy from the moments that made us, stuck on replay. We sat here together. Am lingered on Little that time. There was an unspoken struggle between them. Maybe everyone in the room knew something horrible was coming but me. Little held my hand and promised everything would be fine. I thought she was lying, even then. But maybe she wasn't. Maybe she was playing a different game, or she was just a few steps ahead.

Or most likely, she was just wrong.

There's nothing safe about this place. There's nothing safe about this Am.

She steps before me without a sound. The corners of her eyes gently lift as she smiles. Her glow is undeniable. Her beauty, enough to make God jealous. But where I once felt awe, I stir with disgust.

I cough. She smells like roses. She smells as though she's been bathing in rose water, lathering in oil from their petals. It's far too strong. It's like she's covering an inescapable stench beneath.

She laughs at my discomfort, her smile lingers. At the sight of her teeth, I notice her gap is gone. The feature that made her most alluring, the one that made her more human, has been erased. In place of the small black space are perfectly aligned teeth, the synthetic type you'd see on a celebrity and decide you wanted yourself. Her glowing face is a masterfully crafted mask, and those teeth are the final touch, one last polish.

I imagine chipping away the varnish, gradually shattering the veneer. She extends her hand. I resist the urge to yank her arm and pull her to the ground. That wouldn't go my way. Me versus 21 girls itching for a chance to pull their knives out. I have to see beyond this moment. I have to see the cracks in the façade and follow them. I need to remember I hold no secrets here. I'm not alone in my mind. This is my only chance to hold onto whatever slice of me that's left.

She slides her long fingers between mine, gripping my hand. Her fingers tighten around my skin. She's cold. Lifeless. I wonder what she really looks like beneath the perfection. I remember the image of a winged panther flickering through my mind. Stunning, ferocious. I know this beastly image is closer to her reality than this beautiful projection before me.

But maybe an imposing winged beast is also too generous for her. I'm starting to think her truth is a far more desperate one. Barely clinging to life, I imagine a beaten yet vain vulture, hiding its burnt flesh in peacock feathers.

She guides me to the eye of the compass. She kneels and without delay, I do the same. I'm nervous for what comes next. This is the part in my memory that gets a little blurry. This is the part where I lose myself. This is where I'm most afraid. Not that she'll overpower me. Not that she'll turn the water into death sludge or turn her minions against me. Instead, I'm afraid that this will feel good.

I remember the white. The blinding light. A fresh start. Finally free of pain. Bliss radiating from within. This is how Am wins. Not by scaring us into submission but by filling us with joy. Making us think we've found love. I don't know how to resist something I need so bad.

"Do you remember what I told you when you first joined us here?" Am asks.

I try to remember. I'm coming up empty but then, the thought floats to the center of my mind.

That I was…*that she was—*

*Yes. That*, she interjects.

"That you are me. You are who I can become."

The thought repulses me. She smiles.

"And now we complete what was started. Today, you will fully join us. And all of us, together, can become whole."

I can't help myself. I shake my head. I shouldn't have done that.

She nods hers. *Quiet your mind.*

*You can do this.*

I try to compose my breathing. *Good, good. One breath at a time.*

*We can do this*, we think in unison.

Am scoots herself closer. Our knees knock. She reaches over and cradles my head. Her thumbs press against my temples. Her nails push against my skin.

"Close your eyes," she commands.

I clench my jaw. It's too early to show my hand.

*Far too early. Far too late.*

I grit my teeth. She controls my life. There's no other option.

I exhale and close my eyes. Her coldness turns to warmth in less than a second.

I feel safer…

No. No. I don't want this.

There it is. The white glow, pulsating from my temples and overtaking the black of my insides.

I hear birds chirping behind me. There's a buzzing below that sounds like a TV.

"You know little Scarlett, six years old, she asked me where Jesus lived, and I had to laugh," the TV pastor performs.

*When you're ready…*

I open my eyes.

I'm home.

The sound of the Texan pastor slips up the stairwell, seeping into my attic room. "The easy answer is heaven. But I told her that a piece of the Lord lives in all of our hearts."

Sloped ceilings hover above me. To my left, there's a desk littered with paper. To my right, a bureau with my favorite books stacked on top. I look to the hallway. Across the purple paisley rug is a closed door.

My heart booms in my chest. I stand up too fast. My head spins, sending a chill sliding down my spine.

That door is never closed, I remind myself.

I had almost forgotten this memory. I wish it didn't exist. But now we're back. Back to the moment that started all of this.

I walk across the wood panels, the floor creaking beneath my heels.

"Destiny!" Poppy's voice echoes up the stairwell. "Can you take Tiger for a walk?"

Tiger? I'm flooded with guilt. I forgot about that poor turtle. I lost him three steps into our search party.

And then the craziest thought cuts off my self-reproach. I see a turtle slamming itself against the glass tank then swimming away.

Tiger? Trying to save me?

*Quiet your mind, Destiny. Focus.*

"Where's Lucky?" I ask, expecting the voice to respond.

She doesn't. I know Lucky's not beyond that door. I know that Lucky's here, hidden in this haunted place. But I suppress that. Try to deny what I know. Hide it from myself.

"You tell me," Pop answers from below. "Figured he's at Low's by now."

I lean forward and knock on the door, just below his wishful President Sanders sticker. I grip the doorknob and push the door open. "Lucky?"

The curtains flap in the passing wind. I look down to his bed and he rolls over, covering his eyes from the morning sun. His hand becomes a mask, the space between his hands are the eye-holes.

"Hey bud," his voice sounds like gravel. "This is certainly a first."

"Lucky?" I do my best to sound shocked. "What are you doing here?"

"Well, *here* is my bed," he slides the covers aside. "Where else should I be?"

He lowers his feet to the ground and groans.

He's exactly how I remember him, if this new version of him, swaddled in webs and on the verge of death didn't cut in. His eyes have their signature fatigue, but nothing close to the truth. I linger on his face for a moment too long.

"You're being a little weirdo," he says.

I nervously chuckle, thinking I've been caught. "What else is new?"

He stretches in an over-theatrically way, something totally on brand for my brother. He pretends it's natural until his arms are completely outstretched, then they swoop down, pulling me in for a Lucky bear hug.

I laugh, feeling a lingering smile on my face. The joy I feel is real. I almost believe he is. I wish he was.

I return to the hug, squeezing him back with everything I've got, not spending more than a millisecond wondering what it is I'm actually hugging.

I force myself to believe. He's here. He's back. We're safe.

I push these thoughts to the forefront of my mind. Center stage.

Again: He's here. He's back. We're safe.

Until I hear her whispering back to me.

*He's here. He's back. We're safe.*

"I'm sorry about last night, Destiny," Lucky says.

His cadence is totally off. He'd never say my name like that, at the end of a sentence. But I carry on and smile.

This is perfect, I tell myself.

It's all a—*Stop.* Nope. It's perfect.

I close my eyes, settling into his uncertain embrace. I inhale and exhale, waiting for the white. *This is perfect.*

Still, light flickers beyond my eyelids. I still hear birds outside and still lean against Lucky.

C'mon.

I am complete, I whisper within. I want nothing else.

*We are complete. We want nothing else.*

Lucky's body slips from my grasp. I'm left with nothing. The white consumes the space and I privately pray that whatever I'm trying to do is working.

I feel myself back on my knees and her cagey fingers crowning my head. I don't dare to open my eyes.

"He is safe. He is whole. He is gone," Am says firmly.

I repeat the words back to her. "He is safe. He is whole. He is gone."

I take a deep breath, trying to settle into my private place. I feel the tube pressed against my thigh but don't linger on it. I can't. Hide it, I tell myself. Just watch.

"Keep it up, Destiny," Am encourages. "Just a little more."

*Same as last time.*

I hear shuffling around me. People moving, chatting among themselves.

*This one will be hard. Don't open your eyes until you are ready.*

A massive flutter passes over my whole body. I feel like one giant goosebump. An alien in my own skin.

"Maya, you stay right here," my mother's voice says.

Am didn't lie. This one's going to be harder.

I slowly open my eyes and take in the world before me.

I hate this place. I hate this moment. No one deserves to have this moment.

"I just need to run to the bathroom," my mother says.

She leans down and smiles. She's so gorgeous it makes me sick. My stomach literally starts bubbling.

She reaches for my face, going to tuck a loose strand of hair behind my ear. But I beat her to it, tidying my own loose strands.

Her eyes momentarily go wide like my move shocked her. Like she's been here a million times, on an endless loop, and that wasn't supposed to happen.

Play it cool, I tell myself. No more of that off-script shit. *Relax, Destiny. Just return to the moment.*

I don't know if Am's on to me, but it's no time to panic.

"I just need to run to the bathroom," she says.

I stare at the beautiful stranger that birthed me. I still feel like a tiny girl inside that believes her.

She smiles and her teeth flash through. Now I know we're tooling with the replay. My mother's forced, all-lip smile is imprinted on my mind. This isn't it.

Everything about this smile—if we're comfortable calling it that—is unnatural, unsettling. I cringe. I want to look away, but I can't. With her face slightly cocked, her smile is askew. And those teeth in there don't belong to her. They couldn't belong to any human. Blindingly white, perfectly aligned, they look like they've been carefully arranged by an obsessive-compulsive god.

I stay still as she turns, scurrying off into the bathroom. On cue, she pulls out her phone and brings it to her ear. I wish there were a simple answer to who she was talking to and what they were talking about, but there isn't. It's an accomplice, that much is sure. Perhaps it's a new lover. Standing here now, I hope it's a lover. Maybe they ran off and built the life of their dreams and it all started on this day. But sadly, I don't think she's there yet. She's still just a teenager herself.

This was the last time I saw her. Until the last time I saw her, of course. Which, if Am is sticking to her script, should be in a minute or two. But I don't know that. I have to pretend I don't know that.

I do my part, turning to the fish tank. This cursed fucking fish tank.

The explosion of colors has lost its luster. The swirls of pink and blue, blue and black, yellow and green all bleed together into a lifeless blob. Their insides still glow but my mind turns to what's sustaining them. I remember reading once that a star's shine still reaches us on Earth for like a million years or something after its gone. We'd be dead and forgotten, all of us, before we found out the stars gave up lifetimes ago. Maybe they had the right idea. But these little things? They just keep swimming.

I read the plaque like I'm supposed to. *Pterophyllum.* Pa-tero? Terro-fill-em? Fy-lum? I never thought about its pronunciation before. Why would I? They were, or are, angelfish. I go through my routine to keep Am at bay. Keep myself distracted from my endgame.

I already know the total before I start counting. 22. But I pretend to stumble, restarting several times before tallying. I watch the elusive blue mayor, darting from corner to corner, whispering into the gills of his constituents, running his endless campaign.

I catch my reflection in the glass and choke up.

Sadness swells in my chest.

It's the eve of my seventh birthday. The start of Gigi taking me in, the start of me learning that families could be fixed, but that it's a daily process that needs constant attention. The start of me learning that in order for something to be fixed, it had to be broken.

This is where I broke.

This is where I shattered.

That is why I'm here.

But this time around, the sadness isn't for me. It can't be. There in the glass, all I see is Little. Am stole my image and wrapped her with it, knowing I'd do anything in me to fix that broken girl. I want to bring her back and destroy whatever it is that destroyed her. Long before Am, I wish I could've put out that fire that took everything from her.

I hope that butterflies can fly freely now in her mind. If peace became part of her like the monster promised, she deserves to celebrate them without pain. I'd love to recognize grace in the angelfish again. But I don't think that's gonna happen. Not on this plane. Not with her here.

Quiet. *Quiet.*

I look down at my chipped-yellow fingernails and wonder if they ever turn the knob on the chipped-yellow house again. No. *Shh.* I can't consume my mind with that thinking right now. I've got to follow the steps, scramble for my mother on the run. Pretend this day and my life turned out different.

I remember how I thought I must have missed a direction from her. She must have told me to do something, and I got it wrong. I was the reason the day got ruined. But third time here and I know that's not true. Stay here, she said. Don't move, don't go looking for her. Give her more time to get away.

I ignore the memory of heading to the front desk and calling for Gigi. I head for the restroom, knowing that's what Am expects.

"Mom?" I call across the tile, my voice bouncing off the metal stalls.

Nothing. And I know there's nothing. But I walk through anyway, softly tapping each door until reaching the closed one. Unless my mother's wearing flashing children's shoes with Anna and Elsa, it's not her.

I hear a car horn. A breeze rolls across my arms. There's a window open above the sinks. That's where she got out, I tell myself and Am. I stare at it, hearing traffic rumble by on the street.

She was sick, I think. Mentally bruised and battered. She had no business trying to raise a daughter. Not yet. Maybe I've always thought this, but that doesn't mean I understand it, and it definitely doesn't erase my pain.

I start to shake. There's a tightness in my chest that feels like my body's being pulled inward on itself. I want to cry, just like I have before at this evil aquarium. But this feels different. This is new. I find myself hoping my mother found what she was looking for. I pray it's peace. I hope I find it too, along with the strength to forgive her.

I wipe my tears and let out a heavy breath. My patience is evaporating. I need to get out of this place immediately.

Can an aquarium burn to the ground? I entertain the idea. Images of water on fire flicker through my mind. Admittedly, it feels like an ambitious challenge for the flames to take on the tanks. And to be clear, I don't want anything to happen to the fish. They'd be fine. All of this would happen during one of their monthly tank scrubbings. The fish would be in their mini-tanks, pushed on carts safely across the street.

Ugh. It's not gonna work. It's hard to believe they have the staff to simultaneously clean all the tanks at the same time. Something's gotta give. Fine. An octopus or two are gonna have to meet their end. And probably the sharks. Too many bodies to haul those bad boys to safety. And damn those hippos they've got downstairs.

I sigh. A lot of life would have to be compromised for this wish to come true. I'm not proud to admit it, but the image of this place turned to ash and rubble makes me feel lighter.

I exit the bathroom and she's already there to greet me, a step closer than she was before.

"Surprise!" The heat of her breath slides across my eyes.

It smells like she's been eating grass.

There's no cake in my true memory. There's a dolphin shaped one with glazed blue icing my last go around. But this time, I tighten my fist and clench my jaw.

It's a butterfly. An electric yellow butterfly.

"Happy birthday, my little angel!"

I can't stop looking at it.

There are seven candles stuck across the wings of a butterfly. They look like the pins in the wings of the dead monarchs, saved for science class.

A fucking butterfly.

Is she taunting me?

*No.* No. No. Get that out of your head. Keep going.

My mother reaches her hand down and grabs mine. She

leads me to the nearest picnic table that sits by the logger-head tank. She sits then plops me into her lap. Whoa. I wasn't ready for that. I'd be lying if I said this didn't feel like heaven.

"Okay, baby. Close your eyes and make a wish."

I close my eyes and can't help but think my truest wish of all.

I wish to go home. Most importantly, with Lucky safely by my side.

*Careful,* I tell myself.

Or was that her?

*This is your home, Destiny.*

That was definitely her. Be careful.

I open my eyes and see this perfect butterfly cake.

I wish Little had a chance to leave this place with me and Lucky. But that's a wasted, dangerous thought.

"Go ahead now," my mother pats me on the back. There's an unexpected force in her touch. The type of palm-to-back thrust reserved for a choking baby. A reminder of who's in control.

I gaze at the cake and my stomach starts to spin. The sunshine icing is thick, butter-creamy. A single slice of this thing could hospitalize the faint of heart.

I breathe in through my nose then blow out the candles. Just as the flames extinguish, my mother wraps her arms around me and pulls me in closer.

That blissful wave of white floods my body. I can't control it and I don't want to. I could live in this light. I close my eyes and let it fully wash over me.

*I love you so much*, my mother whispers into my ear.

This shouldn't feel as good as it did the first time. And yet it feels better. Every wound I've ever had suddenly feels kissed, bandaged, healed and left scarless in seconds.

The white has won, completely drowning my thoughts, bringing the inside of my head to a silence.

*Finally.*

I pull in a breath, and I find myself back on my knees. Am clutches my head, my fate in her hands. Her thumbs stroke against my forehead.

*You are almost free.*

Free. If this painless, thoughtless space is peace, take me there.

"We are almost free," I speak. The sound of my own voice startles myself.

I'm joined by a chorus of voices. The rest of the Destinys chant, filling the air:

"We are almost free."   *We are almost free.*   "Warlmost free."
*We are almost free.*   We arlmost free.   *Warlmossfree.*
"We are almost free."   *Warlmost free.*   "Warlmssfree."

Their words bleed together, becoming a ceaseless buzz. This hum envelopes me, moving closer, louder, as their voices blend and boom until they sound like rumbling thunder.

Lightning crashes and my eyes shoot open.

I'm in the kitchen. The lights are below but behind me, Poppy's TV flickers, outlining everything in a neon glow. His favorite tele-pastor presides over the sleeping house.

*"As you know by now, the kingdom of heaven is like a net that was let down into the lake and caught all kinds of fish…"* the Texan pastor reads. *"This is how it will be at the end of the age."*

The door from the refrigerator is wide open. Fluid drips from its bottom shelf, pattering to the ground.

*"The angels will come and separate the wicked from the righteous and throw them into the blazing furnace, where there will be weeping and gnashing of teeth. Have you understood all these things?"*

*Have you understood all these things?*

I peer out the dark window set above the sink. Rain drums against the glass, trying to make its way in. I step forward and my foot splashes against the floor. A 2-liter of Canada Dry lays fallen on its side, its contents completely drained to the kitchen floor.

I stare at the bottle, mesmerized by it. *Something's different.* I don't know what it is. Lightning stabs the backyard, just on the other side of the window, lighting up the whole kitchen. The spilled soda looks like a glowing lake. *Canada Dry.* Gigi never drank Canada Dry—

Breathe. Quiet.

It's a test.

*Just a test.*

Move on. Fast.

Thunder quakes the old wooden house and I hear the dishes rattle. This feels familiar. I focus on the things I know. I know that across the kitchen, beside Poppy's head-of-the-table chair and beneath Gigi's wooden proclamation that

*This House Is Protected By Guardian Angels,* the backdoor is slightly ajar.

My heart rages like the storm overhead.

I want to turn away. I want to go upstairs to my room—my safe space, my private cathedral, my escape pod—and pretend nothing's wrong. A slither of me thinks this is a dream. I force this thought to the front of my brain. That's all this has ever been. Yup. From the moment I woke up this morning, from Lucky to Little to now, I'm just caught in a vicious loop of the moments that created me. But it will pass. It's just a sleep. A deep sleep. It has to be.

I roll my eyes at the childish thought. The idea doesn't stick. Kidding myself won't work. This is real, for I've never had a nightmare as cruel as this.

I step forward through the spill. I have to face this. This is all I have left. I reach the door and grip the handle. Last time, Am made my movements for me. She controlled my steps even when I begged her to make it all stop. But now it's me. All me. This time, as I pull open the door, I still want to turn away, but I don't. My eyes make no attempt at avoiding the horror before me.

The image in front of me aligns with the one carved on the insides of my eyelids.

There's Gigi. Facedown. Her hair floating at the top of the puddle.

Despite knowing she can't be saved, I can't fight instinct. I dash down the steps and pull her body from the puddle. She lands against the wet grass, rain battering her face.

I wipe the soaking hair from her flushed skin. Her royal glow has faded. Yellow and green tints compete for space beneath her sunken eyes.

"Mom?" I shake her shoulders. "C'mon, Gigi."

I pull her forward and she coughs. Water and phlegm dribble down her chin.

She blinks and her sunken eyes come to life. Her emerald irises glisten brighter in the darkness. *This is her.* This is really her.

I smile. My heart can't contain itself. I pull her in for a hug that she returns with the half-force of someone truly confused.

"What's going on?" She scans the backyard.

I take in her face. She's alive this time. Her discoloration drips away in the rain and she becomes her radiant self— a version of herself I haven't seen in years—in mere seconds.

I shake my head, memories of the night pouring back to me. I make no attempt at wiping the tears that are freely flowing.

"We were…celebrating. I graduated and—"

"One too many Gigi Ales," she shakes her head and cuts me off. She moves her hand to mine. "Here, baby star. Help me up."

*Too many Gigi Ales.* It feels good to hear her admit this.

But the phrase "too many" wasn't in her lexicon. Especially in her final year. We spoke plenty about hopes and dreams, but less and less about the demons that trapped us. I wish I didn't run away from her when she got stressed. I wish I sat at the kitchen table and tried saving myself. I think she would have joined me.

"We got into a fight too," I add.

"Don't worry about that, Destiny. I'm safe now."

I clench my jaw. The lie is wearing thin.

As good as seeing her alive feels, I can't keep this up to myself. She's not safe now. This thing before me is not my mother.

"They said you had one of your episodes, Mom."

One of the EMTs thought she must have slammed her head hard against the ground. The ER doctor thought that she must have twisted her neck so severely that she cut off her own airway. The official autopsy declared that she drowned.

"My episodes? You mean one of those seizures?" she scoffed. "I haven't had  one of those in ten years. I'm fine."

She helps herself to her feet then wipes the mud from her arms. She turns and heads for the steps. I linger behind.

"You gonna come in or spend your night in this storm? C'mon in, Destiny. Stop playing."

Stop playing. *Stop playing.* Stop playing.

These very specific words swirl around my head. For a multitude of reasons, I know these words can't be Gigi's. First and foremost, they included the name "Destiny." Gigi never knew Destiny. Destiny didn't exist.

And that word—*play.* The implication that I'm participating in a game feels private. Only one with unfettered access to my mind would know I've been trying to approach this dilemma as though I were playing a game.

And we all know circumstances tend to change near the end of close matches. Final levels get harder. Enemies adapt, and as every move threatens to become your last, the opposition becomes cutthroat.

*Stop playing.*

I take this specific phrasing for what it is—a taunt. The woman behind my mother, controlling her with imperceptible strings, suspects that I've been putting on a mask of my own.

But I can't wear it anymore. The clock is ticking. Every second of this day has felt like a sleepless dark night of its own. I know I can't do this forever. If she knows I've been lying, I'm delaying the inevitable.

Confront Am or die.

*Confront Am and die.*

Either way, I've reached a crossroads.

The game is coming to an end.

I stand taller, a final performance of bravery.

"Don't call me that," the words rumble from deep within.

"Now's not the time to—"

"It's not my name," I say. I feel the thunder rolling beneath my feet.

"Listen," Gigi nods. "I'm sorry I ruined your night. But everything's fine now."

"Nothing is fine now." I step toward her, sloshing in the grass.

I've fully broken character. I don't know if this will work, but there's no turning back.

"You're dead," I say to Gigi's face. I know that's all it is. A false face. "You're not here. You're not real."

"You're talking nonsense. C'mon inside to bed before you get all wet."

Lightning forks overhead, striking on both sides of the yard. For a flash, it's bright as day. In this second, I see through Gigi's green eyes and straight to the black holes hiding beneath them.

"This isn't safe," she waves me forward. "Get in here and we can forget about everything."

The rain pummels down harder.

"I don't want to forget this," I say.

*Your wants are behind us now, girl,* Am's voice bites through the storm.

"We need to change this moment," Gigi pleads. "You gotta make peace with it."

She's right. But not by erasing it.

I unhook the latch on the white leather robe and toss it to the ground. It lands in a puddle of mud with a splash.

"What are you doing?" Gigi steps back into the rain, her nightgown flapping in the wind.

A smirk grows on her face that I've never seen before. The edges of her lips slide too far up her cheeks, like the mouth of a viper. I'm not the only one breaking character. Am's control of the finer details is slipping.

This distorted Gigi steps closer, her bare feet slopping in the mud. I remain planted where I stand, showing her I'm not afraid.

But it's a lie. I'm terrified. I try to steady my shivering hand but it's useless. I reach into my pocket, my fingers sliding across the knife. I feel the etching of the fish on the tip of my index finger.

No, not that. Not what I'm looking for…

"You're not Gigi."

She clenches her jaw, and her jowl muscles shift back and forth. She smiles and my heart drops. There, at the center of her smile, is a black hole. There's a giant gap in her teeth that wasn't there before.

"Identity is relative," Gigi's lips move, but from her mouth comes Am's voice.

There in my pocket, I brush the knife aside and find what I'm digging for. My fingers pull the thin tube into my palm as my thumb tightens my grip. *The golden pen.*

"You won't rewrite me," I whisper.

But she hears me loud and clear. Gigi's face lights up as Am cackles through her, a sound that rattles the clouds above.

"Pure, childish fantasy!" she yelps with glee.

Her laugh continues. It starts high, in both volume and pitch, like a barn owl screeching. It's a noise that sends every hair on my body stiff. But then she dips, bringing Gigi's body hurling back and forth, gagging up the sound. The laugh slowly descends, transforming into a beastly moan. Gigi gargles and grunts, resembling a caged animal with its sights set on freedom.

With a final roar, I take a step back.

*You're scared*, she says in my head.

"And that's okay," I stare into her warped face.

She steps closer, kicking back mud. She's within three feet of me when she winces in pain. Rain splatters against her cheek with a sizzle. Her eyes go wide and her smile disappears. She reaches up for her face.

Smoke slithers through her shaking hand.

*What are you doing?*

The rain is ceaseless against her skin. Everywhere it lands, her flesh starts to drip away. She screams like a calf resistant to slaughter. She wails as though she's just been hacked at the neck but she's not going down so soon. She wobbles, her panic sending her entire body into a shake.

"You thought I was weak. That's why you chose me," I grip my pen tighter, my fingers digging into my palm. "You fucked up."

The skin slides off her body, revealing bloody red muscles shifting beneath. Ligaments rip, dripping down legs and exposing bone. And beneath her skeleton—

She stumbles forward and I step back.

—There's something binding her together. Something I've never seen in any middle school science textbook.

"You're a fake," I spit.

The monster tries to save itself, patching up her holes just as another appears. Her limbs roll and contort as if her bones are made of clay. She turns and curls inward, looking like a snake searching for its own end. Her arms twist behind her torso, reaching down to her ankles. She pulls a leg up and over her shoulder then yanks it back down. She moves faster, and faster, until I can't tell which part is which. In a blur, fingers become a nose, knees become breasts. Her hips spread outward and overhead, almost resembling wings. She's but a blurring whirl with uncountable swirling eyes until suddenly it stops.

She emerges from her mangled dance with her skin fully renewed.

She no longer drapes herself in Gigi's aged flesh but has returned to her preferred flawless façade.

*Am.*

"You're stronger than the rest," her voice shakes. "I'll give you that."

My thumb runs toward the button on the top of the pen. I press.

*Click-click-click.*

I take a deep breath. I'm in control, I repeat. *I'm in control.*

The rain lands against her with an incessant hiss. I gasp. Flashes of Gigi start to bubble atop Am's skin. The beast no longer attempts to compose her exterior. Instead, she allows slabs of her flesh and Gigi's to coalesce. Mom's muddy nightgown burns away. Smoke rises from their shared skin where each droplet has scorched them. Gigi's emerald eyes go wide, clinging to life above an empty wound where her nose should be. Am's mouth comes into shape above an exposed jawbone.

Am nods. Standing before this patchwork of love and hate, death and beauty, she knows I'm terrified.

I take a step back, feeling less brave.

"You need me!" she whimpers. Their vocal cords melt together. Gigi sounds in pain. Am is full of fire. Both are barely clinging to life. "Just like the rest of them!"

She reaches her arms forward, rain burning her hands down to the bone. Am bends forward, digging her fingers into the ground. She gallops ahead toward me, her body falling apart and regenerating with each step.

There, buzzing beneath her spine, I can make out the thing lurking within her. I struggle to process what I'm seeing. Black and white bolts of electricity enwrap atop each other in a frenetic mass. I want to look away, but I can't.

Am darts ahead on all fours. I'm within striking distance. I backpedal, thumping against a tree. I've run out of space.

Am pulls herself erect. Gigi is all but gone, save for her green eyes. Tears have overtaken the bottom of her eyelids. No. This can't be. She's full of fear. Please no. Maybe there is a portion of her in there. Her real self.

"Please no."

Am lunges for me. I side-step but she makes contact, nicking my eye and gashing my cheek with her bare-boned finger. My vision becomes hazy. I reach for my face and feel it spill.

I look down at my red hand. The blood is real. Whatever Am is, she's real.

The sky explodes in light. We both freeze. The strike was just above us. It's followed by a deafening boom that knocks me to the ground. The backyard quakes beneath me as an orange glow flickers overhead. It's suddenly hot. Dangerously so. I look up through my compromised vision. The tree is engulfed in flames.

"Make no mistake. You will die here," Am shakes her head. "There will be no peace. We tried to make things work with Little, but I can see you won't be worth that effort."

I hear a crackling snap overhead. A burning branch falls from the tree. I roll to the left, praying I don't get crushed. The wood lands a foot from my face with a resounding crunch.

The flames from the leaves rip beyond the branches, spreading the fire through Poppy's garden. Petunias are set afire, their flimsy petals scorched in seconds. The tomatoes roast, blackening before my eyes. The fire knows no bounds, raging beyond the garden, working its way up the wooden fence and…

The flames don't stop when they reach the top of the fence. The fire keeps rising, as though there's still something left to burn. But there's nothing. Nothing but black clouds, a starless sky, and a thin line of fire working upward. Like a painted movie backdrop set aflame, or a curtain burning from the bottom, it works its way up, erasing everything beneath it from existence.

I shield my eyes. The light from the fire is blinding, but there's something even brighter. In the fire's wake, there's nothing but white. It spreads until the tree is gone, the garden is gone, and the outline of the yellow home is no more. It's just me and Am in an endless white space, surrounded by—

I vomit. It smells like cabbage and rotten eggs wrapped in mothballs. I take in the source of the smell surrounding me.

No. No. No…

Twenty-one slumped skeletons in various stages of decay surround us.

Most are nothing but blackened bones with cobwebbed ribs. Others still have emaciated flesh, melting into their bare skulls. Am's electric core threads through each of them, connecting each body to the next and tethering them all back to her in a charged web.

I feel a stabbing pain in my chest, sending me completely numb. I reach for my heart and look down. Thin threads of her black-and-white lightning jab through the center of my chest. I choke for air but come up empty. The white world becomes grayer. Hazy.

*I'm not going to—*

Stop. Stay awake!

I pull the pen from my pocket.

*Stay alive!* a voice echoes in my head. It's not mine nor is it hers. She sounds younger…

I feel a soft surge vibrate across my flesh.

"You're not welcome here, witch!" Am roars. Her sound is so violent, her scream so vicious, it rips the jaw from its hinges. It dangles beneath the top row of her teeth before falling to the ground with a slop.

She laughs—her scathing, animal song. She's completely lost it, and staring into my eyes, it's clear that she wants to bring me into her chaos.

With a leap, she throws herself to the white ground and gallops forward. She springs atop me and slams my shoulder to the floor, pinning me to the white. Her blood drips onto my face, mixing with mine.

"Destiny brought you here," her bones dig into my shoulder blades. "We need each other."

She leans closer to me, her face within an inch of mine. Her breath smells like turtle shit.

"Who was there when your grandmother died? Who was there to help you find yourself and start over?"

"I almost jumped off my roof to get rid of you," I scream. My spit lands on what's left of her upper lip. Her tongue crawls forward like a leech and licks it up.

"You fought your truth," she rages. "You're still fighting it."

I pull the pen from my pocket. I want to jab it into the bottom of her neck, but what good will that do? Her body appears to be an afterthought, as she no longer makes any attempt to save it. I look down at the pulsating, painful electric string tying us together. But there's a piece of me she hasn't penetrated.

*Give up. Give in*, she whispers into my head.

I raise the tip of the pen into the bolt between. A spark shoots down the golden barrel, rattling my hand. I wince, but she doesn't appear to notice.

"Give up!" she screams, her blood and stench soaking my face. "GIVE IN!"

I twirl the pen, twisting the electric string around the tip and down to the grip.

"You have nothing without me! You are lost!"

The electric thread is wrapped so tightly, I feel like the pen might rip through my hand.

"It's you that needs me," I shake my head. "You don't exist without me."

And then I tug. I thrust the pen to my side and—

*TWING.*

The electric thread snaps like a guitar string wound too tight.

Am's eyes go wide as her body jerks backward. I gasp for air, suddenly feeling like a boulder's been lifted from my chest and a ceaseless storm has suddenly cleared from my mind.

I feel free.

*Not quite.*

Am shrieks.

"No! No! Ha!" She smiles through her pain. Her animal cackle returns. "Hahahaaaaa!"

She chokes, reaching for her neck. What's left of her skin starts to drip away like burning wax.

"I…will…" There's not much left of her mouth. She struggles to form words.

She's all but gone, her face flattens against the electric ball at her core. Her eyes swell, looking like they might pop…

"…live in you…forever."

And they do. Her eyes burst, red and yellow phlegm flying through the air. What's left of her boneless face burns away with a sizzle against the electric core. Each of her black-and-white threaded legs start to recede, pulling out from the corpses surrounding us. As every electric string returns to the orb, it starts to quake.

It rumbles across from me, like the small ball is holding back an earthquake. For a moment it expands, larger than any body could host, but then it rapidly turns in on itself. I push myself back, looking for something to hide behind but there's nothing.

It explodes in a dazzling white light.

I fall to the ground and shield my eyes.

There's no deafening boom. No loud strike. Just silence.

I open my eyes and white ash flutters around me, falling like snowflakes. Against the endless white, it looks like I'm standing in the center of an endless arctic landscape. There's no sign of Am, only the hell she created.

Still arranged in their perfect circle, the Destinys lay lifeless.

I walk toward the center of them. For a moment, I don't see them as broken bones or rotting flesh. There's no magic moment where I suddenly see their true selves, perhaps their spirits or souls rising from their bodies. But here, in the center of them, I feel stillness.

I don't often pray—I'm too afraid that the wrong god will answer the call—but I do now. Here, I pause and pray that they've finally found peace.

The ash continues to flow, in fact, there's more than before. It's turned into a steady snow flurry. I scan the horizon and try to decide my next step. There's nothing to dictate my course, no sign of where I might go. A blank page.

I look down at my hands. Beneath my whitened knuckles, it's still there. Gigi's golden pen.

*My* golden pen. I'm still gripping it as though my life depends on it. Maybe it does, but I loosen my grip and slide it into my pocket.

Deep in the distance, I think I spot something. I peer but the flurry falling on my lashes makes it difficult to make out anything beyond my nose. I step beyond the bodies and fully into the white terrain. With each step, the ash gets deeper and deeper. I stumble. My foot slumps into the white and a cold shiver runs from my ankle and up through my entire body. My Vans are soaking. I momentarily wish I kept those warrior boots they gave me. I reach down and dig my hands into the white. My fingers instantly freeze.

It doesn't just look like snow, it *is* snow.

I ball some up in my palm and bring it to the wound on my face. I wince but the chill works wonders. Blood soaks through the snowball, making the play thing look like it's been used in war.

I slog closer to the blip on the horizon and thank the heavens that it's no longer a blip. My eyes weren't tricking me. There's something here. Something far larger than I expected. Perhaps a boulder?

I strain harder for each step than the last. I lift my feet to my knees, struggling to make progress. It reminds me of walks in the snow with Mom. The storm when I was eight, when the snow gathered closer to two feet. Gigi held my hand as we marched in the snow. That was the day we found…

How can this be?

I'm almost to the giant rock, but I realize it's no rock at all. I'm close enough to make out its markings. The small cracks and its bright orange stripes.

It's a massive carapace. I know these stripes well. This is Tiger's shell.

I swipe forward through the snow, toward the opening at the shell's front. I lower my head, peering into the darkness. In place of the absent turtle, there's a curled-up body. The ridges on its spine shiver. He must've heard the crunch in the snow behind him. He turns to look at me, ruffling his curly crown of hair.

"Lucky," I exhale.

I step inside the shell. He starts to whimper.

"Hey, hey," I take off my yellow birthday hoodie. "Everything's gonna be fine. We got this."

He sits up and I direct him to straighten his arms over his head. I slide the upside-down smiley over his beaten face, doing my best to comfort him. Way oversized on me, it fits him just right.

I sit beside him, beneath the turtle dome, and hold his hand. He collapses, wrapping his arms around me. I forgot how healing his bear hugs could be.

Neither of us can hold it back.

We don't say a word.

We weep until we've run out of tears and the snow's stopped falling.

By the time we've finally released enough regained the

power to stand, it feels like hours have passed. We bend to exit the shell. We both lay hands on the shell knowing we'll never understand who or what Tiger truly was.

"Thank you," I whisper.

We step ahead into the endless white.

"Where should we go?" Lucky looks around

"Home," I say.

Lucky doesn't ask how I know where I'm going, he just trusts my steps.

Ahead, the white breaks.

Shapes start to form. Familiar ones I know well. There are brown beams with blots of green atop. My heart starts to beat faster. It's the maples on Jefferson. Beneath them, a black strip coats the ground with yellow dashes. A car whizzes by. Above the road, boxes of gray, purple, and orange with square glass stare forward at us. I know these homes. Iyana's house and her neighbor's, the one that used to let us use their pool. And Mrs. Ward's worn old Victorian that pales in comparison to her garden. My hand starts to shake but Lucky holds it tighter.

We step onto the street, no sign of snow beneath our feet. The street is bare. A street light flickers overhead, illuminating the street sign.

We've reached Jefferson Avenue. My heart has never been happier to see those two words.

But there's another green street marker intersecting it, marking the pavement we're standing on that I've never seen before.

I know we're walking where the house numbered 55 should be, but that cursed house is gone, overrun with road beneath our feet.

I step forward, the cross-sign coming into full view.

The white words radiate off the green, making my heart sink.

It reads: DESTINY LANE.

Lucky quickly looks away from it, as though shielding his eyes from a fatal accident. He hardly has the strength to plow ahead, let alone comprehend this impossible sign above us.

But I can't look away. A smaller version of myself would have questioned these white words. Someone was tricking me. Or I was going crazy. But here, now, I know this is real.

A thought floats to the center of my mind. A simple question.

Would I have had the strength to take this road if I had seen these words before?

I'm glad I'll never know. I'm grateful I didn't have to make that decision.

As we turn away from the green sign and head toward our yellow home on Washington Street, one thing is for certain—I'll never go this way again.

# AfteR

**I ALWAYS HATED THE END** of *The Wizard of Oz*, even when I was a little kid. The movie, to be clear. I didn't read the "Wonderful" book until I had already seen the film a million times, so the damage of that ending was already done. Sometimes I'd hit stop or restart when Dorothy got to the third click of her ruby red heels, just before we could see her Aunt and Uncle hovering over her bed.

The return to sepia tone felt morbid to me. But worse than being back on that dusty Kansas farm was the fact that she was immediately told it was all a dream. "A bad dream," to directly quote Auntie Em.

But Dorothy stood her ground. "It was a place," she said with conviction, only to be met with skeptical glances from the men gathered in the small square bedroom.

No one believed her.

"You were there, and you were there," and they all laughed it off.

At the sound of their chirping laughter, even she started to question her reality.

"Doesn't anyone believe me?" she asked.

While Uncle Henry earnestly declared his belief, the rest of the cast just grinned in amusement.

Dorothy's experience couldn't have been authentic. How foolish of this young girl to believe in a land beyond our own, full of great villains and greater friends—friends who were clearly better than their human counterparts back in "the real world."

"Destiny!" Pop calls from below.

My eyes shoot open only to be met by blinding white. The sun breaks in through the triangle window as I shield myself with my comforter. The Supremes' sweet harmony slips up the stairs, slides across the Prince rug, and quakes the wooden floorboards. I don't need to be in the kitchen to see Poppy shuffling across the kitchen tile, bouncing his shoulders like he's in lockstep with Diana Ross.

"Come see about me!" his voice cracks. It's painful but endearing. "See about your baby," he backs himself up.

The sharp smell of canned coffee rises through the vents. I pull back the covers. Maybe a little light isn't so bad.

My feet slap against the wood and I look across the way.

My heart drops down to my toes.

A shiver rolls across my shoulders.

Ahead of me, Lucky's door is wide open and his bed is made. He's nowhere to be seen.

"Pop?" I exit my room and call down the stairs. "Pop?"

"Ah!" he yells up. "The angel rises!"

"Where's Lucky?"

Pop turns down the music, and I'm met with silence. He must have caught the fear in my voice.

*Thunk. Thunk. Thunk.*

Something slowly bumps its way up the steps.

Against my gut telling me otherwise, I step forward. The wood creaks beneath my feet. I poke my head around the corner.

With his head cocked, a cup of coffee clutched between his teeth, and two outstretched arms balancing plates of orange-tinged pancakes in each hand, Lucky creeps his way forward. I reach forward and grab the cup from his mouth.

"Ooh, ooh!" he grunts, "Don't spill."

"Whatever you're doing, not your best idea."

"I was trying to surprise you. Pumpkin pancakes! Last day of summer feast!"

"Looks like you started without me," I point to his chin where a drip of syrup has settled between his stubble. "Can I grab a plate?"

"Grab the window," he nods ahead.

I step forward and slide open the port to our not-so-secret lair. I let Lucky step forward first, crouching through the exit wearing the yellow birthday hoodie. Save for the rare (and I mean *very* rare) shower, I haven't seen Lucky without it. The upside-down smiley looks a lot better on him than it ever did on me.

I follow Lucky out to the roof. The sky is a blanket of blemish-free blue. A gentle wind swirls, sending the rusty weathervane back and forth, the tip of the lopsided fish pointing directly at us. Lucky passes me my plate and we slide against our respective shingles.

"I'm not ready for this to be over," Lucky slops a whole pancake into his mouth.

"I think I am."

"You say that now. This time tomorrow you'll be introducing yourself in Mr. Morrison's English class and trying to pretend you read *The Odyssey*."

"I did read *The Odyssey*."

"Okay, fine. You'll pretend it didn't suck, how's that?"

I poke at the pumpkin-flavored breakfast with my fork, hoping to develop an appetite. The fork rips through one of the pancakes and scrapes against the ceramic.

"I could use a fresh start," I admit.

Lucky nods before looking to the rusted fish or the infinite blue above, I can't tell which. But he gets it better than I can articulate.

Between the roof's twin peaks and the birds singing below, I think about this summer. I think about that day that almost lasted forever and wonder if it ever really ended. The rest of the summer was gone in a blur before I made any attempt at enjoying it.

Lucky looks like he might say something but lets out a sigh instead.

I started writing this story down by hand as soon as I got

home that night. Pop was sleeping on the couch. I changed his favorite droning preacher to one of the classic movie channels in the high hundreds. Some movie called *Bright Road* starring Dorothy Dandridge was on. When Poppy heard us and woke up, he had no idea we were gone all day.

No one came looking for us.

If it weren't for the bleeding scratch across my face, there'd be no sign, no confirmation, that any of the horror we experienced was real.

At the sight of the fresh blood, Pop sprung from the couch and asked what happened.

"Destiny saved us," Lucky said.

Poppy mentioned the idea of a visit to the emergency room—"You might need stitches"—but I insisted otherwise. He asked one more time about how exactly I got the wound and I made up some story about cutting through the woods and getting scratched on a branch. I stuttered and circled back on some of my words. He lowered his eyebrows. It was obvious I was lying, but it was better than trying to explain the truth. When Dorothy returned to Kansas, I saw what happened to a girl who defeated an otherworldly darkness then lived to speak about it. At best, Poppy might label me a liar. At worst, and most likely, he'd probably think I was crazy.

Even if I wanted to tell the truth, I couldn't. Not yet. Not then and there. I didn't have the words to express what had just happened to me.

But I do now. So here this is. Maybe this is just for me, or maybe, hopefully this might help you with whatever you're going through.

I don't know if you or anyone else will believe me, and that's okay. But just as it was when all this was just a blank page, I've still got Lucky.

He doesn't just believe me. He knows what happened is true. He too experienced the unspeakable.

"Looks like it's healing up alright," Lucky nods, his eyes fixed on the thick scar running across my face.

I don't really think about it. Sometimes I forget it's there. I run my fingers across its smooth, slick surface. It glistens in the shining sun, flowing across my left eye like a river.

"What are you gonna say?" Lucky lays down his fork with a clink.

"What? About the scar?"

The wind settles and the birds fall silent.

"No," he clarifies. "When they ask for your name?"

The weathervane creaks overhead and the fish rocks back and forth, finally setting its mark on the sun.

I hadn't really thought about this until now. Maybe I should.

What's in a name? Probably more than any of us care to admit.

"Hi, I'm…Maya?" The words spill from my mouth before I've even processed them.

A creeping smile slowly forms on Lucky's face.

"My name is Maya Lane," I try it on again, this time with a tinge of mock confidence in my voice and my hands on my hips like a pseudo superhero.

Lucky laughs. The sound is healing for both of us.

My name is Maya Lane, I repeat again in my head.

I nod. It sounds good. It feels right.

My name is Maya Lane.

The weathervane whines overhead as the wind brushes the hairs on the back of my neck.

*At least for now.*

# AuthoR'S note

If you or someone you love is struggling, you are not alone.

Support is always available.

Call or text 988 to reach the Suicide & Crisis Lifeline,
or chat at 988Lifeline.org—free, 24/7, and confidential.

# About the Author

**JARED TLC** is a writer and artist from New Jersey. By day, he works as a TV producer. By night, he attempts to astral project across dimensions. He loves Philly sports and AMC Theatres. Some of his influences include Toni Morrison, Clive Barker, and Taylor Swift.